BYUCK

BYUCK

Theric Jepson

Strange Violin Editions
Washington D.C.

FIRST EDITION, DECEMBER 2012
Copyright © 2012 by Eric W Jepson
thmazing.com

Strange Violin Editions
4200 Cathedral Avenue, NW, #702
Washington, DC 20016
strangeviolineditions.com

All rights reserved. No part of this publication may be reproduced or transmitted in any form or by any means, electronic or mechanical or hypothetical, including photocopy, recording, eidetic memory, trained myna birds, synchronized swimming, retired Cold War spy, spinach, or any information storage and retrieval system, without permission in writing from either the publisher or a Donne-quoting federal judge in his or her official capacity, except for the inclusion of brief quotes in reviews, tattoos, subpoenas, letters to the editor, rock-opera lyrics, weepy tirades, or spam.

ISBN 978-0-9837484-8-9 (original trade paperback)
ISBN 978-0-9837484-7-2 (e-book)

Library of Congress Control Number: 2012955567

Printed in the United States of America!

Pragmati Cataloging-in-Publication Data
Byuck / by Theric Jepson
Summary: Dave, Curses, and Ref try to write a rock opera, but life gets in the way.

Official Stance of the Pragmati

The above summary (which, it should be noted, was supplied to us *by the author* and therefore *cannot be construed* as a *fair or accurate assessment*), fails to represent this novel honestly. *Byuck* is not only about three deviants deciding that writing a rock opera is a sensible use of their time, but is also about such things as Lexi, injuries sustained from lacrosse, an improper combination of snack foods, blind mermaids, road trips, candlelit ceremonies, a person who does not like lobster, a keyboard, a guitarist with a shady past, a guitarist with a shady present, a giant thumbtack, and gross overusage of the word *byuck* as well as its derivatives *byucky, byucker,* and equally mindless others. Just what the heck is *byuck* supposed to mean, anyway? And didn't *anyone* at Strange Violin have enough sense not to name this book something a little less inane?

On top of these grave flaws, we the Pragmati feel constrained to point out that this book has certain irredeemable traits which put it in direct opposition to everything we stand for:

1. It has already caused the following reactions in readers: laughter; offense, recognition, anger, tears, crushes. All of these reactions are quite contrary to Pragmati ideals. Although we will excuse anyone for being angry at this particular book.

2. This book, like so much fiction, claims to tell truths while making stuff up left and right. The absurdity of this is dealt with more fully in Pragmati Publication 12B.4, available from your local agent. We urge you to read it instead of this.

3. Although there is nothing in this book to suggest that Brigham Young University is anything other than an absolutely crackerjack institution of higher education, it does suggest that some of the people who attend that storied home for scholars are silly, weird, or possibly even jerks. This insinuation is categorically and demonstrably false and highly insulting to boot and a good example of why we disapprove of this Jepson character. Not that we have any more official connection to the university than Jepson, but we admire its choice of a dark respectable blue for sweatshirts and ballcaps.

4. It has jokes.

Finally, the Pragmati officially denounce this seditious book for alleging support—from its very first chapter—for chasing rainbows. It is a well-established fact that if even so few as 0.01% of Americans were to behave in such an unrestrained manner, the very fabric of our society would tear; within twelve months of reaching the 0.01% threshold, buffalo will roam the deserted streets of Boston, glaciers will destroy Detroit, and three of four human babies will be born with Neo-Synephrine addictions.

The Pragmati thank you for your wisdom in turning to our assessment first and then flinging this book from your person with all vigor and running screaming from the bookstore. You will be much happier popping that *Best of Punky Brewster* DVD back in for one more view. Don't miss the Very Special Episode with the refrigerator. That one will teach you useful facts about what happens to the lighthearted *in real life.*

KAMSA

Byuck *was born in 1999 as a feeling and a handful of scenes under the banner* Byuck: A Play. *My first thank you also dates to '99 when Donlu Thayer read character sketches and early scenes printed off my old 386 and told me they were good but maybe I wasn't quite ready to write this yet. She was absolutely right.*

Byuck awoke from hibernation and wrote itself all licketysplit-like just in time to be nurtured and loved by Fob: Ben Christensen, Kari Ambrose, and Arwen Taylor.

Among the other people who have read the book (or portions thereof) and given me feedback are Dean Hughes, Kyle Jepson, Tom Lowery, Christian Sorensen, the Quinner, Jessie Christensen, Arwen and her crew (Valerie Snyder and Erin Hallmark), Sherri Lowery and her crew (Steph Stitt Burt, Angela Davies, and, yes, even Linda Pope), and Mandi Tinnel.

Thanks also to Preston McConkie, who spent countless hours helping me polish my prose.

And to Therese Doucet of Strange Violin Editions, the first person crazy enough to see Byuck *all the way into book form.*

Above all others, thanks go to Lynsey. Without her I would not be motivated to breathe, let alone string words into books. This book is for her, because it was first her gift to me.

To Build a Fence

a public service message from
The Institute for Marital Concerns
Brigham Young University Chapter

© 2000

As all you returned-missionary gospel scholars know, erstwhile prophet and to-the-moment namesake of our great university Brigham Young once said:

> I will give each of the young men in Israel, who have arrived at an age to marry, a mission to go straightway and get married to a good sister, fence a city lot, lay out a garden and orchard and make a home. This is the mission that I give to all young men in Israel.

This presents us with a distinct problem, if we 1) do not want to get married, 2) don't want to get married, or 3) would really rather not get married. If this sounds like you, then rest assured that we at the IMC are here to help you get out of what, at first glance, seems like a direct commandment from a prophet of God to get married.

Living in the post-Clinton era as we do, we have the right to demand strict word definitions and to nitpick on how they fit together. Being exactly the sort of "Young Man in Israel" that Brigham Young was speaking both to and about, it is necessary to build excuses for ourselves. But a bad excuse is self-damnation and really good excuses are hard to come by in this dispensation of the fullness of times, so in order to stall for time, we need to demand some definitions while we strive to understand the "deeper" meaning of this prophetic utterance.

To the neophyte, defining "straightway" may seem our best starting point, but like any bomb, picking the wrong wire (or in this case, *word*) can make the whole thing go off in your face. Be warned: "straightway" is such a potent word that it may, in fact, actually be impossible to completely disarm. In cases like this, where the obvious is not the ideal, it is wise to open the abstract mind, allowing fresh, clean, and clear thoughts to fall in from above like so many bird droppings.

In the case of this phrase ("go straightway and get married"), the best place to start is probably "get." To those unfamiliar with the fine art of advanced word refinement, or *clarification*, "get" may not seem so great, but as every wise word clarificator knows, "get" is the word clarificator's best friend. For one thing, it is of that rare tribe of word safe to look up in the dictionary! Dozens upon dozens of wildly disparate definitions for the choosing! "Get" can make a sentence mean anything you please! "Go straightway and succeed in coming or going married!" "Go straightway and achieve as a result of military activity married!" "Go straightway and be subjected to married!" (Er. Bad example.)

But before we get *too* happy about discovering "get" just where it could have best been found, let's look at a larger portion of Brother Brigham's sticky speech:

> I will give each of the young men in Israel, who have arrived at an age to marry, a mission to go straightway and get married to a good sister, fence a city lot, lay out a garden and orchard and make a home.

All right, clarificators, here we go! First of all, why do we *need* to refine this statement? Because it is presenting us with a *mission* – or, in other words, it's handing out (heaven help us) *responsibility*; and if there is one thing we *don't* need (or at least *want*), it's responsibility! Brigham *couldn't* have meant for us to have *more* responsibility! We've had enough of that! We're returned missionaries! Are you with me? ARE YOU *WITH* ME?!?!

BUT WAIT – *who* is he giving this mission to?

> . . . each of the young men in Israel, who have arrived at an age to marry . . .

Ah ha! There's an out right there! Who's to say what "an age to marry" is? Or whether we have "arrived" at such an age? I don't know, but I'm *sure* that doesn't include me!

But that's *too* easy, and not completely satisfactory. Here's why: I can't go around saying "I haven't 'arrived at an age to marry' yet" all of my life. Also, unless I can point to what I *am* doing to *obey* President Young rather than my reasons (however valid) for *not* obeying him, then the focus will remain on what I'm *not* doing and no amount of pious explication is likely to save me from the judgmental frowns of others. So let's look once again at this quote of Brother Brigham's, and this time, let's pay Close Attention to the *commas*:

[The mission is] to go straightway and get married to a good sister, fence a city lot, lay out a garden and orchard and make a home.

It doesn't take a prophet to realize that President Young has offered us young men in Israel who've arrived at an age to marry three options:

1. Go straightway and get married to a good sister
2. Fence a city lot
3. Lay out a garden and orchard and make a home

The first option is what we kinda wanna avoid and the third is an awful lot of hard work. Therefore, the only option I can see left for us (short of apostasy) is to fence a city lot. If we can get oh, say, six thousand of us young men in Israel together some Saturday afternoon, we should be able to fence a city lot in no time! And then we can go home knowing we have been faithful in following the commands of the prophets! A major plus of this plan is that we will be able to carry around a Polaroid of our fenced city lot – our pride and joy – to show anyone who may ask us why the only ring we're wearing is our well-worn CTR.

"You see, Brother XYZ," we might say, "while *you* were off getting married to a good sister, *I* did the thing most wouldn't. *I* built a fence." That should shut them up.

And hey! It almost sounds heroic!

ONE

Simple Faith

DAVID THEM HAD NOT EXPECTED "To Build a Fence" to be such a success. He had thought it was funny when they wrote it, but never imagined it would fly out of control like it did.

His roommate Curses thought the wild reactions were great and wanted to turn their essay into a book. Dave didn't necessarily disagree, but he didn't really think they could write a book in one crazy evening like they had "To Build a Fence." He also didn't figure that one freak hit necessarily meant there was a book market for smart-alecky, byucky commentary.

"To Build a Fence" reached its first audience when Curses read it at a ward party. Everyone loved it. Several of the guys asked for an electronic copy to electronically mail to their electronic friends, and before the week was out someone had e-mailed Dave a copy of "this hilarious new thing going around e-mail." By the end of the month *The Daily Universe* had done an investigative report on who the authors really were. The reporter was Curses's older sister's former roommate, and the story had been Curses's idea, but the article inspired a spate of controversy over the appropriateness of the essay's sentiment. For almost three weeks, the letters to the editor page was bogged down with wildly disparate commentary. Dave's favorite letter made the inevitable suggestion that those who want to build fences would be better off attending another university. His second favorite was a failed but heartwarming attempt to start a fence-building club.

Simultaneously, both Dave and Curses started getting e-mail from people they had never met. Apparently their fellow students were taking the news story, looking them up in the BYU directory, and finding their e-mail addresses. They received date offers and accolades from people who had liked the essay, and self-righteous ramblings and confused threats from people who had not liked it.

Dave had been too freaked out by the bulk of attention to write back, but Curses had used the text from the e-mails he received as content for the new "To Build a Fence" website he set up with help from their roommate Peter, a computer science major always on the lookout for some new bait in his endless quest to attract the fairer sex to the apartment.

After everything calmed down, Curses dropped the book idea but made a suggestion that actually appealed to Dave – it seemed much easier. What about writing a play?

That evening, Dave's hometown friend Martha "Referee" Plantree dropped by right after lacrosse practice; her longish, brownish hair was still wet from the shower. She often stopped by since Dave's apartment complex, Draftwood, right next to the westernmost stadium parking, was across University Avenue from Sierra de Provost, where Ref lived, right between the intramural fields and Wyview. But late fall? And with wet hair? All the way from campus? Dave shook his head and tut-tutted.

"You really shouldn't be walking around in the cold with your hair like that, Ref," he said. "I told you I'd give you a ride if you needed one."

"Thanks, Mom," she said. "Is Peter here?"

"No."

"Good. Then I'll come in." She walked in and whipped her wet hair so it hit Dave in the face. "Hey, Curses."

Curses waved. "Hey, Ref. Nice smack."

"Thanks. What are you guys up to?"

"We're writing a play."

"Oh no. About building fences?"

Dave shut the door and walked back into the conversation. "Ha ha ha. No."

"What then?"

"Actually," Curses said as he moved some papers off the red and blue plaid couch to make room for the lady, "it's Dave's idea."

"Oh? What is this idea, Dave?"

"The idea," Dave said, pausing to clear his throat artistically, "is that there are people out to despoil the dreams and ambitions of young people, those still unjaded by the worldliness of the world. They're called the Pragmati."

"Scary."

"Isn't it great?" asked Curses. "The play was my idea, but this Pragmati thing is fantastic. Of course, it's a love story at heart."

"Of course," said Ref, "love being your expertise. When did you guys decide to write a play?"

"Recently. But it is a love story. Also: it's a mystery." Curses glanced over his shoulders then whispered, "We know all about mysteries."

Dave sat down on the floor, across from Curses and Ref. "It's a terrifying mystery, too. I don't know who's actually part of the Pragmati and who's just been brainwashed by their soul-stealing antics, propaganda and whatnot, but I do know that their power on campus is strong. Take a look at the letters to the editor page."

Ref gave Dave a look and uncrossed her arms. "Is this a play about BYU? And wouldn't secret combinations be against the Honor Code?"

"Yes and good question. I don't think they're specifically mentioned. Curses?"

"Not that I can remember. But there must be some sort of 'other' category it would fall under."

"You would think so." Dave gasped. "Unless – unless – unless the Honor Code Office has been infiltrated! What if they have become the enforcing arm of the Pragmati! Oh my!"

"This is getting better all the time," said Curses.

"Oh my, yes," Ref said as she rested her head on the back of the couch.

"And maybe those who continue to dare to dream –"

"Like yourself?" asked Curses.

"Like myself, are turned over to the Honor Code Office to be 'dealt with' and 'dismissed.'"

"Yikes," said Curses.

"You guys will never get this produced on campus if you're accusing the Honor Code Office of secret combinations."

Dave looked at her. "Are you saying you're Pragmati?"

Ref smiled that smile girls smile when they think they're being naughty. "Maybe."

Curses: "Now I'm really yikesing."

Ref turned to him. "Okay, Texas boy, what's your major?"

"Communications."

"Exactly. And you, Dave?"

"English. You know that."

"I did, but I'm proving a point. The Pragmati have won over us all. We're not in our most majoriest of majors. I should be with a musician and a writer right now, not a communicator and an Englisher. Sellouts."

"Right, but see, we're writing a play. It's rebellion against the Pragmati – following our dreams, et cetera. We've started living the dream."

"Oh, I gotcha." Ref put her feet up on the hot-chocolate table. "I just read an article that said Christian death metal is rebellion against our secular society."

"Did it have a pie chart?" asked Curses.

"No."

"Never believe anything in a magazine that does not have an accompanying pie chart."

Dave sighed and turned to Curses. Sometimes it was so hard to hold a serious conversation with him in the room. "Curses, you're crazy."

"Me, Curses? Crazy? Curses Olai, crazy? Curses?"

"Do you see anyone else here named Curses?"

"No, but curiously enough, there is another Curses on campus. She's from Jamaica."

"Really?" Ref asked.

"Maybe."

"So you made it up."

"No! Her name is Curses Maybe."

"Really?" she asked again.

"Sure!"

"I don't believe you."

"Well, you may be right," Curses conceded. "She may be graduated by now."

"Anyway," said Dave, putting equal emphasis on the *any* and the *way*, "this isn't Christian death metal, but, um, Mormon rock opera. And besides, it's not rebellion. Rebellion is petty and childish. This is art and education."

"Whatever you say, of course," said Ref. "What do you call it? *Madame Pragmati*?"

"What? No, it's called *Byuck: A Rock Opera*."

"What's Byuck?"

"It's like BYU, only it's Byuck."

"I don't get it."

Dave looked at Curses and Curses shrugged. "No one does," said Dave.

"Then why are you calling it something no one gets?"

Dave opened his mouth a few times. Finally he said, "Simple faith."

TWO

Stanisplatusky Junior

"**I** CAN'T BELIEVE I DON'T have to work today," said Dave over his bowl of not-as-exciting-as-they-sound Rilly! Nütrishus! Snuggle-O's!

"Why? It's a national holiday." Curses cut up his sausage with a plastic knife he had kept from his last Wendy's run. "You know, I believe this sausage has the exact same diameter as a dime."

"It also stinks. Where do you find that stuff? You're a Texan – why can't you just eat normal hearty Texan sausages rather than that stinky stuff? Anyway, I usually have to work on national holidays."

"That's what you get for calling people on the phone for a living. Besides, this stuff's cheaper. It's an Authentic Filipino Sausage."

"Says who? You've never been to the Philippines. And it's not like I'm selling stuff – it's just surveys."

"I did serve my mission in Hungary, and there is a secret subterranean tunnel that connects the mission homes in Budapest and Manila. We had food exchanges."

Dave drank the last of the milk from his bowl before answering. "Would you be this nuts if your parents had named you a nice healthy name like John?"

"Probably. I have an Uncle John, and he's as crazy as the day is long. I can say someone is as crazy as the day is long because I'm from Texas. Don't mess with Texas, Thumb."

"I won't, thank you. And it's *Them*. Not thumb. Not them. The *t-h* of the first and the vowel of the latter. And I know you know that, you know." Dave pushed away his empty bowl and watched Curses down the stinky sausages. "As soon as you're done, I want to hear this song you kept me up all night praising."

Dave stood and walked to the sink, then washed out his bowl and six or seven other dishes off the pile. "Whose dishes are these?"

"Well," said Curses, "the orange plate is mine, but the rest must be Peter's."

"Or X's."

"No," said Curses. "I'm not sure if X eats at all, but if he does, I'm sure it's not here. We were up till one last night and he still wasn't home. And when I walked out to get my CDs from your car this morning, I saw him driving off. He's never here."

"He should have built a fence."

"Yes, he should have. Who knew girls were such trouble? Should I start to fall in love, just remind me of the terrible situation X is in. What's it called again?"

"Engagement."

Curses shuddered. "The very word!" he exclaimed, throwing his knife in the very general direction of the sink. "I'll get that later." He walked into the front room to plug in his keyboard. Dave kicked the knife towards the sink and followed him.

Curses removed the keyboard's dust cover and switched it on. "Hey, pretty baby," he said, stroking the keys from treble to bass.

"Now, Dave, we start with a stirring chord progression. This one, to be precise." Curses demonstrated the progression. "Meanwhile, our choir's backstage singing, *Rock on . . . Rock On . . . ROCK ON!* Then, suddenly, supercool and without a noticeable entrance, our hero is onstage and sings the opening number.

> *Brigham Young University's where I want to be*
> *Where all the babes are hotties*
> *And the ice cream grows on trees*

It took Dave a moment to realize Curses was finished. "That's it?"

"Yeah!"

"You kept me up all night bragging about that?"

"Well, yeah."

"I thought you had written an entire opening number."

"No, but that should be enough of a start for you to finish it, don't you think?"

Dave didn't know what to say.

"It's really quite the killer chord progression," Curses volunteered. "You've got to admit that."

"Yeah." Dave paused. "What were those lyrics again?"

"Brigham Young University's where I want to be / Where all the babes are hotties / And the ice cream grows on trees."

"Well you know, although I don't really like all that talk about babes and hotties, I think the Referee will hate it. Second, isn't our hero already at BYU?"

▟

REF FELL OFF the couch she was laughing so hard. "Sing it again," she gasped.

Curses sang his three lines again, this time with more confidence.

"Oh, that's great! That's great!" she said from the floor, panting.

"Dave said you would hate it," said Curses.

"I did not!"

"You did so," said Curses.

"I did not say that, Curses." Dave turned to Ref. "I didn't say that, Ref."

"Well," said Ref, "I think it's hilarious, but isn't he already at BYU? I thought this took place on campus."

"That's what I said," said Dave.

"And this is what I answered," said Curses. "Do you remember when Dave made us watch *Singin' in the Rain*?"

"Sure," said Ref.

"Well, remember that weird dance sequence where the guy goes to Broadway 'cause he wants to dance or something? Well, our man wants to go to BYU."

"Does he have a name?"

Dave elbowed Curses before he could say "Stanisplatusky Junior."

"No," said Dave.

"Well, he needs a name," she pointed out.

"Yes," said Dave, "but it's hardly urgent."

Nov 13, 11:47 P.M.

Okay, first, Curses wrote kind of a scandalous opening to Byuck and Ref likes it. Which means she's less of a feminist than I am, and I have a chromosomal disadvantage. Next, Curses is still on that "Stanisplatusky Junior" kick – sounds like a Russian spitting, he says. But even if that's true, I don't know why that makes it a good name for our hero. But what can you expect from a guy named Curses Olai? Ref hasn't had any ideas, but since she chooses to be called Referee, I can't expect much from her either.

So anyway, we're trying to do Byuck, and Curses – never mind. I guess I shouldn't complain: I haven't done hardly anything for the play yet. But it's tough, you know? Posterity, if you ever decide to write a play, make sure you have more than vague ideas. Evil Pragmati and falling in love is kind of overbroad, I'm deciding.

And my best ideas all come from real life. I think how funny a cross between Peter and Curses would be on stage, but I can't come up with anything really original. If I'm not careful, I'm going to end up writing a rock opera about writing a rock opera about writing a rock opera.

But at least I didn't have to go to work today. That was nice. Veterans Day off? That's not like them at all.

THREE

Bearer of Estrogen

As often happened on Tuesday nights, Dave returned from work to an empty house. He sat and ruminated on that day's call-center hijinks. Usually work was like a dreamland in that, when he left, Dave could barely even remember having been there. But this time he was thinking of the little kid who picked up the phone and proved to have as vast a command of vulgarity as anyone Dave had met at high school or while a missionary or anytime else. Dave had written on a scrap of paper by his monitor that "This kid was raised by the telephone wolves" and stuck it in his pocket. It was sitting in front of him now as he ate a sandwich, and he read it over and over. "This kid was raised by the telephone wolves." Something about the sentence was very attractive to him and he was trying to figure out just what that attractive quality was.

He was distracted, however, by the front door flying open and crashing into the newly repainted kitchen wall. Peter walked in, and, with one foot in the front room and one in the kitchen, wailed.

"Hi, Peter."

Peter was still recovering from his wail. Dave could tell that he had come from the gym because his hair was distinctly rust-colored – when it was dry it was brown, and when it was wet it was dark brown, but for some reason when it was sweaty it turned to rust.

"Dave!" cried Peter, causing Dave to choke on a piece of bread. "The wench has sent me another letter!"

Dave coughed up the wayward bread onto his plate. "What? Who?"

"Sister Earnshaw!"

"Oh, your missionary?"

Peter took a step into the kitchen and leaned into Dave's face. "If she was mine, she wouldn't be a missionary! And when she gets my last letter, we'll hear no more from her."

"Right. Sorry." Dave leaned back until Peter stepped away.

"You," said Peter, "got *another* one." He threw down a square white envelope on the table and tapped his toes in melodramatic impatience. When he realized Dave intended to continue eating his sandwich, he leaned forward again. "Open it."

"All right, hang on a second."

Dave popped in the last bit of his sandwich and drank some milk. Then he slowly and methodically cleaned his peanut butter knife and laid it down on his plate. After inspecting his fingers and flicking stray crumbs, he wiped them on his pants. Peter, meanwhile, was starting to dance.

Dave picked up the envelope. "Let's see here . . . no return address – so mysterious! My, my, my! Who could it be?"

"Just open it!"

"Okay, okay. Just trying to enjoy the mystery a little."

Dave opened the first envelope and removed the second, then opened the second and removed a third. Inside the third was a wedding invitation.

Peter tried to read the invitation, but Dave turned it so he couldn't.

Peter whined. "What does it *say*?"

"It says, 'The parents of Matilda Mae Averburn –' Wait, I don't know any Matilda Mae Averburns." Dave flipped through the layers of vellum in search of a picture. "Oh. Well, no worries, Peter. It's just my cousin Eddie from Salt Lake."

"Again? Another cousin?"

"Looks like it, poor sap."

Dave started to put the invite and picture back into the envelopes, but Peter snatched them away. He yanked out the picture and glared at it. Suddenly he seemed to be racked with acute abdominal pain.

"Ohhhhhh," said Peter, holding his gut. "She's so beautiful."

"Mmm." Dave took the picture back and inspected it. "Yes, she's a very striking girl." Dave tossed the picture back on the table and Peter fell into one of the ratty old kitchen chairs, which responded with a phenomenal squeak.

"Peter?" No response. "Peter?"

"Dave?" Peter sniffed. "When will I get married?"

For a terrible second, Dave thought Peter was going to cry. He wasn't sure what to say. "I don't know?"

Peter wailed again.

"Hey, hey! You date *all* the *time*! I mean, you're the only one of us with a date Saturday, right?"

Peter brightened right up. "Oh yeah! That's right! Janice! She's hot!"

"See? That's nice."

"Nice, nothing! It's wonderful." Peter sighed the sigh of the saved.

"I'm glad," said Dave, though he wasn't. Few things were less likely to make him glad, but to Peter, glad was the only appropriate response to hot. Dave had learned this the hard way.

"She's hot," Peter said again.

"Well, there you go. Have you seen Curses today?"

"Who?"

"Curses. Our roommate. How many Curses do you know?"

"Oh, him. No, I haven't. Why?"

"No reason. Just need to tell him something, that's all."

▥

"YES, I'M SERIOUS," said Dave for the tenth time in seventy-three seconds. "That's exactly what he did." Dave was starting to think he would have been better off not telling Curses about Peter's latest outburst. He didn't need Curses doing something crazy about it – like the time he made the sign that still hung over his bed:

BEARER OF

ESTROGEN

WANTED

APPLY ANYTIME BEFORE CURFEW

FEMALE APPLICANTS

=ONLY=

If accepted must visit at least once a week.

PAYMENT: All the lovin' you can handle, honey!

The sign had been inspired by one of Peter's moments of madness, and it had taken Dave three days to convince Curses that putting the sign on their apartment door was further madness. Curses thought it might teach Peter something. Dave thought it would ruin everyone's chances of ever getting invited over for brownies ever again.

"Maybe we should write a play called *Peter's Follies*," suggested Curses.

"Maybe not. I'm worried that kid's going to get us in trouble."

"Could be. But I welcome trouble. I am a man of trouble."

"Amen." Dave looked back up at the sign on the wall. "Amen."

An Introduction to David Them's BYU Memory Book by the Man in Question, David Them

On my mission there was a tradition among the sisters that I always thought was kind of cool: they would make pages for each other's "memory books" that they compiled over their eighteen months. The pages essentially consisted of a bit of text (I am so-and-so and remember when this-and-that?) and, say, a photo and some stickers or whatever. I was cajoled into making pages for some of these books myself.

By the end of my mission I was wishing that I had been making a memory book too. It seems like it would be a nice record to have . . .

With this thought in mind, I have decided to institute a David Them BYU Memory Book (of sorts) in this here 79¢ spiral-bound notebook. I'll get my friends to write a paragraph re: who they are, and voila! I shall never forget them. The following is the sample entry for you, my friends, to observe and follow. Hearken!

DAVID THEM

My name is David Them – the TH as in thumb, the EM as in them, but my name is not Thumb as in the digit or Them! as in nuclear ants, but Them as in somewhere in between. I shan't be explaining this again.

I am from Fresno, and thus have known you, Dave, oh illustrious owner of this book!, for most of our lives. I can remember kindergarten, but if we go further back than that I cannot tell.

I am an English major and an overall swell guy. Also: I'm awesome. Also: I love you. Also: You better give me back my twelve bucks or I'm breaking your legs.

FOUR

Tag, You're It

"Knock, knock."

Dave and Curses looked up from their crayons to see Ref standing in their doorway.

"Why is your door open?"

"To expedite the entrance of lovely young ladies," said Curses. "Do come in."

"Thanks. What are you guys doing?"

"Our new favorite Friday night activity." Curses held up his drawing of a menacing pair of eyes and three noses. "You like?"

"You see," said Dave, "we walked down to the video store and read the backs of horror movies until inspiration struck."

"You're kidding. Inspiration?"

"No. Check it out: A kid gets a birthday card that says something like, 'It's your birthday! Let's have a masquerade party! Pick out some eyes.' Then it shows a bunch of loony eyes. 'Choose your ears.' Ditto ears. Then it shows some noses and says, 'Pick your nose,' then you turn the last flap of the card and it says, 'Eww, gross! You shouldn't pick your nose!'" Dave gave half a laugh, then asked, "Have you ever seen a card like that, Ref?"

"Actually, I think you gave me that exact card when we were, like, fourteen."

"Oh. Sorry about that."

"Water under the bridge. But what's that got to do with horror movies?"

"Well," said Curses, standing up, "a kid gets that card and thinks it's hilarious, and while he's laughing his head off –"

"– nose off –" said Dave.

"– a gas tank explodes or something and he loses his nose and they replace it with a detachable one."

"Then," said Dave, "when he gets to be like twenty-four or -five or so and surrounded by coeds, he starts killing people and taking their noses so he can have a different detachable nose every day of the week. He's crazy. Loco."

"Choo-choo-rific. But," Curses paused to consider, tapping his own nose, "we're not sure if he's possessed by demons or anything."

Dave shrugged. "Neither of us have actually seen one of those slasher flicks, so we're not sure if that's a requirement."

"The boxes aren't clear."

Ref gave them a Look. "That's sick."

"And lame?" suggested Dave.

"And lame," conceded Ref.

"That's what we were aiming for!"

"But we're not sure what to call it," said Curses.

"I like 'Night of the Living Nose-Picker.' 'Living' optional," said Dave.

"Or just plain 'Nose-Picker,'" said Curses.

"Or 'The Picker of Noses.'"

"'Nightmare for Nose-Pickers.'"

"'The Nose Watcher.'"

"Or how about 'Well Picked'?"

"Or, 'The Picker.'"

"'Nosebleed.'"

"'Bloody Nose.'"

"'Bloodier Nose.'"

"'Bloodiest.'"

"'Bloody Nose 8: the Final Nose Bleed.'"

"Stop," said Ref. "You're disgusting."

Dave pouted. "You should read the boxes."

"Should I really?"

Dave and Curses considered.

"Well?" Ref asked.

Dave sighed. "No, I guess not."

"She got us there," said Curses.

"Unless I'm the next Wes Craven."

"I knew Wes Craven," said Curses, "and you, my friend, are no Wes Craven."

Ref blew him a kiss. "So. Enough blood and gore. How's the play?"

"Oh yes, glad you asked." Dave started putting his crayons away. "I got this whole box at the thrift store for seventy-five cents, you know."

"That's nice."

"Anyway, Curses has the music for the Noticing scene."

"Wait," said Ref, "Noticing's first, right?"

"Yes, Noticing's first."

"No," said Curses, "Awareness is first. But there's no song for that."

"Right, I thought that's what she was asking."

"That's all right, Dave," said Ref. "So Awareness is first, then Noticing, then – ?"

"Tension!"

"Yes," said Curses, "and Tension'll get a *dundundundundundundun*-type song. Really intensive."

"Then Movement?" asked Ref.

"Yeah," said Dave, "but I'm not so sure about that one."

"I am," said Curses.

"I know, I know," said Dave, "but I'm just not sure Tension and Movement can be separated. I mean – where does movement by magnetism end and movement by gravity begin?"

"How would I know?" Curses shrugged. "I've never been Involved."

"Which is the next step," said Dave.

"Exactly." Curses slammed his fist into his hand for emphasis. "But that reminds me. I haven't asked you, Ref, if you've ever had a boyfriend. Are you, in fact, the expert among us?"

"Not really." Ref sat down on the couch and put her feet on the hot-chocolate table. "I sort of had this boy in the dorms, and I even was going to let him be my missionary for about thirty seconds until I realized that was stupid."

"What was his name?" asked Dave.

"Um, Ned."

"That was a fake um."

Ref smiled. "Maybe. But let's hear that song."

▥

DAVE AND REF sat in the dark on opposite ends of the couch while Curses stumbled to the back of the apartment to flip the breaker back on.

"I told him those amps were a bad idea," said Dave.

"Where did he get them?"

"Some yard sale." Dave exhaled and put his feet up on the hot-chocolate table. "Remember when we sold all your dad's garden tools at our own little yard sale?"

Ref laughed.

"What did he do, anyway? Did he ever get them back?"

"I don't know. I doubt it. How could he have?"

"So he just bought all new?"

"I guess. I don't remember." She paused. "Actually, I don't remember doing yard work after that for a couple years."

Now Dave laughed. "Man. I loved being a kid with you, Ref."

"Yeah." Ref sighed. "Yeah."

From the back room, a crash. Dave and Ref both jerked up straight. Then Curses yelled "I've found it!" and they both slouched back down and put their feet back on the table.

The lights came on and Dave was startled to see how close Ref was sitting. "You're a lot closer than I thought."

"I'm clear on the other side of the couch."

And the other end of the couch is about seventy feet closer than I realized, thought Dave.

He looked down at their feet. Their toes were less than an inch apart. He stared at them. He turned to look at her. He looked back at the table and tapped her foot. "Tag. You're it."

The Love Progression

a public service message from
The Institute for Marital Concerns
Brigham Young University Chapter

© 2000

A recent study conducted by ourselves in connection with our colleagues at Love Sure Is Nice (LSIN) reveals that most of the students at our university have no concept of what Love is or what it means to be in it. In order to address these concerns and prevent the merely Aware from marrying mistakenly, we at the Institute for Marital Concerns have put together this brief description of the Love Progression for your use and edification.

Stage One: AWARENESS
Love is not possible without the two people in question first becoming aware of each other. It must be noted that being Aware of someone is not the same as just being aware of them. Say you're a boy named Sue and you know a girl named Clarence. That's nice. But you are not Aware of that person till you have developed an Awareness that Clarence could potentially be someone to hold and to cherish, to kiss, yes, and even to love. Awareness generally arrives suddenly, but need not and may not be a permanent state. Awareness can be fragile, gone in an instant, but it can also be impossible to destroy.

Stage Two: NOTICING
Ideally, Noticing is Stage Two, but it can precede Awareness or occur simultaneously. Noticing consists of discovering another person's Awareness of yourself. Proceeding along the Love Progression without Noticing is risky indeed to the old blood-pumper. But sometimes proceeding is the only path to Noticing. Ah, the broken hearts that lie along the road betwixt Awareness and Noticing!

Stage Three: TENSION
Beware of false Tension! True Tension occurs when both parties have Noticed the other. False Tension arises from one Aware mistakenly Noticing the person he or she possesses Awareness of. Oh, the poor souls. True

Tension is the source of fine memories, as courage is built and forays into friendly territory are gradually attempted. This is the magnetic attraction spoken of in Meg Ryan movies and romance novels. An irresistible force, pulling. But only when both parties put themselves within range of this irresistible force.

Stage Four: MOVEMENT

Movement is an acceleration of Tension. Tension still exists and is recognized and embraced. Gravity takes over and a sense of inevitability is achieved. Further progress along the Love Progression seems the only possible fate.

Stage Five: INVOLVEMENT

Pretenses are set aside and a relationship is recognized and admitted to. The flurry of senses and emotions is dizzying, but reality also peeks through from time to time, testing the strength of the Involvement. Involvement can last years or minutes, and the older it is, the more likely it is to be mistaken for the final step along the Progression. But never so mistake it! Disaster will follow! Involvement is, make no mistake, a (snort) beautiful thing. But it is still a step and only a step, no matter how much it looks like a plateau.

Stage Six: LOVE

We at the IMC have no idea what Love is. But it sounds nice. Maybe you'll get there someday.

FIVE

A Really Funny Ring

WOMEN'S LACROSSE HAD AN EXHIBITION game at five to stoke fan excitement for the coming season, so Dave and Curses went and watched. Five minutes from the final buzzer, Ref was squashed between two Colorado players. The man sitting behind Curses was so angry he spit a mouthful of caffeine-free cola down Curses's back before standing and yelling at the black-and-white-striped referees. His anger was not unwarranted; player number 23 Plantree was one of BYU's leading scorers, and in a close game like this one – even if it was preseason – there was every reason to suspect demonic involvement on the part of Colorado.

Curses was uncomfortable enough with colored sugar water down his shirt that he forewent the last five minutes to go clean up. Dave tried to get down to the bench to see Referee, but was turned away by security. "Man, we wouldn't let you down there if you were married to her. Go sit down."

BYU scored two quick goals before the game ended and the crowd dispersed happily. Dave waited until most everyone was gone, then walked as near to the bench as he could manage. They had taken Ref off the field, but some of the other players were still lingering, number 13 being the closest. Dave wasn't sure how to address the victorious female athlete. Number Thirteen? Miss Coulter? *Sister* Coulter? Finally he settled on Pardon Me.

"Yes?"

Number 13 Sister Coulter turned around and looked at Dave. Her head was haloed by the field lights and she looked like a sweaty angel.

"Is Referee okay?"

It took her a second to get what he meant. "Oh! Plantree!" She laughed.

"Yeah, she's fine. Just a couple bad bruises on her thigh I'm guessing." She narrowed her eyes and raised half her top lip. "And *whom* may I say is *calling*?"

Dave was unnerved by the innuendo and said something ridiculous. "A friend."

The angel laughed. "Okay, I'll tell her a 'friend' called."

"No, wait. I'm sorry. Hang on. My name's Dave and I was hoping I could give her a ride home."

"Dave?" The angel crinkled her brow. "Are you the guy with the weird name?"

"Them?"

"That's the one. Good thing your parents didn't name you Tom." She laughed. Dave bit his lip. His brother's name was Tom. "She still has to shower and whatnot, but if you want to wait, maybe I can talk her into not washing her hair." Coulter seemed to think this was funny. Dave had no idea why but he laughed politely and said he would wait.

▥

REF SAT ON the couch with her legs up on the hot-chocolate table. She was wearing her lacrosse shorts with towels over her legs and ice on the towels. She hadn't seemed terribly excited about coming over, but apparently she was glad enough Dave and Curses had come to the game to make an attempt at good humor.

Dave took up the story where Curses had left for the bathroom. "I wanted to come see if you were okay, but first, there was this security guard who told me I couldn't see if you were okay even if we were married, which obviously we're not. So I waited till after the game ended, then I talked to Little Miss Thirteen –"

"Coulter," said Ref, with her eyes half closed.

"Coulter, yes. She –" He stopped because Ref was half laughing. "What is it?"

"Sorry. It's just that last night my roommates and I," she said, yawning, "were playing that game, you know the one, where you get the ward list and try on different boys' last names? And it just occurred to me that 'Martha Them' has a really funny ring to it."

"Oh," said Dave.

"So if we ever get married, I'll just have to stick with Referee."

"Well, I'm glad that's settled."

"Anyway," said Curses, who appeared to have no interest in Ref's story, "the play. Dave's got some new scenes."

"Anyway," said Ref, who appeared to have no interest in Dave's new scenes, "I'm sore and tired. Let's do this later. Give me a ride home, Dave."

Dave and Curses didn't have a prepared rebuttal, so Dave got his keys and drove Ref across the street to her apartment.

"I'll see you tomorrow?" asked Dave.

"I guess so," said Ref. "But don't call me until eight."

"See you then," Dave said, but Ref just closed the door.

The Mysterious Game
by David Them

Five girls sat in a huddle on their apartment floor. The carpet was green and black, and the flickering apricot-scented candle lengthened their eyebrows into startling screams across their young, collegiate faces. After Marilyn had married and moved out of the apartment, the girls had prepared for a new roommate. But they had not expected a freshman would transfer out of the dorms and into their lives.

Natasha spread out the ward list in front of them. She had lived in apartment Q-240 the longest, and it was her responsibility to lead the night's agenda. She nodded at Minerva, who quietly stood and went into the kitchen to scoop ice cream. As she brought in the cool addictive treat, Natasha began to explain the nature of the game to their nervous freshman friend, Polly.

Polly had thought that transferring out of the dorms would give her life a sense of normalcy that constant freshman intrigues had denied her. She was a good girl with aspirations to medical school, and the puppy love and panty raids of dorm life had been a constant and unwelcome distraction. But now as Natasha laid out the rules, Polly was not certain things had changed for the better.

"This is the ward list," Natasha was saying. "Each of us has a pencil and one hundred uniform scraps of paper. We will begin with your name, Smith, and starting with the boy directly under you, we will match your first name with every boy's last name. We will each vote, on a scale of one to ten, which names best mesh with your own. We'll add them up and post the top five scores in the hall by the mirror." Natasha looked at the other roommates who nodded. "Marilyn," Natasha said under her breath with a gothic intensity, "married number three on her list."

Polly gulped. "But I'm a freshman," she whimpered.

"Then pretend this is a game. Now first," said Natasha through a mouthful of burnt almond fudge, "Polly Tarkin." The girls scribbled on pieces of paper. Minerva gathered them up and tallied the votes. Polly sweated. Natasha raised a questioning eyebrow to Minerva, as she set down her pencil.

"Thirty-five."

The girls nodded happily. It was about what they had guessed, maybe a little higher.

Natasha checked off Ed Tarkin's name. "Polly Thomson," she said.

The girls handed in their slips and Minerva added them.

"Eighteen point three three eight nine three."

Natasha sighed and put her head in her hand. "June. Don't."

"Sorry," said June.

They reached D before "Polly Daring" beat "Polly Tarkin" with a score of forty-five. "Daring's a great name," one of the girls told Polly. "He's on all our lists."

"Polly Paulsen" got a score of forty-eight, which set June whistling. "That's the highest score ever!" She winked at Polly knowingly.

The next name was John Quibfigg, a cute boy Polly sort of knew from her home stake. He had moved into the singles ward the same week Polly had, and said hi to her at church. Polly smiled, remembering.

"Polly Quibfigg," said Natasha. The girls couldn't hold it in, and busted out laughing. They laughed and laughed. And laughed some more. One of them knocked over the candle and spilled wax on the carpet, but they were laughing too hard to clean it up.

Minerva added up the numbers. "Two," she said. Five roommates, and the best they could come up with was two.

When they finally finished, Natasha mumbled something mystic about a virtuous woman and burned the edges of a yellow piece of paper, then handed it to Polly. It was her top five:

Polly Paulsen:	48
Polly Daring:	45
Polly Pennilson:	39
Polly Red:	39
Polly Limond:	36

At first Polly was sad John hadn't made the list. But then she thought about it. Quibfigg was not a name she wanted to carry with her through eternity. And besides, she pointed out to herself as Minerva turned on the light and gathered up the ice cream bowls and tut-tutted a wax stain that would outlive them all, it's not like I'm planning on getting married here anyway.

SIX

Pointless Episodes

DAVE FIGURED THERE WERE AT least six things he had to apologize for, and lack of consideration for Ref's injuries and the resultant pain were, respectively, numbers one and six. He recited the order to himself once again before knocking on Ref's door. One of her roommates opened it, and Dave realized he didn't know her name. Or any of Ref's roommates' names.

"Hi, um, is Ref here?"

"Hi, Dave," said Ref, slipping past her roommate and out the door. "See you later, Liz." Ref wrapped her scarf around her face and neck another ten or twelve times. It was a long scarf. "Chilly," she said.

"Yeah, I –"

Ref held up a hand and paused before the stairs. "Dave, look, I'm sorry about laughing at your name last night; I know you get that all the time, or did anyway, and I'm sorry."

"Oh. Thanks." They continued on down the stairs, and Dave struggled to update his plan. "I should be the one apologizing, though." He decided to start with number three. "I was pretty insensitive."

"Yeah, I guess you were." She laughed. "Jerk."

Dave nodded. "Right. Exactly." Since she already knew that much, he decided to forgo the rest of the apology and get down to business. "Anyway, so the semester's about over, and –"

"No, Dave, the semester *is* over. And thanks, by the way."

"No problem." Dave unlocked Ref's door and left it open while he walked around to his own door. After he put on his seatbelt he asked, "So where are we going?"

"Just up the canyon. There's a park not very far up. I've borrowed a tough-guy flashlight from Mr. Camp-Every-Weekend in my ward, so hopefully the fact that the sun set three hours ago won't hinder us."

Dave turned left out of Sierra de Provost's parking lot onto University Avenue. "It's not like you to leave stuff to the last minute like this, Ref."

"I know, I know." She sighed and rummaged in her backpack. "I totally forgot about it. I feel stupid. I don't know why I thought a Local Ecology class would be fun in the first place. I mean, do I want to graduate or don't I?" She pulled out a sheet of paper. "I just need seven legally harvested leaves from native flora. And I have a list of stuff that isn't native. Hopefully this won't take too long."

Not far into the canyon, Ref spotted the park to their left; they parked between two cars with fogged windows and walked into the native flora.

"So I guess you know the names of all these plants, right?"

"Eh. Where I'm at, Dave, is the stage where this is due tomorrow morning at nine, and something's better than nothing."

"Right. Been there. How can I help?"

Ref pulled off her backpack and took out a dictionary and a roll of paper towels. "You press."

"Right. Check. Full court or man-to-man?"

"Don't make sports jokes, Dave."

"Right. Oil or wine? Or printing? Haha!"

"Don't make jokes, Dave."

"Right. The time is far spent." Dave pulled off some paper towels, and as Ref brought him leaves he distributed them throughout the book. He watched Ref's head, the seeming source of a beam of light, bob through the bushes and picnic tables and trees, coming and going and coming.

"What are we at, Dave?"

"This turns it up to eleven."

"Okay. I ought to have at least seven natives then. Let's go back."

She turned off the flashlight and Dave nodded invisibly in the dark. They walked to the car and Dave let her in. As they pulled back onto University Avenue, Dave said, "We just spent two hours doing something neither of us really cares about."

"Mm."

"Why is life composed of so many pointless episodes?"

Ref looked out her side window at Borders welcoming them back to civilization. "Is it pointless," she asked, the quiet words misting on the glass, "just to be alive?"

Dave shook his head and Ref turned and smiled at him. They drove the rest of the way home in silence.

REFEREE PLANTREE

*If you don't know who I am by now, Dave, you're an idiot. And if you need me
to be pithy so you can remember me ten years from now then you don't deserve to
remember me. In fact, you better send me a letter of apology. Pronto.*
  Punk.

*Editor's note: Though, yes, Ref is caustic and cruel more often than not, we are
friends, really. Here is a documented example from my sacrament-meeting scratch-
pad, affixed with acid-free glue, culled from our recent stake conference, which
demonstrates how witty she is and how mean she can be:*

  — *Stake Conference in Nov with the skies a lovely gray.*
  — *How poetic.*
  — *Provo Tabernacle must have a stake conference every single Sunday.*
  — *Probably. Except General Conference weekend.*
  — *Speaking of, when is my Conference* Ensign *going to get here?*
  — *You have a subscription?*
  — *I think it starts this month.*
  — *Oh — I know this girl. She's in my ward. I think she's in the Relief
      Society pres.*
  — *How does the pres feel about her being in there?*
  — *I meant PRESIDENCY.*
  — *Like the old woman who swallowed a fly.*
  — *Shut up, Dave.*
  — *Who wriggled and scribbled and giggled inside her.*
  — *Why don't you listen to her talk?*
  — *I'm not talking.*
  — *You're not listening either.*
  — *Neither are you.*
  — *Yes I am.*
  — *What'd she just say?*
  — *This is almost the same as the lesson she gave last week about charity
      and covenants.*
  — *Charity + Cov'ts. That about sums up Relief Society.*

— *What's that supposed to mean?*

— *Oh, you women. Always being nice and righteous and so on.*

— *It's hard to catch sarcasm on the page.*

— *Okay, let's practice. Let's try this one: You're a dumb math major.*

— *Nice try, but I'm not.*

— *Dumb?*

— *A math major.*

— *I thought you were.*

— *I was when you transferred, but not now.*

— *I thought you changed back.*

— *Oh yeah. Forgot. Anyway, I changed again.*

— *Again?!?! Ref!!!*

— *I know, I know. Amen. Anyway, it's dietetics now.*

— *How many majors have you had?*

— *I don't know.*

— *How many minors are you going to have?*

— *Just two I think.*

— *Figure it out.*

— *Okay. First major: Spanish. Minor? Ha. Then Biochemistry. No minor. Horticulture. Maybe a class or two. Marriage Family & Human Devmnt. Minor. Elementary Education: Coaching. No minor. Math. One class to minor. Physical Therapy. Don't know. Dietetics. Major, I hope.*

— *Ref, Ref, Ref. What, afraid of commitment?*

— *No, just graduating.*

— *Haha!*

— *We're running out of paper.*

— *Any last words?*

— *Pay attention.*

SEVEN

Angst on Campus

"CURSES. CHECK THIS OUT."

Dave was home from work early tonight because there were no surveys to be done. It could spell bad news for rent and groceries, but Dave was always glad to leave.

"It was kind of dead tonight, and I worked up this." Dave handed Curses some sheets of paper.

"What is it?"

"Our first few scenes. They need some work, of course, but you start putting that song on the other page to music, and we should have ten minutes worked up by this time next week."

"Sweet."

"See, as I was sitting there, I got this idea about our hero, right? He hasn't been at BYU long, and so he's adjusting. The stage is split in half, and on one half, we see what he imagined would happen when he came, and on the other half we see what really happens. We might need twins to play the part of the hero."

"Twins?"

"Or the lighting could change between the set halves and he could just walk across or something."

"Okay."

"Now, here he's imagining people proposing all around him as he walks about, and girls spying on his left ring finger with telescopes as he goes to class. Then, on the other side of the stage, as he walks to class he gets trampled by a bunch of singing freshmen late for biology."

"That's funny."

"Thanks. I got a couple more ideas, but you need to come up with some too."

"Got one," Curses said.

"Oh?"

"We've got a guitarist on the way."

"What?"

"A guitarist. To audition."

Dave still wasn't sure he had heard Curses correctly. Then: "Oh. Your website. Terrific. Did you tell him we don't even have a score or anything yet? Or a script?"

"Yeah, I told him," said Curses. "He should be here any second now. Where's Ref?"

"She should be here any second now, too. I just called her a couple minutes ago. But why are you having this guy over? We're not ready for musicians!"

"Well, he told me that it was good we hadn't finished, 'cause he knew the true story of BYU and would happily share it with us."

"What's the true story of BYU?"

"Dave, he'll share it when he gets here."

"Terrific." Dave went into the kitchen to get a glass of water. As he was picking a dried-on piece of rice off the bottom of a "clean" cup, Ref came in. "Hi, Curses," she said.

"Hi, Ref."

"Hi, Ref," said Dave.

"Hey, Dave. Are you getting water? Bring me some too." She walked to the couch. Dave filled the rice glass and the second cleanest glass (just some dried-on Nesquik) and followed her.

As they sat down, someone banged on the door and Curses jumped up and opened it to an unshaven lout with a guitar and no hair above his troglodyte eyes. Ref made a face and tried to blow the odd odor he brought out of her nostrils. "Who's that guy?" she asked.

DAVE, REF, AND Curses sat in dead silence. No one knew what to say. "I see," Dave finally managed.

Ref cleared her throat and rubbed her knees. "So you're saying the guy blows a hole in a window at the Swicket with a sawed-off shotgun after having a perfectly normal and healthy conversation with his professor, then, notwithstanding his many wounds from the ricocheted buckshot, leaps out, plunging head first, ten stories to his death?"

The odiferous guy nodded. "Right, right. It's the angst, you see? All the angst on campus."

"All the angst on campus," Dave repeated. "I do see. And just how much angst *is* there on campus" – he paused – "Garth?" He had a hard time believing the guy's name was Garth.

"Oh man! So much! You can, like, feel it! Like, in the air! You know?" Garth demonstrated and took a deep breath through widened nostrils. "It's putrid, man, putrid."

"I think I smell it," muttered Ref.

Curses slapped his knees and jumped up in a sudden show of enthusiasm. "Yes! Well! I think that's just the angle we've been looking for! You're so right! Angst! That's just what BYU's all about! Angst." He turned to Dave and Ref for agreement.

"Yes," Ref obliged, "I feel simply relieved now that I know what my problems have been all this time." She looked at Garth, then added, with apparent sincerity, "Thank you."

"Yeah, welcome. Thanks for listening. Don't forget I play guitar."

"We won't," Curses assured him. "Of course, with your input, we may just have to start all over. We may never finish!"

"Dude." Garth was sympathetic. "I know just how that is."

The three of them shook his hand and showed him out with a host of thank-yous, then Curses turned to them. "Angst on campus, anyone?"

Ref looked at him. "I can think of one guy."

Curses nodded. "And let that be a lesson to you."

Byuck: a rock opera

(another scene somewhere in the middle)
by David Them

JAMESON (swirled about by black rainclouds led by Hank).
The angst!? What do you mean the angst?!

HANK.
The angst!

CHORUS. (offstage).
The angst!

HANK.
The angst!

CHORUS.
The angst!

HANK.
The angst it creeps along along
The angst!

CHORUS.
The angst!

HANK.
The angst it sings a horrid song
The angst!

CHORUS.
The angst!

HANK.
The angst it creeps and steals your soul
And the songs it sings are the first to go
And we'll all lose faith when
Our lives are filled with angst!

CHORUS.
Our lives are filled with angst!

JAMESON.
I don't believe! I can't believe! This life is not just angst!

HANK.
It is.

JAMESON.
And faith in God and other folk tain't's futile as you think.

HANK.
Oh no?

JAMESON.
(Something clever and witty that dispels the clouds and turns the chorus angelic once more and also works with the established rhythm. Darned if I know what.)

Note to Curses: Okay, I know – not so good. But I think we can work a character like this in. You probably noticed that Hank's song goes to a certain American standard, which you have to admit is pretty witty. If we turn that song creepy, this scene might work. Otherwise, throw it away and pretend I never gave it to you.

(signed, dave)

EIGHT

Home in Time for Dinner

FINALS. OY VEY.

Not that Dave had been having a particularly hard time with them. Victorian Novelists had been a joke. "Thackeray?" Dave had scoffed when Ref had asked him how it went. "Thackeray! Ha! We don't need no stinkin' Thackeray!" In Family History he was supposed to have turned in a paper re why his dad's dad had changed the family name from the perfectly respectable Jones to the no-one-can-pronounce Them. But the court in Pennsylvania wouldn't release records to him – at least not at the procrastinator's last minute – and definitely not to nonfamily members (and he was no Jones) so he had written instead about how his parents met. It had been shabby work, but he felt he had aced the final at least. Now he was standing on the ground floor of the testing center, watching a television screen, waiting for it to display the last four digits of his social security number and his biology score.

The semester was over and Dave still hadn't forgiven his enemies in the administration building, those who had cursed him to take biology. When he was at Fresno Community College he had taken anthropology, which would supposedly fulfill any biology requirement at any four-year school, but BYU had negated *that* foolish dream. And so Dave had taken biology, and it was essentially just a repeat of high school biology, except the teacher bore daily testimony that whatever *you* decide about evolution, God's still real, and personally, *I* think it's a true principle.

Dave didn't care. He had no stake in the validity of Darwinism.

The result of Dave's irritation at having to take the class was zero hours spent studying. He had done fine anyway: high eighties, low nineties on his tests, a near perfect on his "Changing Views on the Morality of Animal Vivisection, 1700–1950" paper (he had chosen the topic for the gruesome anecdotes and illustrations he felt well demonstrated his disdain for the class), but he was uncertain about the final. Now that it was all over, it was easy to think he should have applied himself more – and Dave *was* thinking that – but too late now.

"Ah, here it comes."

4435......................................84

Dave shrugged. Not great, but he hadn't tried really, so what was there to complain about? Thank education for grade inflation. Dave shifted his backpack on his tailbone and left the testing center. It had snowed slightly the night before, first snow of the season, and it was mostly gone now, but the air was still crisp and Dave liked that. At least, he liked it in twelve-second increments. He walked the fifteen feet to the Joseph Smith Building and weaved his way through sprawled out backpacks and legs of studying/snoozing students to another twelve-second increment of cold and the Benson building, and worked his way to the Fishbowl.

The Fishbowl was a round room, with windows to the outside making up maybe three-quarters of the walls. It was meant for studying – and during finals week that was certainly what it was being used for. There weren't any unoccupied tables, but there was a corner seat available at the one nearest Dave; everyone else at the table seemed engrossed in chemistry texts, so he sat down and hurriedly took out a notebook and pen.

He wrote "BYUCK" at the top of the paper, circled it, and put the cap of the pen between his teeth.

When Dave had entered the actual, all-extraneous-paper-must-be-stamped-by-a-testing-center-employee part of the testing center, an idea for a lyric had come to him, and by the time he had sat down with his test he had had quite a bit of song worked out. Now it was simply a matter of re-creation.

Let's see . . .

Dave closed his eyes and imagined walking into that room. Big and tall, great and spacious, really high ceilings. Nice wood paneling. Probably one of the nicest rooms on campus – too bad it was endowed with such a demonic purpose.

Dave remembered remembering that some people have church in that room. Had that been his inspiration – the juxtaposition of testing center and chapel, test-taking and sacrament-taking, fear of score and fear of God?

Dave clamped down hard on his pen cap and it shot out of his mouth and bounced over the book and into the lap of the person sitting in front of him. She looked up, wide-eyed. "Hexabromobiphenyl," she said.

"Better living through chemistry," said Dave.

"Sixties counterculture."

"Fifties plastic advertising."

She blinked, and her head dropped back to her book.

Dave wasn't sure whether he should ask for his pen cap back.

HE WAS ALMOST home when he suddenly thought the phrase "mechanical pencil" seemed familiar. He crouched down in stadium parking, pulled out his capless pen and notebook, and wrote "mechanical pencil," then looked at what he had so far:

> the study dance
> more prayers than anywhere
> something about headaches only funny
> ninjas
> the temptation to cheat – with marbles!
> mechanical pencil

He shook his head. Ninjas didn't seem right anymore. He sighed and looked up towards his apartment complex. He was going to have to face it: he had forgotten the stupid song.

"GOOD NEWS, DAVE," Ref said as she came in the door. "Is Peter here?"

"No."

"Well good news, then." Ref had her hair pulled back in some sort of yellow contraption that looked barbaric and painful. She shrugged off her backpack and sat next to Dave on the couch. "My professor finally e-mailed my stats grade and I don't have to take the final after all. I've got a ninety-six point two."

"What did you need?"

"Ninety-five point seventy-nine."

"Ninety-five point seventy-nine?"

"I know. Imagine what the class was like. But at least if I stick with dietetics, it's the last math class I'll need."

"But you'll still take one."

"Well, I'm really interested in number theory, but I haven't taken all the prereqs yet. Anyway, you want to leave tomorrow? If we leave early enough we could be home for dinner."

"Okay, only because it occurs to me that if we leave early enough, we might could be home for, like, dinner."

"Right."

"And what's even better is, if we left early enough, we could even be home in time for dinner!"

"Oh, shut up." Ref hit his arm and it hurt. It wasn't fair – she worked out. "But, so, shall we?"

Dave nodded. "Sure, sounds good. And Twinkies are on sale at Macy's."

"Joy." Ref rolled her eyes – slowly, so Dave could not possibly miss her dietetical disdain. "What are you working on?"

Dave looked down at his notebook. Ref picked it up and started reading. "'Maybe the ninja has a headache because he has to take a test and he's praying so hard, and he's got a –' What's this?"

"Mechanical."

"Mechanical what."

"Pencil?"

"Dave, this makes no sense."

"Let's leave tomorrow." Dave took his notebook back, closed it, and threw it frisbee-style clear onto the kitchen table. "I need a vacation."

"Right, because, like, if we left tomorrow, you'd be on vacation."

Dave nodded. "Right."

DECEMBER 19TH ~9PM

Does Kwanzaa start today or after Christmas? I can never remember, but it's a week long so if it's before it probably starts today, which reminds me, I need more stamps.

I ehhed my biology final today, but just before I took it I had this great idea for a Byuck number — something about ninjas in the testing center, or maybe angels, I can't remember. It had something to do with how pretty the room is but how ugly the test-taking torture within can become. I think.

("Test-taking torture." That's pretty good.)

Ref and I are leaving tomorrow since she doesn't have to take her stats final, and it's official for Curses: His parents and a sister are coming here to visit another sister and him. Or, more accurately, sister visits sister, parents visit sister's daughter, Curses ends up babysitting both sisters' kids. The local sister/daughter combo is named Lorraine and Lorene. I can't remember which is mother and which is daughter. I'd ask Curses, but he's actually studying and I don't want to break the spell. Besides, he's so tired he might not remember himself. (Of course, if his parents had named his sister a nice normal name like "Weirdo" or "Death to Squirrels!" like they did for Curses, remembering her name might be easier.) The other sister's name starts with an E I think, and is somewhere between Lorraine/Lorene and Curses on the weirdness scale. Anyway, who cares?

At least he'll have our place to himself. Peter's flying to Massachusetts. I guess his dad just got a condo in Cape Cod or something. Or do you say on Cape Cod? And no one's seen X for a couple days at least, so we figure he's gone too. Curses is thinking about letting his parents stay here, but I'm not sure that's "allowed." His mother, after all, is ♀.

It's only nine, but Ref claims she'll be waiting for me to pick her up at five a.m., so I'm turning in now. Right after I find out what happens next in the exciting adventures of Ivanhoe. That's the last time I bet a professor I won't like some dead Scottish guy.

Bonne Noelle, Lassie.

NINE

That Barren Wasteland

DAVE WOKE UP WHEN HIS alarm went off at four thirty and staggered across the room to turn it off. Good thing he'd decided to leave it on his desk.

Dave next woke up in the shower, not remembering getting there. "Stupid Scott," he said. He'd stayed up till one – well, almost two . . . two thirty . . . okay, three . . . maybe later, he wasn't really sure – finishing that stupid *Ivanhoe*. "Stupid, stupid, stupid," he said.

Dave poured himself some Fruity Pebbles and was adding the milk before he remembered he didn't *like* Fruity Pebbles, that these were *Curses's* Fruity Pebbles; that, in fact, Fruity Pebbles were the *foulest* thing in Creation. "Boy. I'm not sure I should drive."

"Love your enemies, bless them that are cheerful," Dave thought as he saw Ref bouncing down the outer stairs from her apartment, carrying her two little suitcases, one baby blue, one yellow.

"Hi, Dave!" she gushed as she opened the passenger-side door. "Can you pop the trunk?"

Dave did, and got out to help.

Ref closed the trunk as he arrived. He looked at it, trying to figure out why she had closed it.

"Okay, I'm ready. Shall we go?"

Oh. She'd already put her bags in. She should definitely be the one driving. And hey – it's *cold*.

"Ref. Would you mind driving? Just to Nephi or so? I'm really tired for some reason. I could use a couple more zzzs."

"Wow, Dave – are you okay? You look really tired. You seemed fine yesterday."

Dave didn't want to talk about that stupid, stupid, stupid kid who'd stayed up all night reading. "I'm fine. I could just use another h –" But what he could use another h – of was lost in a massive yawn. He put one hand against the car to steady himself.

"Yeah, yeah, okay. I'll drive. Sheez, you look rough."

"Fruity Pebbles," he said. "But not as bad as Cocoa." Dave wondered at himself. Was he really so tired as to sound this stupid, or was he playing it up now? "Stupid," he said. But he crawled into the passenger side, put on his seatbelt, leaned the seat back and was asleep before they left the parking lot. He didn't *really* wake up until the cold winter sun was high in the sky. Dave adjusted his seat and tried to get his bearings.

"Where are we?"

"About ten miles from St. George."

"Wow, I'm sorry, Ref. You should have woke me up. Do you want me to drive?"

"At St. George. We need to stop and eat. All I had for breakfast was half a bagel, which was dumb. Like I'm really going to want the other half when we get back to school."

Dave laughed and stretched. "How's she driving?"

"Fine. I guess you know it shakes till you get past sixty."

"Yeah, weird, huh? Doesn't exactly encourage safe speeds." Dave yawned and asked, "Did you get those Twinkies?"

"No, Dave, I didn't."

"Well no wonder you're hungry."

Ref took her eyes off the road just long enough to give him a withering smile.

▥

DAVE WAS ALWAYS glad to leave Vegas behind. The freeway was always packed and crazy and he had a hard time not looking at all the signs. He asked Ref to read them to him so he could focus on not getting them killed. But the real reason he liked passing Vegas was because it meant they were almost to California, home sweet home.

It would still take the rest of the day to get to Fresno, but the rest of the drive always passed quickly for Dave. First, those crazy hills where it seemed like every five miles you pass an elevation marker – *1000 FT, 3000 FT, 5000 FT, 2000 FT*. It didn't feel like so much up and down to Dave, but who was he to argue with the wisdom of the signs? Then Baker, with the world's tallest thermometer, and a sideline through the Mad Greek's drive-thru for baklava (hard to eat while driving, but worth it), the mysterious Zzyzx Road, good ole Barstow, the super-deluxe abandoned waterpark among the Joshua trees, the Amazing Disappearing Freeway in the Middle of Nowhere (Hey! Where'd the *freeway* go? Oh, *there* it is!). Tehachapi – which was actually better to pass through at night this time of year because one of the myriad windmills would be decorated like a *Blade Runner* Christmas tree.

Of course, if you drive through at night you miss the rusted-out hulk of the *S. S. Minnow* abandoned off the side of the freeway, and you can't see the orange orchards coming into Bakersfield either, though you can still *smell* them. But then, if it were night, Visalia would be a sea of blue lights – or so it would seem from the freeway. Then the grapes of Selma (and the wrath of Louise, heehee), and before you know it, you're getting off the 99 onto Shaw and you're almost home.

Dave took the trip in his mind as they hit State Line and its Last Chance Casinos and headed for the first great uphill. "We're almost there."

Ref laughed at him. "We're almost halfway there," she said.

"You know, Ref, I don't know why, but I really like driving home."

"Wouldn't you rather fly?"

"Mm, probably. Usually. But sometimes it's good just to see all this."

"Gotta love that barren wasteland." Ref laughed again. "No, I know what you mean."

Dave looked around at the desert and smiled. It was nothing like Fresno, but it still felt like home.

TEN

Caught in the Middle

THEY HAD MADE GOOD TIME, and so even with their stops, they still pulled up at the Plantree home by five thirty. Ref stood up, laced her fingers behind her back, and stretched. Dave popped the trunk and took out her bags. "You sound like you're in pain, Ref."

She tried to stick out her tongue and yawn at the same time. The experiment wasn't a success.

Dave led the way to the door, carrying both Ref's bags, but Ref ran ahead at the end and opened the door for him.

"Ref!" squealed Marjorie née Pokey, the youngest Plantree, and she ran up and gave her sister a hug, complete with squealing. She had started high school this year and dropped the pigtails and nickname, but she still looked ten to Dave. At best.

Ref's mom came in from the kitchen, holding her hands up like they were weapons primed to go off. "Hi, honey, Dave," she said, smiling at each in turn. "I'd hug you, but I'm making caramels, and we might not be able to get apart if I did. Your dad's out getting more nutmeg and Ryan and Suzy are with him."

"Have you heard from Clipper?"

"Not for a couple weeks. His ship's headed to the Philippines. But Ref, honey, I wasn't expecting you till tomorrow. What happened?"

Ref followed her mother into the kitchen, and Marjorie approached Dave. "Have you got a girlfriend?" she asked, same as she had been asking since his sixteenth birthday.

"No."

"Sheez! You're never going to get married this way!"

Dave affected his French accent. "I em waiting for you, Marjorie, ma pet."

She blushed and he suddenly wondered if she was too old for that joke now.

"Well," she said, "you and Ref have gotta get married, and you don't even have a girlfriend yet. I bet Ref doesn't either."

"Have a girlfriend?"

"*No, a boyfriend.*"

"But – it sounded like you said –"

"*Dave! Stop it!*"

"You're right; I'm sorry. I don't think she has a boyfriend."

"You don't *think*?"

"That's right. Has Ryan got his call yet?"

"*No*, he just *sent* them."

"Oh! He did? When did that happen?"

She shrugged.

"Well, Poke –"

"Marjorie!"

"Right, what I said, Marjorie, tell everybody hi for me. I haven't talked to your dad in a long time. But I better go home and see my family." Dave walked over and stuck his head in the kitchen. "Bye, Ref. Bye, Sister Plantree."

Sister Plantree was rolling caramels and Ref was wrapping them in wax paper, twisting the ends. Sister Plantree looked up and smiled again. "Bye, Dave. You'll stop by again, won't you?"

"I imagine I will."

"Take a caramel with you."

Ref held one out and Dave took it from her and unwrapped it. "Wait – if I eat it now, can I have another?"

Sister Plantree laughed and Ref stuck out her tongue as Dave grabbed another one, tipped an imaginary hat, and raced Marjorie to the door, where she stood and waved goodbye.

<hr/>

NO ONE WAS home when Dave arrived. He found the key in the keyrock and let himself in. That no one was home wasn't too surprising. It was just after six on the nineteenth of December. School was still in session, but only barely, and they might be at a band at the high school or something. Dave went to the kitchen and started inspecting the fridge for leftovers.

"Chili? Maybe. Slimy old green salad. Some sort of casserole?" Dave sniffed it. "Hard to tell. Ooh! Potatoes au gratin! Looking good!" Dave set the potatoes on the counter and opened another container. "What in the – ? Whoa! Smelly!" Dave replaced the lid. "Moldy something. No." He put it back in the fridge.

When he finished the inspection, he pulled the chili back out and made a plate of potatoes, chili, and some mysterious chicken he hoped wouldn't kill him.

After dinner, Dave put his dishes in the dishwasher and walked over to the answering machine and recorded a new message: "Hi, this is Dave. I don't live here. But if you wanted to speak to some other Them, you've reached the right number. Oh, *boy* have you." Then he went into the living room and sat down on the couch.

The living room was not only clean, but tidy. There weren't any books or magazines out, no shoes on the floor, nothing. Weird. Dave rubbed his arms. Not much twilight was making it through the shut curtains, and Dave realized the house was cold. And that he was tired.

He walked to his room and opened the door. The conversion to a game room was in progress, but his bed was still there. He could squeeze past the ping-pong table and take the boxes off the bed and get in, go to sleep. So he did. He hadn't brought in his stuff, so he just took off his pants and got into bed. His eyes were feeling heavy when he realized he had forgotten to say his prayers, brush his teeth, wash his face, read his scriptures, write in his journal, recite the works of Dickens (no wait, don't need to do that anymore), tell himself he'll do some pushups tomorrow, update his checkbook, close the bedroom door – in fact, his entire going-to-bed routine had been blown to pieces. He was just moving from that thought, to deciding to go out and at least get his scriptures and toothbrush, when the phone rang, he fell asleep, then realized it was morning.

▥

CONSIDERING HE HAD neglected to pray for a good night's sleep for the first time in who knows how long, Dave felt very refreshed when he awoke. He decided to pray his thanks before doing anything else, but then changed his mind and put on his pants – just in case someone walked past the open door.

Dave squeezed back past the ping-pong table and walked out to say hello to his family, but no one was up. Or rather, he discovered after wandering through the house, no one was *there*. He ended up in the kitchen scratching his head and looking at nothing and wondering where everyone was. Then he noticed the blinking light on the answering machine. He punched the button.

"Hi, this is Grandma Snow! When did Dave record that new message for you? It's so cute! Anyway, I just wanted to let you know that everything is fine; Murray called and said he will be able to put you up after all. I'm just going to stay with my sister. So you come see me.

"But, I guess you've already left. Can't wait to see you all! Bye!

"Bye? Is nobody there? Okay, bye then!" Click.

Dave stared at the phone. His Uncle Murray lived in Provo. He wasn't sure where all his grandma's siblings lived, but at least two of them were also in Provo. Dave had a bad feeling. A feeling that told him his family was trying to surprise him.

Dave looked at the calendar. Under the nineteen was written "Leave for Utah." "Dave Arrives" was below the twenty-one. Dave looked at the blank day in between. "I'm caught in the middle," he said.

ELEVEN

Exactly What It Was

DAVE HAD BEEN TRYING TO call Carol or Janice or Janet or some other local who went to BYU when Carol's mom finally picked up and told him Carol and her sister had gone over to the Plantrees.

"Did Carol drive home?"

"Yes."

"Great, thanks! Merry Christmas!"

Dave hung up and the phone rang, so he picked it back up. "Hello?"

"Oh, Dave," his mother said.

"'Oh, Dave' is right," Dave replied. "Where has that kid gotten himself off to now?"

"I'm sorry."

"That's okay. I'm trying to arrange a ride back to BYU for Ref right now, then I'll drive back."

"We wanted to surprise you. We thought you were coming later."

"Well, I was. But I wanted to surprise *you*. Surprise! How's Provo?"

"Dirty! They just had one of those filthy gicky snows that makes everything feel gritty. Can you afford the drive back?"

"Well, yeah. I was going to have to drive back eventually anyway."

"Oh, Dave, I'm sorry." She sighed and Dave knew she was pulling on her perm, looking for all the world like she was inspecting for split ends, but really just feeling guilty and avoiding eye contact. His mother tended to blame things on herself. "If only I had called first!" she would likely say next.

"If only I had called first!" she said.

"It's okay, Mom, no big deal. It was a lovely drive; we stopped in Baker for baklava and looked at the brass lawn ornaments in Kramer Junction – it was fun. And since Ref's not coming back with me, I'll be able to play my music loud. Maybe I'll even buy a new album for the trip."

"You don't buy albums, Dave, you buy CDs."

Dave had known this word choice would replace her guilt with irritation.

"No, Mom. An album is a collection of songs, by an artist, arranged artistically. It has nothing to do with the recording technology."

"Dave, you always say that, but it's not true, as you well know. An album is the same thing as saying a vinyl record. They're synonymous. I don't know why you always do this."

"Filial piety, I imagine." Dave laughed, although frankly even he knew it didn't qualify as a joke. "Well, Mom, tell Uncle Murray hello for me." She said she would and he said he'd see her tomorrow.

DAVE KNOCKED AND voices yelled "Come in!" so he did. Ref was standing by the front door and she threw an arm around Dave as he came in and squeezed his shoulders.

"Hey, Dave. I was wondering when you would show up. I was starting to think you thought you needed a special invitation. Carol's here." She gestured and Dave could see Carol and her sister coming from across the room, though he had to look through Ref's family and their 457 closest friends to do so.

"I know. I actually kind of came to see her."

"Well! I never! Is this where I get jealous and stamp my feet?"

"Hey, what about me?" Marjorie glared at her sister – rather inexplicably, Dave thought.

"Okay, okay. You be the jealous one, Pokey. Stamp away."

She blushed. "Don't call me that," she said and ran from the room, into the kitchen.

Carol and her sister arrived. "Hey, Dave. Why don't we ever see you out at the Y?"

Dave shrugged. "Because you live south of campus?"

"Lame reason."

"Hey, can I talk to you three real quick?"

"Sure, Dave," Carol said. "What's up?"

"Guess where my family is right now?"

They shrugged and looked politely attentive.

"Provo. They're in Provo."

No one was quite sure what to say.

"Wait, wait," tried Carol's sister. "I learned about this in freshman english. That's *irony*, right?"

That's exactly what it was.

"Anyway, I wanted to ask if you two could give Ref and her cute little bags a ride back to school."

Carol nodded. "Yeah," she said, turning to her sister. "We should have room, right?"

"Sure. Unless Mom gets us that treadmill. Which she's not going to do."

"Thanks," Dave said. "Sorry for ... whatever this is."

"No," Carol said, "it's fine."

Ref smiled at Carol, then frowned at Dave. "Hey, Dave, will you come with me for a second?" Ref grabbed his arm and led him down the hall, just past the bathroom. "Dave, you should be gone. I could've taken care of a ride."

"Yessss . . ." This had not occurred to Dave.

"Yes, what?"

"I guess I felt responsible?"

"For what, your parents being sneaky?"

"I don't know exactly."

"Exactly." Ref leaned against a wall. "Anyway, thanks, Dave. I appreciate it."

"You're welcome. You're right, too. I should be gone already."

"Yeah." Ref straightened up and looked at Dave. "I'm sorry you have to go."

"Me too. But at least I'll be chuckling all the way to Utah."

"Yeah, but –" Ref looked at Dave's breast pocket as if trying to read the fine print. "How weird."

Dave tried to look down at his chest. "What?"

Ref raised her eyes and wiggled her head. "Nothing. Just – hum. I'm just bummed you're leaving."

"Well, thanks, Ref. I'll miss you too." Dave leaned in for half a hug, but she offered her hand instead. He shook it.

"I'll miss you," she said, as if that emotion was akin to discovering Tutankhamen's tomb.

Dave laughed. "I'll miss you too, but I want to hit the road before nightfall. Besides, it sounds like they need a Referee out there."

Dave wasn't kidding. The dark hall they stood in gave an illusion of quiet, but somewhere in the background, the unseen hordes were laughing and whooping it up. It sounded about sixteen seconds from full-out riot.

"Right."

They abandoned the hallway and Dave started goodbying everyone. It actually only took a couple loud ones to do the job, but fielding the return goodbyes took minute after minute after minute.

"You know, Dave," said Sister Plantree, "you wouldn't have to go if you were part of the family."

"I know! I keep saying you should adopt me."

"There are other ways to be part of our family, you know."

"Sure, but I can hardly afford to adopt all of you. Maybe Pokey. I bet she doesn't eat much."

"You might be surprised," said Sister Plantree over a squeal from across the room.

"Don't call me that!"

"Sorry!" Dave laughed. "And tell your truant husband I was here –" Dave checked his watch "– oh man, almost an hour, so it's his own fault he missed me."

Sister Plantree agreed and hugged him and Dave walked to the door where Ref and Carol were standing.

"Thanks, Carol, for giving Ref a ride back. I know she can be a handful. Just remember the magic word."

Carol narrowed her eyes after the manner of those who hold deep suspicions as to the validity of magic. "Sure. And what might the magic word be?"

"'No, Ref! No!'" Dave cracked himself and no one else up. "I guess that's more of a phrase, really." He smiled in apology. "Anyway, gotta go." He winked and he and Ref walked outside.

"So you're leaving now?"

"I got to run home first; I left my toothpaste and scriptures there which is really funny for reasons I won't tell you or you'll lose all respect for me."

"Oh, I doubt that."

"Yeah, I figured it was too late." Dave unlocked his door and opened it. Ref stood on the other side, as if waiting for him to unlock her door. "Well, I'll see you, Ref."

"Yeah." Ref tilted her head and looked at Dave in a way that made him feel like a rare, perhaps previously undiscovered sort of bird.

"What is it?"

"I'm just – I don't know." She shot herself in the head with her finger. "I'll see you next year, okay?"

"Okay." Dave smiled. "I was planning on witnessing the new year's arrival with you, but I'm sure it'll come anyway."

"I hope so. Anyway, Mom said the stake's having a New Year's Eve dance, so I'll probably go to that. Next time you see me I'll be hopelessly in love."

"Uh-huh. I have this great thing I should e-mail you. It's for guys, but you might like it."

Ref slowly walked around the car, then renewed the bruise in his arm.

"*Aaooch.*" Dave rubbed his arm. "Hey! That was premeditated!"

"Whoops."

"You keep saying you're going to stop doing that."

"Forgot."

"You've been forgetting off and on for years now."

Ref wrinkled her nose at his frown and gave him a hug.

"Oh, so there's more to being your best friend than just getting hit now and then?"

Ref held on a little longer, then took a step back. "I thought Curses was your best friend."

"What, that crazy Texan? No way. I like people with nice normal names like Referee."

Ref nodded and looked at him like she was reading the classifieds. Maybe all the classifieds. Maybe the classifieds and the personals as well. And the financial report. It made Dave nervous and he cleared his throat.

Ref blinked and walked back to the curb. She waved a hand. "See you later, Dave."

He waved back and laughed at her. "Bye."

He got in his car and with a final wave drove away from the sunset.

TWELVE

Too Many Mormons

STRANGELY, IT FELT GOOD TO be back in Provo. Dave hated Provo. Or, more accurately, he liked a lot of other places better. For one thing, there were too many Mormons in Provo. A weird thing for a Mormon to feel, Dave knew, but he couldn't help it. Of his Provo acquaintances, only one and a half weren't LDS, and that made Dave feel slightly useless. Saints love everyone, but Dave didn't feel he had much opportunity to work on that in Utah.

Also, Dave thought as he slammed on his brakes as a late-model Cherokee ignored a stop sign and pulled in front of him, these people can't drive. Dave would take LA over Provo any day. You might never *get* any-where in LA, but at least you'd be nowhere *and alive*. Dave preferred San Francisco over Utah cosmopolia, too. He even preferred the Silicon Valley's driving, and that was saying a lot.

"Crazy Utahns," Dave said, and immediately repented. He had once broken down in Cedar City and had spent the day walking around that fair city and being amazed at how courteous their drivers were. "For all I know," Dave humbly admitted, "Cedarians are the norm and Provofolk are a weird (and unfortunate) aberration." Besides, Dave's mom was a Utah girl, and most of her family still lived within a couple hours of Happy Valley.

But whatever the reason, he was glad to be back. It felt weirdly like home.

Dave had driven straight through and wasn't sure if he should go home and sleep and make everyone worry or go on over to Uncle Murray's for love and attention and noise and somnambulism. Then he missed the Center Street exit, and since his apartment was now much closer than his uncle's house, he decided to go to his apartment and call his mom's cell phone (which would probably be turned off) and tell her he was taking a nap. That way he couldn't be talked into coming over, but when she started freaking out, she would immediately be able to dip into the cooling well of Don't Worry Mom I'm Fine. It was a good plan.

Except Curses was at the apartment with a napping two-year-old and a crying baby so his sisters and their husbands could go with his parents to dinner and the temple. Who knew thirteen pounds could make so much noise?

"Daaaaaaaave," said Curses, when Dave walked through the door. "What are you doing here?"

"Funny thing: my family is in Provo."

"That *is* funny. And it also explains why they hung up on me when I said you'd already left." Curses stood from the couch and started bouncing his knees. "These baby things are loud. So, whatcha been doing?"

Dave gave Curses an overview of his vacation so far, and Curses gave him an overview of his vacation so far. "And so here I am, stuck with Esmerelda's budding opera singer," it finished. "But at least *she's* adorable," he added, pointing to the sleeper.

Dave excused himself to leave a voice mail for his mom and to attempt a nap. He lay in bed and stared at the ceiling. He lay that way a long time, desperately tired, not the least bit sleepy, listening to the baby turn off and on. The ceiling never got any more interesting, so he finally sighed and sat up. He put on his shoes, then stood and left the room, heading for the front room where Curses was on the couch, burping the baby.

"I love being encouraged to encourage an impressionable young mind to make impolite noises," said Curses. "Tell me how jealous you are."

"My jealousy knows no bounds. I can't sleep."

"Bet the baby can."

"Lucky baby."

"Please. It's not all so rhapsodic. I mean, the kid's got to sit in her own crap all day. Well, unless someone changes her diaper. But maybe that's my point."

"I'm not sure rhapsodic was the adjective I was going for."

"What then?"

Dave shrugged. "Babiriffic?"

"No."

Dave sat down on the couch, projectile distance away from Curses, and stared at the wall. "I guess I'll just go over to my uncle's."

"Banana grove?"

"No, Curses, his house."

"Oh. I should have guessed." Curses looked down at the baby now sleeping in his arms. "I feel strangely domestic."

"Women's lib has hardly touched you."

"You know, I have a lot of these niece and nephew things, but each one's still amazing."

"Mm." Dave had his doubts about babies. Even young children were suspect. He could accept ten-year-olds okay, but eight was iffy and six-year-olds were downright mythological. And yet, here was a baby, right here. And a toddler, right there. Amazing. And real. "Ex nihilo est absurdum," he said in a game attempt at Latin.

"Yeah," Curses agreed. "Yeah."

DAVE SHOWED UP at his Uncle Murray's before anyone thought to worry about him. The place was in a state of utter chaos – nihilo would have been an improvement. ("Be nice," Dave reminded himself.) Uncle Murray's sixty or so daughters behaved like excitable nuclear particles at the best of times, but the presence of the Thems seemed to release megajoules of hitherto unimagined energy. Any agnosticism Dave retained as to the reality of children encountered a barrage of hard physical evidence. "Stalky hairless birds?" one might try – and the resemblance was inarguable – but one would be fooling oneself. And not even that so well.

Uncle Murray was always difficult for Dave to describe without falling into Santa Claus imagery. He had no beard, but he was round and jolly and when he laughed (a robust ho-ho-ho-type thing), he shook very much like a bowl full of jelly. When Dave was a kid he had suspected the real Santa had a fake beard and lived not at the North Pole but in Utah and was actually Uncle Murray. He still had his suspicions.

Dave's mom came to meet him at the door. Her recently degrayed hair struggled to frame a face featuring a lipstick job that could generously be described as skiddywompous. Orbiting her like electrons from a fifties textbook were three of Uncle Murray's daughters – eight, ten, and sixteen, but they all looked the same age, more or less. In fact, except for his oldest daughter, now on a mission, all of Uncle "It's a Girl!" Murray's daughters looked barely the age of accountability. These three had makeovers matching his mother's and giggles reminiscent of a herd of angry buffalo on helium.

"Hi, Mom."

She hugged him, noted the bags under his eyes, whispered a Utah joke into his ear, and led him into the living room, which was overrun with immature estrogen. Somewhere through the hormone haze, Dave saw his father and uncle sitting on worn orange velour recliners, talking.

Dave tiptoed his way over Barbies and tea sets and plastic ponies and gave his dad a hug, shook his uncle's hand, fielded a couple of apologies, and escaped to find his sister.

Dave liked to pretend he had a hard time remembering he was the oldest in his family. Everything he read about birth order suggested to him that he was the one with the characteristics of the middle child and his brother Tom was more like an oldest. Tom was on a mission in Serbia now, which meant no more Tom Thumb jokes for two years and perhaps even no pronunciation confusion in Slavic languages, who knows? Also, no more arguments on how best to shorten Thomas. Dave always said he should keep the *H*, because Thom Them maximized symmetry, humor, and confusion. But Tom was very much the no-nonsense type of person, and the no-*H* type of Tom.

What there was no doubt of was who was the youngest. And that would be Julie, a mere fourteen, if disturbingly womanly in appearance.

Which was why it relieved Dave to find her on the swings, surrounded on the ground by a gaggle of little girls in coats as she went back and forth and back and "Dave!"

She leapt from the swing and ran over and gave him a big hug. "I'm so glad you made it," she said.

"Well, I took the scenic route from my apartment. You know, California."

Julie laughed and playfully grabbed the bruise Ref had left on his arm, then leaned against him. The other girls took over the swing set and Dave and Julie watched them swing back and forth, back and forth. Back and forth. Back and forth.

Back and forth.

"Dave?"

"Huh? What? Sorry," he said, rubbing his eyes with one hand. "Tired."

Julie nodded and led him into the house and into a back bedroom where she pointed out a floor mat and a couple pillows under a crib. "Naptime," she said. "I'll put up the Do Not Disturb sign. It's, um, sacrosanct. Which was the only word I spelled wrong on that stupid vocab test. Did you have Ms. Blackwelder?"

"You know I did."

"Well, I hate her. Sacrosanct. That's not even a real word."

"You just used it, didn't you?"

"I was being *sarcastic*, Dave."

"Right."

He climbed on his hands and knees, then realized he was still too tall. So he took off his shoes and lay on his back and scooted under the crib like he was about to check out its pesky oil leak.

"'Night, Dave," said Julie. "Do you want me to wake you for games?"

Dave shifted in the Kix crumbs and thought about Uncle Murray's peculiarly democratic version of Trivial Pursuit. Or the way Aunt Wilhelmina always freaked out when she had to take her Chance in Yahtzee. Or the way sixty thousand girls can react to a competitive game of charades. All of which, Dave had to admit, was a lot more fun than it sounded.

He fluffed up the faded She-Ra pillow and said, "Yes. Of course."

But when she woke him he fell right back and slept through to the ice cream: big tubs of vanilla with sprinkles and syrups and nonpareils and marshmallows on the side. And, judging from one little girl's bowl from across the room, Flintstone vitamins? Dave turned away – just in time to see another little girl spooning on the brown sugar.

"Brown sugar!" Dave surprised himself by saying it aloud. He could remember doing that. Gross. He watched her and remembered. Gross. Maybe children were real after all.

Gross.

TWENTY-FIVE LINES BEFORE SLEEP

by that guy we call Dave

1. *I enjoy spaghetti*
2. *Tell me when it's ready*
3. *I enjoy linguini*
4. *So pass it you big meanie*
5. *And now for something completely different:*
6. *Fish!*
7. *Thank you Salvador Dali*
8. *I once had a sister named Julie*
9. *Whose growth spurts were rather unruly*
10. *She looks all grown up*
11. *Though she's just a young pup*
12. *Get close and I'll clock ya, ya bully*
13. *Halfway point*
14. *Beware the jabberwock, my son,*
15. *His grading's harsh, his finals long*
16. *He gives out papers, calls it fun,*
17. *Tell me, don't you find that wrong?*
18. *Beware the jabberwock, my son,*
19. *Next semester he's teaching American Heritage*
20. *Five!*
21. *Four!*
22. *And now a haiku:*
23. *A thousand blonde girls*
24. *Tadpoles erratically swim*
25. *Fueled by brown sugar*

THIRTEEN

Time Immemorial

THE THEMS HAD AN UNOFFICIAL tradition held all day December 23, Joseph Smith's birthday: Christmas shopping. This year, Dave took his sister to one mall while their parents went to another. Dave finished his shopping in under an hour, including a present for himself – *Three Men in a Boat* – then parked himself on a bench and started to read his present.

Dave had to go buy himself another present – a Discworld book – that afternoon and was almost half done when Julie found him and was ready to go home. She was carrying fewer and smaller bags than Dave was.

"Are you done?"

"Yep."

"You know," Dave said, "I hate to stoop to gender stereotyping, but I was done by ten and the girl took all day."

"Huh. Interesting." Julie rolled her eyes, much as you might expect a fourteen-year-old girl to do in this situation. "But –" and here Julie stuck out her tongue – "I'm the only one who collected phone numbers from six different college boys."

Dave frowned at her and shook his head and was really glad he was just Julie's brother and not her parent.

Any Christmas Eve traditions the Thems might have normally enjoyed were swallowed up by the traditions of the Murray and Wilhelmina Snow family. Which was fine, actually; it was all very Christ-centered, which Dave appreciated, but when, in classic Book-of-Mormon-Christmas-style, the wicked Nephite Barbies were preparing to slay all the righteous Nephite Barbies if the sign didn't appear, Dave excused himself to use the kitchen phone.

He dialed the number then hung up. No sense Uncle Murray getting charged for this. He dialed up his phone card, then punched in the number again.

"Hello?"

"Agent Pokey, this is Q9-47. How goes Operation Merry Christmas?"

"Hi, Dave. My name is Marjorie."

"Oh great, Marge, thanks. You just blew both our covers over an open phone line. Thanks a lot. Is your sister there?"

"Hang on."

Dave heard her calling Suzy.

"Hello?"

"Hi, Suzy; Dave here. Is *your* sister there?"

"Of course, you were just talking to her."

"Ref."

"No. She and Carol went with my mom and some people to go caroling. Wait. That's funny. Carol. Caroling. Get it?"

"I do. Did you come up with that yourself?"

"Shut up, Dave. The point is she's not here."

Dave could hear Luke's nativity starting from the other room. He hoped against hope no Barbies were involved. "Well, Suze, tell Ref that I –"

"Hang on, Dave. My dad wants to talk to you."

"Oh, good. That'll work."

"Hello?"

"Hello."

"Hello. Dear me, is this David?"

"It sure is. And whom do I have the pleasure of addressing?"

"This is Brother Plantree, Dave. How are you?"

"Oh, I'm good. You?"

"Fine, fine." Brother Plantree cleared his throat – his let's-talk-about-state-politics throat clearing, not the let's-order-a-pizza one. "I'm sorry I missed you while you were here – wait – you are gone now, right?"

"Gone as can be. I'm sorry I didn't see you, too."

"Me too, me too."

Dave really was sorry. Besides being his best friend's father, Brother Plantree had always been a good friend himself. Once, after Ref had gone to BYU, Dave and Brother Plantree had taken the Boy Scouts up to Shasta Lake together. It was a miracle they had survived the Scouts' brilliant (if misguided) Flaming Mosquito Brigade. And since the first grade Dave had viewed the Plantrees' home as a dinner refuge, when his mom's zucchini started coming en masse.

"So they just up and left, surprise-style, eh?"

"Yeah, apparently." Dave sat down at the kitchen table and wondered at the chorus of laughter coming from the other room. "They sure got me."

"There's a fine line between showing love and being sneaky. If there's a line at all."

"Sure." Dave hoped this was an appropriate response.

"Martha tells me you've acclimatized well to BYU this year."

Martha? It took Dave a second to realize who he meant. He'd only ever heard him call her Referee as long as Dave could remember. Same as everyone else.

"Didn't I tell you you'd like it better than Berkeley?"

"You did."

"And you do?"

"I guess we'll never know."

"What?"

"Well, I've never attended Berkeley, so it's hard to compare."

"Oh, I'm sure you like BYU better, Dave."

"You may be right."

"Oh, I am. Dave."

"I'll take your word on it."

"You do that."

Dave tried to figure out who he was talking to. It wasn't Dinner Host Brother Plantree. It wasn't Scout Leader Brother Plantree. It wasn't Manic Sports Fan Brother Plantree. Even Stake Executive Secretary Brother Plantree had told a joke when Dave came in for his Melchizedek Priesthood interview. Who was this guy?

Dave realized the phone had been silent for quite a long time and suddenly felt a need to fill the silence. "Um, thank you." He waited. "Brother Plantree?"

"Oh, yeah. Sorry. Look, Dave." Brother Plantree cleared his throat. "So . . . when does the new semester start?"

"January third, I think"

"The third! So soon! How was your mission?"

"My mission? It was fine . . ."

"Oh good, good. Look, Dave, let's see, look, I was wondering . . ."

"Yes?" Dave heard a sound vaguely like hyperventilating and vaguely like rubber bands shooting, but no words. "Go on."

"You know my daughter?"

"Marjorie?"

"No, not Marjorie." Brother Plantree paused. "Haha!"

Dave waited, then offered: "Oh! You mean Referee!"

"Yes! That's the one! That's the one! You know her, right?"

For some reason, the old photograph of Dave kissing Ref at her fourth birthday party jumped into his head. Did he know her?

"I do."

"Good, good. She's my daughter, you know."

"Yes." This was getting too weird.

Brother Plantree took a deep breath that sounded like a radio sound effect. "Well, whenyouseeherIF! I mean *if*! When the semester starts, *if* you see her – why don't you ask her out?"

Dave was dumbfounded. The fact that Brother Plantree had to know that Dave and "Martha" had been hanging out all year made the request seem not just odd but redundant. Go out with her? Of course he would! Every week! They'd been hanging out together since time immemorial, and he thinks that's suddenly going to change? Dave looked down at the telephone receiver in his hand and raised it back to his ear. "Okay," he said.

"Oh, great, great, great. Great. Thank you."

"Sure. I'm glad we had this talk. We'll have to do it again sometime. Thanks."

"No, no, no! Thank *you*, Mr. Them!"

"Um. You're welcome." Dave hung up the phone but continued standing by it for several long minutes, head cocked, eyebrows pushed down over his eyes. When he finally shook his head and turned to leave the room, all he could think was that Fresno was not any saner than Provo after all.

FOURTEEN

A Very Byucky Christmas

ONLY FOR THE GREATER GOOD had Dave allowed himself to be talked into camping out in the same room as the Christmas tree. It certainly wasn't for his own peaceful slumber. At a quarter to five by the Santa clock over his head, the youngest five Snow girls jumped on him and screamed "Merry Christmas!" as if being awoken by girly screams was the merriest thing in the world.

I have an attitude problem, Dave realized, so he grabbed a cousin over each shoulder and ran them around the room, yelling something about the Christmas Ogre Who Eats Little Girls, then he dropped them on the couch and they all laughed together.

Better, thought Dave.

By the time a quarter past five rolled around everyone was up and Uncle Murray was ready to give some opening remarks.

"Merry Christmas," he said, and the girls cheered. "Of course, what with the pagans and everything, Christmas isn't really held on Christ*mas,* which I guess must mean birthday or something, but even so, it doesn't hurt to take a moment even in winter to remember why somebody started Christmas in the first place long, long ago." Uncle Murray smiled and pointed to the much-glued ceramic nativity set on the piano. "Two thousand years ago, the Son of Man showed up so we would all be nice to one another and not steal or lie or cheat –"

"Or kill anybody," said the little blonde-haired cousin with her head on Dave's left shoulder.

"That's right, Mary, or kill anybody. But he knew we'd make mistakes. So do you know what he did?"

"He died," said another cousin.

"So we can repent," said another.

"That's right," Uncle Murray said. "And that includes?"

"Grandma," the girls chorused sadly.

"That's right. She's coming at noon, remember. And that's what Christmas is all about. So the least we can do now is be nice to each other." The girls nodded but were looking at the tree. "Well," Uncle Murray asked, "should we have breakfast now?"

"No!" chorused the girls.

"But what else is there?"

"Presents!"

"Presents?"

"Yes!"

Dave had a feeling this catechism was part of the sacred Snow tradition.

"Okay, then." Uncle Murray paused for dramatic effect. "Presents!"

The girls leapt for them, but instead of a flurry of unwrapping paper, as Dave had expected, he realized each girl was not grabbing the presents *to* her, but *from* her. It took him a while to figure this out. Then, when everyone had the presents they were giving, they gave. And another little girl would say thank you. Then they all had the presents *to* them. The whole thing made Dave feel a little dizzy.

"*Daaaddy! Daaaddy! Daaaddy! Daaaddy! Daaaddy!*" the girls began chanting. Uncle Murray approached Aunt Wilhelmina, closer, closer; the chanting got louder and faster and more frenetic. Then he kissed her and the unwrapping began, madcap, like a zillion angry butterflies. Dave watched all this and tried to imagine how such a tradition ever got started. He auditioned a number of possible scenarios, each more ludicrous than the last.

"Dave!" Julie sat down next to him. "This is for you." She handed him a boot box–sized package wrapped in yellow candy-cane paper.

"Thanks, Julie. Yours is under the tree somewhere. I hope." Dave ripped the paper off slowly but not carefully. Then held up a box with a pasted-on photo of, apparently, a gumball machine. But the type said Used Bubble Gum Receptacle. "You've got to be kidding me."

"Funny, huh."

Dave looked at her. "Where did you *find* this?"

She shrugged. "The mall. It says it comes with a booklet thing telling you what you can do with all the used gum."

"But I don't chew gum."

"I know. That's why I got you this." And she handed him a pack of Juicy

Fruit. "That's why I had to go with Dad last night when he was buying Cool Whip."

"Thanks."

"Now, next year I want to see some, I don't know, bubble-gum swans or something. I'm gonna go get your present to me, okay?"

"Sure. Get Mom and Dad theirs too."

Julie distributed the rest of the Them presentry and Dave set to checking out his haul.

His dad had given him a bicycle repair kit, apparently for the bicycle he'd wrecked right after getting off his mission and was now sitting in his parents' garage desperately requiring the repair a bicycle repairman with this very kit could give it. If that bicycle repairman were in Fresno.

Bicycle Repairman!

There were sixteen packages from his mother, nine of which, he could tell without opening, were funny-looking pairs of dress socks. Pink stripes, that sort of thing. Dave smiled. If there was anything his mother knew it was how to make her oldest son happy. With nine new pairs, Dave would never have to feel shy about crossing his legs in church again. He set them aside, preferring to save the thrill of first sight for one Sunday morning at a time.

The other seven gifts proved to be subtle hints to get married. A John Bytheway tape, presumably about why being single is, like, totally lame – and funny! A box of cologne samples. A twelve-pack of normal black "church" socks. Dave went through them quickly and set them on top of the bicycle repair kit, with the unopened nine by the side of the couch.

Dave looked over at his parents. His dad was setting aside Dave's present of *60 Sexy Sandwiches* and *Tie Your Own Fly You Nimrod You*. It wasn't a very good present, Dave knew, and Dave couldn't even be sure his dad would remember the time he mysteriously told Dave "Fly fishing's for sandwich makers," but *Dave* remembered. Besides, he had included a gift receipt so he could exchange them for something he would like – *Primary Causes of Death in Argentinean Agricultural Accidents, 1845–1859; Proper Wearing of the Kilt; Davey Jones' Locker: Lost Pirate Treasure Since 1975*; or something else equally unpredictable. Dave had tried buying books his dad would like, but there was just no telling. He remembered when he was Julie's age, getting his dad *The Pictorial History of the Modern Submarine* for his birthday and thinking it was a real winner, then not even getting a smile. At least this way Dad reacted. And it was more personalized than a gift certificate. Dave put a lot of thought into picking out the books his dad would like least.

His mom was already laughing as she thumbed through *The Big Book of Utah Jokes* he'd given her, and Dave was glad she'd be back in California soon. As long as he could remember, she'd told at least one Utah joke a day, and most of them he was pretty sure she'd made up. Example: How do you tell a Utahn from an ear of corn? You can't! They're both too corny! Dave was never sure if she told them because she missed Utah or because she was glad to be gone.

"What is this?" Julie sat down again.

"A book."

"Well, duh. I mean, it's a journal, right?"

"Right."

"Oh." Julie considered this. "Thanks, but a journal isn't very funny. I thought you'd get me something funny."

"Oh, I did."

"Really? What?"

Dave pulled a little black plastic box with a red button out of his pocket and showed it to her. She took it from him. "What is it?" She turned it upside down then back. She pushed the button and a horrible sound made everyone turn and look. "Julie!" Dave said. Julie blushed. The Snow girls giggled and turned away.

Dave leaned into Julie and whispered, "Now you have something to write about."

"Jerk." But she laughed.

⛩

DAVE WALKED DOWN the street from Uncle Murray's house and watched the sun setting. Or rather, the clouds, suddenly pink and orange. "Clouds make sunsets spectacular," Ref had once told him, which reminded him why he was out in the street in the first place. He bit the middle finger of his right-hand glove and pulled it off. He fished his mom's cell phone out of his pocket with the other hand and punched in the Plantrees' number. Then he switched the glove for the phone's antennae in his mouth and tried to get his glove back on before anyone answered.

"Hello?"

"Do'nang uh!" Dave yelled.

"What?"

Dave pulled the phone out of his mouth. "Hi, it's Dave."

"Hi, Dave," said Ref. "I was hoping you'd call. How's Christmas?"

"Madness. Fun, but madness. Girls everywhere."

"Girls, huh? Well, I'm glad you don't have to miss me too much."

"Are you kidding? Ref, you are no mere girl; you are an oomahn. In fact, I even wrote a song for you."

A pause on the other end, then, "Really?"

"Yeah, but don't go thinking it'll make your day or anything."

"Okay."

Dave put on his lounge lizard voice. "Awright, shweetheart, this little number's coming to you all the way from Provo, home of the BYU Cooougars. Hit it, boys.

> *Have yourself a very byucky Christmas.*
> *Make your yuletide byuck.*
> *From now on, your troubles will be out of byuuuuck!*
> *And have yourself a very byucky Christmas now."*

Ref laughed. "Oh, Dave. It's better than I imagined."

"Well then, I'd say you need a better imagination."

▓▓▓

DAVE ARRIVED AT his apartment at a quarter to midnight. On the porch were the still-smoking remains of long-stemmed roses, evidence that someone angry and passive-aggressive didn't know Peter was out of town. Dave kicked them aside, unlocked the door and had just finished closing it behind him when he heard someone yelling, "Hey!" He reopened the door and there stood Curses.

"Sheesh, Dave! Didn't you hear me running up the stairs after you?"

"Nope. Merry Christmas?"

"Yeah, I suppose. This makes nine years running I didn't get any toys though. I'm starting to think no one loves me."

"You should go through the Wish Book and make a list of everything you want and their page numbers."

"They don't publish the Wish Book anymore."

"Oh. I'm sorry."

"What about you?" Curses asked.

"My sister gave me a prechewed bubblegum holder."

"Serious?"

"It looks like a penny machine."

"But it holds ABC gum?"

"Yes. Precisely."

"Why?"

"Arts and Crafts."

"Serious?"

"Best I can tell."

Curses took off his coat. "It's cold in here."

"Yeah. I'm going to brush my teeth then go to bed." Dave took off his coat as well and they both threw their coats on the couch. "Hopefully by the time I'm done with my scriptures and chronicling the day, it'll be warm enough to sleep in."

Curses yawned. "When's your family leaving?"

"Day after tomorrow."

"My parents and everybody are flying back tomorrow. My sister's taking them to the airport. My brother Blight's supposed to pick them up. His family held off on Christmas for Grandma and Grandpa. Those kids must be going insane."

"I would've assumed they already are."

"Oh, likely. But postponing Christmas morning till Boxing afternoon – that'd push even me over the edge."

"Too late." Dave laughed. "Or is that what did it to you?"

"You'll have to ask the bodies buried in the basement."

"But dead men tell no tales."

"Well, there you go then."

Dave rubbed his teeth with his tongue and could tell they were still under attack from a full day of Christmas candy. "Well, I'm brushing."

Curses nodded. "You certainly are."

OLAI, CURSES

Hi. I'm Curses Olai (co452) from San Antonio (not the one in Chile or any nation other than my Lone Star home. Yeah. Texas. Don't mess.)

I'm here at BYU as part of a family tradition started by several of my elder brothers and sisters (I'm tenth of twelve: bgbgbgbgbbbg – or possibly gbbgbgbgbbbg [long story involving twins, fathers, and hospital records]). I'm majoring in communications, which is reasonably cool and I, at this moment, hope to produce cable television, which would be a better career than sinusologist. Yeah, I may not be rich or famous, but I'll supply the crap that'll make other people rich and famous and that's saying something.

I met Dave last, what? January? We were in physical science together, him because of some GE screw-up, me because I was barely not a freshman anymore. Speaking of Dave, I suppose it's only fair I tell you this straight up: he writes crap like this (pulled from our trash can this very night):

WHAT A BRUSHING YOUNG MAN
by david them

Everywhere Jameson went, folks said, "My! How brushing!" And Jameson couldn't deny it. He certainly was a brushing young man.
The end.

Just so you know, I didn't put him up to it. And I'm going to stop encouraging him.

FIFTEEN

Plantree Hug

DAVE WAS UNUSUALLY PLEASED TO be welcoming a new semester into the world. Part of that may have been that he had finally gotten that Isaiah class to fit into his schedule, and part may have been that he had three classes in a row in one room, which meant a record low amount of walking over the next fourteen weeks, but mostly he realized it was because Ref was back.

Funny, because, frankly, he hadn't missed her much the year she went to BYU, at all during the two years of his mission, or the year after as he finished up at Fresno Community College. In fact, Dave had hardly talked to her between high school graduation and arriving at BYU, and now he was missing her. I suppose missing is the sign of a good friend, Dave thought, then forgot all about it because he noticed on his bookstore receipt that he had been charged twice for the twenty-pound *Brief History of the English Language*. He was sure he would have noticed had he just carried two copies of that thing home.

School started on a Tuesday and Ref had arrived in Provo with Carol and Carol's sister at one o'clock that morning. Ref managed to make appearances in both her classes that day but, as she put it, "I wasn't *there* there."

"Right," Dave said, "but you must have some idea if it'll be a good semester."

"What I want to know," said Curses, "is why skateboarding is always viewed as being on the fringe. I mean, why don't jocks board?"

"That has nothing to do with anything, Curses," said Dave.

"I know, I know, I was just thinking about that on my way home. Sorry. I need some sausage." Curses walked into the kitchen.

Ref yawned. "I'm tired, Dave. Will you give me a ride home?"

"All the way across the street? Sure, but you're going to have to pay for gas."

"I've been up over twenty-four hours, Dave."

"Yeah, I know. I did it too when I came back. Sometimes I think someone ought to invent a building that you could, like, sleep in. You know, to break up your trips into more manageable sizes. They'd make a killing."

"Well, Dave, such a hotelopia wouldn't have saved me from Carol's last-minute rush. And if we'd stopped, we'd still be en route."

"Crazy Carol."

"Crazy Carol."

"Shall we go?" Dave asked.

For an answer, Ref stood up.

Then Dave smelled the sausages and stood up too.

#

DAVE HAD PARKED below Ref's apartment, but they were still laughing and yelling "Go Dogs!" at each other.

"Go Dogs!"

"Go Dogs!"

"Go Dogs!"

"Go Dogs!"

"Go Dogs!"

They were reliving old Fresno State Red Wave memories, attending games on campus with Ref's dad. They remembered Ron Cox hitting quarterback after quarterback, and they remembered Trent Dilfer leading the Bulldogs to Freedom and Aloha. They remembered Dave's very first game, when Kevin Sweeney passed that incredible touchdown after nearly being sacked for a loss, and Dave getting sandwiched in a giant jumping-up-and-down Plantree hug.

"You know, Ref," Dave said, calming down a little, "I have never enjoyed sports unless there was a Plantree involved."

"Well, lacrosse season is starting soon. You'll be there, right?"

"Every game."

"Good. Go Cougs!" Ref yawned. "You know, I am pretty tired." She yawned again, which made Dave yawn, which made her yawn. "Thanks for the ride." Ref opened the door partway and stuck one foot out. "I loved it," she said. She pulled herself out, then closed the door and walked up the stairs to her apartment, one step at a time.

THE MEMOIRS OF DAVID THEM: THE RED WAVE

My first ticket to a sports event played by people older than twelve was paid for by Ref's dad. The three of us went to see Fresno State play football – against Washington, I think, because I have always viewed them as the Ultimate Enemy, and I don't know why else I might feel that way.

We were pretty high up in the stadium (which was more fun for a second grader anyway) and Ref's dad bought us hot dogs and soda. It was early afternoon, early fall, and early on in the game it was evident I had no sense of football whatsoever. They took turns trying to explain the rules, and by the end I had a working knowledge of the two Fresno quarterbacks' different styles and how much it would suck to be a lineman. And where the bathrooms were. Sixty-four ounces of sugar water has a way of passing through a boy.

That first game was the start of a long tradition. Whenever Brother Plantree's work buddy didn't need one of his tickets, little David Them got to attend a game. My mother let me spraypaint an old pair of slacks with holes in the knees red, and I got my own hat with the Bulldog on it. And the pants and hat weren't just for football either – the three of us did basketball, baseball, water polo, and every single women's sport the Bulldogs played.

We, by which I mean Ref and Dave only, had played sports together too when we were little – t-ball, soccer, and so forth – but I got tired of it. Once I realized the only part of playing sports I liked was getting a Capri-Sun after it was over, I started complaining till my parents said I could quit.

But I didn't quit going. I liked cheering. So I went and cheered for Ref. Every game, so long as I wasn't sick or we weren't on vacation. All the way through high school.

But that sounds like another entry for another day.

The point of this one is, Go Dogs!

SIXTEEN

The Ring of Revelation

"JUST BECAUSE SOMETHING IS URGENT does not make it an emergency. This," Dave said, because he knew Curses would never get it through his thick Texan skull if he didn't repeat himself several times, "is not an emergency."

"Not an emergency?"

"Right. It's not even urgent, really. And even if it was, it still wouldn't be an emergency."

Curses nodded. "I guess that makes sense. If it were a real emergency Ref would have been here, right?"

"Perhaps. But lacrosse is in full swing right now. They're traveling to Vegas this weekend."

"She's left us for a bunch of women in hockey gear."

"It's not as bad as all that." Dave pulled a stack – a small stack – an *embarrassingly* small stack – of papers off the top of the TV. "This is all we have thus far for *Byuck: A Rock Opera*," he said. "Three halves of songs, a couple paragraphs on the Pragmati that we've already decided to cut, a list of the steps in byucky relationship development, and five blank pages to add bulk. At this rate, we'll have a working rough draft sometime between the Apocalypse and the Millennium."

"Great! Then it can play for a thousand years!"

"Really, I don't think *Byuck* is Millennial fare. We should shoot for earlier."

"I don't know why not. What about how all the babes are hotties and the ice cream grows on trees? Sounds like the Millennium to me."

"Curses, please! You're going to get this place torpedoed by lightning and burnt down with me still inside! Do you mind?"

"I assure you, Dave, that wasn't my intention."

"Anyway, we need a plan." Dave collapsed in the couch and threw the papers on the table.

The phone rang. Curses went to get it. "Stupid phone," said Dave.

"It's for you, Dave."

Dave sighed and pulled himself back off the couch. He trudged over to the phone, said hello, and was greeted by a horrible noise, girlish laughter, and a click on the other end. Dave hung up.

"Who was it?"

"My sister."

"I wrote a new song while you were on the phone:

> *Welcome to BYUUUUUUUUUUUU*
> *Some people call it a zooooooooooo*
> *So what else can you dooooooooooooooooooooo*
> *But get hitched at BYUUUUUUUUUUUUUUUUU*
> *And I've got the girl for youuuuuuuuuuuuu*
> *Her name is Marilouuuuuuuuuuuuu*
> *She wants to love you toooooooooooo*
> *Welcome to BYU! Dun dee dun!*

"Did you get that Dave?"

"What?"

"The song. Did you write it down?"

"No."

"Great. Another masterpiece gone. Lost forever!" Curses collapsed into the couch. "It's no wonder we still haven't finished."

▓▓▓

"THE PROBLEM YOU guys are having," Ref was explaining after unexpectedly (for Dave and Curses) dropping by and unexpectedly (for her) being subjected to their whining and moaning, "is that you're the to-build-a-fence guys. You're experts on staying single trying to write a play on getting married."

This had the ring of revelation to Dave. "You're right! You're absolutely right!" He paused. "But it wouldn't be a very entertaining play if it was about nothing happening." Dave scratched his chin. "I guess we need to learn how to get married."

"Another problem," said Curses, "is we don't have a number with 'Mr. Roboto'–like grandeur to build the rest of the play around. If only we could find our 'Mr. Roboto' – !" Curses turned to face his keyboard and started playing "Mr. Roboto," which Ref took as her cue to go home.

"I've been here almost an hour," she pointed out, "and I still have my homework to do. And besides, Styx sucks."

"Actually," said Curses, turning to face her, "it would be grammatically proper to say 'sticks suck,' but in fact, sticks don't suck. They just sort of sit there. Being sticky. Achieving ever higher states of stickness."

"Goodbye, Curses," Ref said with mother-like finality. She looked back at Dave and graced him with a smile. "Bye, Dave." She nodded, stepped outside, and before the door shut they heard her explode in a half-second giggle.

"That girl," said Dave.

REFEREE PLANTREE

No, Dave. Write your own introduction for me if you really must have one. This is the best you're going to get.

SEVENTEEN

Of International Significance

THE NEXT NIGHT, AS HE and Ref were walking down the stairs from his apartment, Dave tried out a new tongue twister he had found in the Book of Mormon that morning. "It's from Jacob," he said. "Wherefore, welfare. Wherefore, welfare. It's pretty hard. You should try it."

"Simple minds," Ref said. "Curses with the puns, you with the tongue twisters. I have got to find some grownups to hang out with."

Dave laughed, but Ref didn't. Was she kidding? He couldn't be sure. She was behaving less like a friend and more like a girl all the time. By the time they reached the parking lot, Ref seemed decidedly glum.

"Ref, are you all right?"

"Oh, Dave, shut up." Ref sighed. "Sorry. I've had . . . a lot on my mind lately."

"School?"

"No. I mean sure. Yes. No. Maybe not really. Oh, okay, it's school."

Well, I'm glad we at least have that settled, thought Dave.

Dave unlocked the passenger-side door and opened it for Ref, then walked around to his side to let himself in. He had put on his seat belt, started the car, was reaching for the parking brake and opening his mouth to let out an attempted witticism, when he noticed Ref frowning at him, her stare stapling itself into his head.

"Why do you always open my door for me, Dave?"

"Um." Dave had never thought about it before. "I have to unlock it anyway, so why not open it while I'm there?"

"Why don't you just unlock it from the inside and let me open it myself?"

"It doesn't seem polite?"

"Hm." Ref seemed satisfied by this and sunk back into her seat. "Where's Curses?"

"I'll tell you if you promise to believe me."

"I promise."

"Doing homework."

Ref shook her head. "I'm sorry I promised; it was rash." She put on her seatbelt. "Let's go do this thing."

DAVE HAD RECEIVED an e-mail from his friend Marie Llewellyn, telling him that her roommate's MFA opening was Friday and do come. Refreshments provided.

Dave had immediately imagined a ritzy New York-esque gallery opening with slimy French cheese on Belgian crackers and BYU's version of wine, walking around and saying nice things about bad paintings in Tony Curtis's voice from *Some Like It Hot*. So he had talked Ref and Curses into going along with him, and now here he was with Ref, entering the fine arts building to the sounds of cello, viola, and violin. They walked in slowly, and Dave looked for anyone he knew. He had hung out with Llew and her roommates a lot when he had first transferred, but it had been a while, and he didn't see any of them now. So he just struck off for the nearest refreshment table, Ref in tow.

"Dave!" said a girl with long straight muddy-blonde hair and glasses that could judiciously be described as goofy. She was wearing a long black dress, straight and formless, putting her body at a strict perpendicular to the freckles splashed across her nose and cheekbones.

"Llew! I was just looking for you!" Dave stepped over and gave her a one-armed hug. "How are you?"

"You know, dancing." Llew turned to Ref. "Hi," she said.

"Hi," said Ref.

"Are you the Referee, Dave's best friend in the whole world, whom I cannot understand why I have never before met?"

"Yeah. I guess so. Nice to meet you."

"Come on, Dave, you've got to meet Miranda. She can finally get her degree now. She's very happy." She took Dave's hand and pulled him off. Dave grabbed Ref by the arm and the three of them wormed through the crowd. Dave watched Llew glide before them, her legs and feet not seeming to move. She flowed. Like a ghost. Or like she had a Segway hidden under her dress.

Miranda was talking to a trio of gentlemen wearing black turtlenecks under their suit coats. "Gallery owners," Llew whispered. "From Park City." Miranda saw them and waved, but didn't break away. "Paintings?" Llew asked, then floated off.

Dave and Ref and Llew were staring at the central piece, an enormous canvas almost eight feet tall and half as wide. Llew had her hands clasped and was quivering. Dave and Ref were frowning.

"It's a thumbtack," said Dave.

"It's called *Of International Significance #45*," said Ref, squinting at the title, printed on a speckled piece of gray paper mounted beside the painting.

"This one's my favorite," said Llew.

"It's a thumbtack," said Ref.

Dave enjoyed visiting galleries, and he would happily admit that *Of International Significance #45* featured neither eye trauma nor naked people – his two least favorite subjects – but somehow giant thumbtacks did nothing for him.

"I like, the, ah, veracity of, you know, how it really looks like a thumb-tack," Ref said.

Llew nodded. "That's the first thing that struck me, too," she said. "Before she even finished working on it."

"You're both absolutely right," said Dave, and turned to the next painting.

Dave liked the rest of the show much better, and when Miranda swung by to say hi he could honestly tell her how much he liked the triptych of Washington, Lincoln, and a jack-in-the-milk-jug. Not only was it kind of funny, but the strength of the colors made it rise above the silly. Anyway, it felt more significant than, say, a giant thumbtack.

Llew stuck with Dave and Ref through to the refreshment table, which was covered in tiny sandwiches and mint brownies. Dave took two brownies and immediately stuffed one in his mouth so he would seem to have taken only one.

Llew tugged on his sleeve and leaned in close. "There's sunshine," she said conversationally, "in my soul today, more glorious and bright."

"Oh?" Dave said through the brownie.

"Yes," she said, and pressed a floppy disk into his hand. "When the peaceful happy moments roll."

"What's this?"

"We're all on there, Dave. Our lives, in abstract, as requested. Roll with the sunshine." She held up her palms – fingers wide, like a mime caught in a box – then laughed and walked away.

Dave watched her go as he chewed, then swallowed and walked over to Ref and the sandwiches. "Did you enjoy the show?" he asked.

"Yeah. I really did."

"What do you think of Llew?"

"Is she crazy?"

"No. Stranger than usual. Maybe she's in character. I think she's in a play soon. She was one of those trashcan dwellers from *Endgame* for two whole months once."

"I often think that about Curses."

"Curses." Dave smiled, and bit into his second brownie.

DENIZENS OF 784 NORTH 900 EAST

Jill Sanchez

Sorry this took so long. You would think e-mail would make it easy for me or something. Dave! How are you! What a darling idea, a memory book. I love it, I hope it works well for you.

So, me! I remember you coming by, sure. It was nice because I had big-time senioritis, and you were a good/fun distraction. And it was nice to have someone else bringing a boy over for a change. You were coming by like once a week there for a while, weren't you? And you had a funny story about a fish or something on your mission and I think maybe it stunk? That was funny.

So I guess you're still going to school then? That's cool. Glad to know you want to remember me. Study hard. Tell everybody hi for me,

Jill

Marie Llewellyn

Hello. My name is Marie Llewellyn. I go by Llew (pronounced the American way, loo, not the Welsh way, which might be something like thloo). I believe this is because when I was a child growing up in Boston, being called Marie made me feel Catholic. Most of my friends were Catholic, and two of my best were named Marie. So maybe now that I think of it, I really started going by Llew in order to keep us straight. One of my friends thought of it, and I just liked it.

Maybe that's the only reason.

This is also much of the reason I wanted to attend BYU. I was the only Mormon for most of my growing-up years. There was Jeff for a few years in elementary school, but he did this snorting mucus thing in and out of his nose that creeped me out. I wanted to know what it was like to just be one of the crowd.

I've decided I don't like it. It was nice being The Mormon, knowing that everything I did, people judged my faith by. That responsibility made me strong and courageous. It was easy to say no to the slightest impropriety because I was The Mormon. But now? No one cares. I want what I do to matter.

And what I do is act. I am also Llew the Thespian. There's an incredible magic about the stage that is indescribably beautiful while being deathly frightening, and I can't escape it. I want to spend my life on the stage. It's where I belong.

As for David Them, he's a friend who claims he has an addictive personality, and if he got on a stage just once here at BYU, he would never leave. He's silly. He also has my rhyming dictionary. Or, rather, it's on an eighteen-month mission to Themland. Don't forget to come home someday, dear thing.

Love,

iLLEWsion

ps: right now i am a hypocrite desperately seeking solace in the word, but i've tried to keep this out of your book, that it may have that timeless, shakespearean quality

Miranda Richardson

I met you two weeks after my grandfather died. I was trying to buy his old duplex from the estate. I was also trying to fire my agent, who was an idiot, but a good friend. I still don't have any new representation. I met you, in fact, during the worst three months of my life. I lost $2,500 on a bad stock tip a couple weeks later. You were Llew's contribution to a string of disasters and bad luck. I mean that in a nice way.

Come by sometime. Llew's contributions are always welcome.

Anna Hargrove

David Them used to hang out at our place a lot his first semester at BYU, then he stopped. I don't know why.

I remember once I sat down next to him on our couch and got my hair in his ice cream.

I'm not very tall.

I had leukemia when I was a kid which I guess makes me more interesting, but people always say oh, how sad. Why is it sad? I didn't die.

Sometimes I feel I'm too short to have to walk to campus.

I'm from Oregon.

That's all.

Lina

Sweden

Unkind to kittens

EIGHTEEN

Generalized Punishment

DAVE WAS WAITING TO TURN left into his apartment parking lot after dropping Ref off. Waiting, that is, for Peter to make a right in. The girl in the Lexus with him was familiar – in the ward. Dave had never met her, but he knew she was fairly new and had a pleasant laugh. She was in the passenger seat, and as Peter turned in, Dave's headlights flashed on their faces. Peter looked grim, like he had just inherited the national debt, but his date was red. He couldn't tell if she was mad or crying or had just laughed too much, but with Peter Dave doubted it was the latter.

Dave turned in after them and parked only a few spots away. As he got out he heard the girl saying "ever again" and it was definitely tears she was talking through. He watched her storm off, then turned toward their apartment and hurried to intercept Peter.

"What happened?" Dave asked.

"I don't know. She's very . . . emotional." Peter was trembling, like he was about to lose control of himself. Dave decided to be sympathetic. "You two've been seeing each other long?"

"First date."

Dave wondered why so many of Peter's first dates ended in disaster. And second dates. And thirds. Come to think of it, Friday he'd broken a plate over breaking up with his "girlfriend" Mandy who lived on the first floor. And if Dave remembered right, that had been after only the second date.

They started up the stairs. "I'm sure you'll find someone, Peter."

"Shut up. You don't know what it's like to have a righteous desire."

Dave was a little surprised by this assumption, but shrugged it off. One couldn't take everything Peter said personally. In fact, it was best to take nothing that Peter said personally.

Peter pulled out his keys and sulked to his room, punching the wall on the way. After Peter had slammed his bedroom door, Curses looked up from his textbook. "I hope your evening went better than his," he said.

"They always do." Dave sat on the floor by the couch and started sorting through the stack of old *Ensigns* Curses had picked up at the thrift store. "I can't believe they let people wear clothes like this on the cover of an official Church publication. I mean – *look* at those lapels!"

Curses shook his head. "The seventies, Dave, were a decade of bacchanalia and other sins, most of which involved fashion, and from which the Church was not totally immune."

"Thank goodness we're marching steadily towards Zion."

"Amen." Curses closed his book and tossed it on the hot-chocolate table.

"How's the lesson going?"

"Fine. Your mom called."

"What'd she say?"

"'Get married.' Then she laughed."

"Well, it's good advice, Curses."

"Thanks." Curses leaned back in the couch and yawned. "I saw X today."

"Really? I haven't seen him in a week, at least. I figured he was married."

"He said Peter had a friend who might want to buy his housing contract."

"X is moving, then?"

"I guess." Curses shrugged. "Engaged people do tend to get married."

"And married people don't want to live here – not even with their old pals."

"Single people don't want to live here, Dave. Old pals merely make it bearable. Anyway, byuck?"

"No."

"Dave! You promised!"

"Did not. And you got to prepare that lesson anyway. Here's a good article: '"Old Dead Book" of Job.'"

"Actually, the lesson's on the Liahona."

"Well, these are *Ensigns* you bought, not *Liahonas*."

"Haha. Brilliant wit you display, my young friend. Anyway, the lesson in the book's good – with some mustard I mean – but there's something about the Liahona that's kind of bugging me."

"What's that?"

Curses grabbed a spare Book of Mormon off the couch and waved it at Dave. "The story goes like this: Lehi wakes up one morning. Outside his tent is this ball of curious workmanship that tells them where to go. Right? A little spindle pointing the way? Words written now and then with additional instructions?"

"So I've heard."

"Correct me if I'm wrong, but the spindle only worked when they were righteous, yes?"

"Sure."

"But Nephi, bless his heart, was *always* righteous. And most of them were, most of the time. But if a rebellious faction rose up –"

"*When* a rebellious faction rose up."

"*When* a rebellious faction rose up, it ceased to work. For all of them!"

"Yeah?"

"That's not fair."

Dave leaned back on his hands. He'd never thought of the Liahona in terms of fairness before. "It happened again on the boat. The storm's about to capsize them all, even innocent little Jacob and Joseph. Not just Laman and Lemuel."

"You're right!" Curses grabbed a notebook and jotted something down. "But what does it mean? For us? Today?"

"I don't know. I never thought about it before. But the rain rains on the just and the unjust alike."

"Yeah, but this isn't rain. We're talking about the direct consequences of other people's sins affecting the righteous. Like when the teacher made the whole class write lines when only one kid threw the paper airplane."

"I hated that teacher. I hated that kid." Dave looked up at Curses. "I'll bet that kid was you."

Curses waved the accusation away. "Not important." He dropped to a whisper. "But I'll tell you what I think it means for us."

"What?"

"Peter's heartbreaking exploits are smiting us all. When was the last time girls brought brownies over here? Or invited us over for ice cream? The whole female half of the ward shuns us."

"X is engaged."

"Grandfathered in. Look, Dave, that's the lesson of the Liahona for us, today. We have to be responsible for each other's sins. Peter's punk factor is bringing down a generalized punishment."

"I don't know . . ."

"I'm talking to him."

"I don't know, Curses . . ."

"Tomorrow."

Curses nodded grimly, gathered up his books, and headed down the hall. Dave waited till he heard him brushing his teeth before he got up to follow.

NINETEEN

A Blood Factory

SATURDAY NIGHT, AND DAVE AND Curses sat stretched out on the front couch, mesmerized by Curses's new lava lamp. Dave attempted to sit up a couple angstroms. "You know who I think you might like?" Dave said, as he and Curses slipped deeper and deeper into a catatonic state.

"Who?"

"My friend Llew."

"That actor girl?"

"Yeah."

"I dunno, man." Curses stretched and repositioned his left leg under him. "Isn't she a little weird?"

"Weird?" Dave scratched. "No, not really."

"You had to think about it. You mean she's not really weird – more of a total freakshow? Is that it?"

"No, compared to you she's not too weird."

Curses smirked. "Right. Thanks. You saying I'm the freakshow?"

"What? No."

"No, that's exactly what you're saying, Dave. You think I'm a screwball who's got no chance to get himself married so you're trying to hook me up with a fellow lowlife."

"What? What are you talking about? Llew's a good girl."

"I bet. Gots a sweet spirit, huh? You're probably just trying to get her off your back, and I look like your patsy." Curses was suddenly up and pacing.

Dave watched him walking back and forth. "You talked with Peter."

"I don't need Peter to tell me I'm a loser; I've got you."

"Hey now –"

"Hold it, Dave. I know what's up, and it's a nationwide conspiracy."

"Okay, now you're sounding crazy. What are you –"

"Will you shut up for just one second!"

Dave sat still. Curses was mad and Dave had no idea why. No idea what to say. So he just watched Curses turn and storm towards the front door, stopping within doorknob distance and taking a deep, deep breath.

And the door exploded open into his face. Peter fell in. "Oh, I just had the most terrible night," he wailed.

"My nose ... my nose ... my nose ... my nose . . ." Curses said.

"My gosh," said Dave as he jumped over to Curses. Curses was holding his hands under his nose, but they were already filled, with blood dribbling down his arms.

"What happened to you?" asked Peter.

"Get him to a sink," said Dave.

Peter took Curses by an arm and led him down the hall to one of the bathroom sinks. As Curses bled into the sink Dave tried to clean up the blood on the door, carpet, and kitchen floor with the last two paper towels. After a few minutes Dave went down the hall.

"How's the bleeding?"

"Fantastic," said Curses.

"The man's a blood factory," said Peter.

"Ha, ha," said Curses.

"Have you tried pinching it?" asked Dave.

"It hurts too much."

"He says it hurts too much," said Peter, as he lifted an eyebrow and pursed his lips at his reflection in the mirror.

"You're going to pass out if we don't get that stopped." Dave took two steps in every direction. "What's the name of that girl in our ward who's a nurse?"

"Isabel?" yelped Peter.

"Right! Isabel! Isabel Porter! Be right back."

"You're not going to get *her*, are you?"

"Sure, why not?"

Peter's lower lip quivered. "She ruined my life."

"She did? When?"

"Only tonight."

"I didn't know that."

"I tried to tell you, but Curses was bleeding. She was terrible! Cruel!"

"Shut up, Peter," said Curses. He wiped some blood out of his mouth.

"Go call her, Dave."

Dave turned to Peter. "Look, when she shows up, just go to your room. If she asks, we'll tell her you cried yourself to sleep."

"What? No! You can't do that!"

"Well, you figure something out." Dave walked to the phone and picked up the ward directory. He tried to block out Peter and Curses:

"Curses, what am I going to do?" Peter moaned.

"I dunno, Pete."

"She ruined my life."

"It's happened before, Pete."

"But never like this."

"I know, I know. Can you hand me the soap?"

"Sure." Peter kicked the wall. "I'm never dating someone from this ward again. Another bad date and I'll have to move."

"Too bad. Can you hand me the soap? And see if I got any blood on my pants."

"No. You got any prospects outside the ward?"

Curses sighed. "Dave wants to hook me up with his friend Llew."

"What a pretty name."

"I guess."

"Lou Stanley. Has a nice ring, don't you think?"

"Actually, Llew's her last name, Peter."

"What's her first name?"

"I don't know. Danielle, maybe? Something like that."

"Danielle Stanley. That sounds heavenly domestic."

After the fortieth attempt to dial without getting distracted by his roommates' chatter, Dave finally got Isabel's apartment.

"I don't think she's going to want to talk to you, Dave," said one of her roommates. "Did you hear what Peter did?"

"Not yet, but Curses is bleeding everywhere and we could use her help."

"All right. Just a second."

It only took a couple minutes for Isabel to arrive, but by that time Curses was sitting in the living room with his head thrown back on the couch. The blood on his shirt was starting to dry.

"Wow," said Isabel. "Chest wound?"

"Bloody nose," said Curses. "But I washed my face. Do you think it's broken?"

Isabel and Dave walked over to Curses, and just as Isabel was reaching for his face Peter walked in.

"Sorry to interrupt, but can I speak with you, Isabel?"

"Hi, Peter," she said without looking around. "No."

"Okay. I just wanted to say that I appreciate the time we had together and that you hurt me deeply, but I've got new prospects and I think I'm ready to move on."

"Go away, Peter," said Dave.

"Fine," said Peter, and he walked away to slam his door.

Dave wasn't sure what to do. Even from his position he could see Isabel's eyes tearing up, and if the situation got any worse she would probably be dropping them on Curses any second.

"I'm sorry about Peter," said Curses. "First date?"

"Yes," she whispered.

"The guy is so stupid. You should see what he does to people on the third date."

"Curses –" Dave started to say.

"No, Dave, wait. I'm sorry about blowing up at you earlier. Peter was reading my e-mail, and you know how my dad's always sending me updates on the girls in my ward? Well, guess what. So much for civilized conversation. From now on, I'm warning every girl I know about him." Curses yelped as Isabel prodded a sensitive spot on his face. "I'm sorry, Isabel. I wish I'd decided this yesterday. And Dave, I accidentally mentioned Llew to him. Watch out."

"Who's Llew?"

"A girl I know," said Dave. "A really good girl, but I think she doesn't know how to relate to most of the people around here."

"Yeah," replied Isabel. She looked up from Curses's nose into his eyes, and Dave suddenly wished he were in another room. "It can be hard to find someone you can really relate to around here." Her eyes had cleared of tears.

"I know," said Curses.

The silence that followed was much too long. Dave wished Isabel would take her hands off Curses's face.

"Um, how's the old schnozz?" asked Dave.

After a pause, Isabel jumped up and away from the couch. "I think it's fine," she said. "But I think you're going to have quite the shiner in the morning, Curses."

"What should I do?"

"Just keep some ice on it. Maybe I'll stop by tomorrow and check on you. I get off work at five on Wednesdays."

"Don't come here," Curses warned. "Peter might be here. I'll stop by your place half past."

"Okay."

Dave walked her to the door, and after it closed Curses kept his eyes on it.

"What are you doing?" Dave asked.

"Watching her walk home."

Dave looked at his friend. The blackness was already filling in under his right eye. Curses looked to be in a trance. But then he came out of it and shook his head. "Ohh," he groaned, and a couple drops of blood fell onto his ruined shirt.

"So I guess you found the cure for her broken heart, hum?" Dave said.

Curses didn't answer. Dave was about to try another approach when Curses snarled, "I just wish we could find a final solution for that nut in the other room."

"Mm."

"And, Dave?"

"Yeah?"

"Sorry."

Dave nodded, shrugged, and left the room.

TWENTY

Tick Tick

"**D**ANCE, MONKEY! DANCE!"

Dave wasn't quite sure what the strangest three words to hear upon entering one's apartment were, but he considered these to be definite contenders for the title. Curses came down the hall carrying cymbals to see who had come in, and Dave was startled by his face. The skin under his right eye had turned black, and tendrils of black crept over his nose. But Curses's hair was wet and combed and he was wearing his maybe-I-don't-*want*-to build-a-fence shirt that Dave had only seen out of the closet twice before. Dave took off his backpack and headed for the cupboard, praying his mac and cheese had transmogrified into fun-size candy bars while he'd been at school. "Aren't you going over to see Isabel?"

"Yes, I am."

"Have fun."

"Thanks." Curses set the cymbals against the wall and smoothed his shirt. "How do I look?"

"With your eyes."

"Even when they look like this?"

"Even when."

"Excellent. I got that one right on my bio test, then."

Curses grabbed an apple off the kitchen table and headed for the door. "An apple a day," he said, turning his back to Dave, "may keep doctors away, but an apple for dinner makes you a winner. With nurses."

"What's this about dancing monkeys?"

"I thought you'd know, Dave. Monkeys are good luck. Especially dancing monkeys. Oo-oo-ah-ah and all that."

Curses left the apartment and Dave turned to look at the box in his hand. "Would you say it's more of an orange or a peach? A peach or an apricot?" he asked himself. They were doing a forty-five-minute survey on towel colors at work this week. Dave dreaded going in. But it couldn't be helped. He rooted around under the cupboard, but the only clean pot was big enough to boil a turkey in. Dave angled it under the faucet anyway.

"Is Curses gone?"

Dave jumped but didn't turn around. "Hi, Peter. Yes he is."

"I can't believe he's trying to steal my girlfriend."

Dave didn't reply.

"What about you and that girl?"

Dave paused. "Ref?"

Peter snorted. "I don't know how you can seriously consider a girl who would take such an unfeminine nickname."

Dave set the pot – nay, cauldron – on the stove and turned it to high. "She's my friend. Has been."

"Right." Peter came and stood next to Dave and watched him salt the water and try and fit the battered lid over the top. "How do you keep her coming back? I don't think you've kissed her – you wouldn't have the guts. You have some stealth method, don't you?"

"What? No! She comes back because she's my friend. Friends hang out. That's what they do."

Peter leaned over the sink and tapped his chin. "But getting them to think you're friends takes time. I mean, that's okay for you because you've known her since you were young. But at my age, to start that way, well, it's not very time effective."

"Listen to yourself, Peter."

"What do you mean?" Peter turned to Dave and held a hand to his chest. "I do. I wish more people would."

"Girls are people too. *Women*, Peter. Women are people."

"Duh, Dave. I'm not stupid." He turned back to face the wall.

"But sometimes you treat them like, I don't know, rats in a maze, trying to get them to do what you want." Dave turned from his watched pot and looked at Peter's profile. It wasn't the best view. "They're *people*, Peter. Like you and me."

"Oh, shut up, Dave. You're starting to sound like Curses. And people are just big animals. They can push buttons for cheese as well as any rat. Not to say I like your metaphor." Peter turned towards the front door. Then stopped. And turned. "Dave, if you really are 'just friends,' can I ask her out?"

"No." Dave tried to think of something Peter would understand. "Dibs."

"Fair enough." Peter turned and walked outside, putting his head back in before closing the door. "But tick tick. Girl can't wait forever."

Dave took off the lid and looked at the almost boiling water. He frowned, then turned to pick up one of the cymbals. He looked at the lid and cymbal. He clanged them together. "Dance, monkey, dance," he said.

a scene o' byuck
by david them

The Predator enters the swimming pool – what? Too expensive you say? Okay, cheapskate, The Predator enters the . . . dance floor, dances a girl offstage, returns for another. Four or five times.

I don't know where in the story this falls, so I don't know if Jameson has encountered his love interest / potential love interest yet, and, come to think of it, I'm not sure that's even important. Let's make it his sister. Of course, Curses, that means a whole new and potentially important character . . . Write a theme!

Anyway, "she" (whoever "she" is) is with Jameson (for some reason) and up comes The Pred.

Now, two options:

1. Jameson stutters and freezes and "she" disappears. With the Pred.
2. Jameson sweeps her away onto the dance floor. Either before the Pred arrives, or after interrupting him and saying, "No, she's with me," or something. Probably the latter.

Like I said, I don't know where in the story this comes. Somewhere. You tell me.

--d.

TWENTY-ONE

Really Nice

"**D**AVE!" SAID REF, NEXT SATURDAY afternoon, bursting through the door, hair unbound and out of breath. "Ryan got his call!"

"It's about time."

"No! You don't understand! The envelope was all ripped up and even had tire tracks on it. It arrived in a plastic bag with a note from the post office saying 'Sorry, not our fault.'"

"What?"

"It was *late*, Dave. Not sent late, but it should've arrived *weeks* ago. He goes into the MTC Wednesday!"

"Oh. Gosh. MTC. Training. Missionary. MTC. Center." Dave stood and stepped towards her. "Do you – MTC! – want to sit down?"

"No, I can't! I gotta I gotta I gotta I gotta I gotta...I gotta I gotta..."

Dave took Ref's arm and led her to the couch and sat her down.

"You gotta what?"

"He's going Wednesday! They just got his list!"

Dave understood. "You gotta go shopping?"

"Yes!"

"Wait. How come the bishop and stake president didn't get their notices? There's plenty of redundancy in the system. And how's he going to write in his acceptance?"

"I don't know, Dave. Does it matter? This all happened far, far away in California. Oh! I gotta call my mom!" She stood up and pulled out a stack of cards rubberbanded together: BYU ID, driver's license, debit card – "Ah ha!" – calling card. She ran to the phone and started punching numbers.

"Hi, Pokey, is Mom home? What? No. I'm sorry. Just – aargh! – Go Get Her! Marjorie! Thank you."

By the time Ref got her mother on the phone and they had settled each other down, Dave had gone to check the mail, had a peanut butter sandwich, and finished watching Curses's bootleg copy of *Rubin and Ed*, which they had restarted for the half-dozenth time last night. Oh, that cat!

Ref hung up the phone just as Dave was deciding whether to trim his toenails next or make a much-needed ice-cream run. Ref came over and sat next to him.

"So, what's the news?"

Ref took a deep breath. "Well, they're going to get everything they can the rest of today and Monday. They'll leave Tuesday afternoon, which really means Tuesday night –"

"Wait."

"What?"

"Where's he going?"

"Who?"

"Elder Plantree."

"Oh. Korea."

"Cool."

"Yeah."

"So, leaving Tuesday . . . ?"

"Right. Go into the MTC on Wednesday. My parents aren't sure they'll be able to get more than just Wednesday off on such short notice, so then it may fall to me to complete his shopping and send him the stuff."

"Great. I'll be your wheels."

"Really? You don't mind?"

"Not at all. Anything for you, my dear. Besides, it can't take all that long."

"Thanks, Dave."

"What, you think I'd make you walk? Ref shalt not walk whilst Dave is about."

Ref leaned back and looked at Dave. "You're nice," she said.

"I've always been nice."

"Yeah, but –" Ref looked away and studied the dusty cobweb line trailing down the wall. "You're really nice," she said.

"Stop it – I blush. Perty young thing like yourself can make a man quaky in the knees for bashfulness."

But it was Ref who blushed. And it was Dave who laughed at her. And Ref who punched him in the arm.

"Hey!" he protested.

"I'm not sorry."

DAVE HAD TESTS Wednesday, so he missed breakfast with the Plantrees, but he did rendezvous with them after they dropped off the first Elder Plantree known to history. He had never seen such a red-eyed crowd. And when he asked "How was it?" they all burst afresh into tears. "Sorry," Dave said.

They stood outside the Chuck-O-Rama as per Plantree trip-to-Utah tradition. They were all in Sunday clothes and Dave felt strangely underdressed as they entered the buffet. Brother Plantree paid and they headed for the food. Suzy and Marjorie accompanied Dave to the fried chicken and pizza.

They both looked older than they had the month before, and Dave was struck by how much they looked alike. They both had their father's squint, unlike the Referee, and except for the foot difference in height, different colored blouses, and Marjorie's purple scrunchie they were almost indistinguishable. It had to be those Plantree noses.

"Are you missing anything at school?" Dave asked them.

"Tests," shrugged Suzy. "No big deal."

"Marge?"

"Nope. Freshman year's a piece of cake." Marjorie poked through the chicken until she found a fourth drumstick, then piled mashed potatoes over the rest of her plate.

Dave nodded, took a breast, and scooted over to the lettuce. In the middle of the eternal kidney bean debate – to put on your salad (because they are good for you and tasty in their way) or not to put on your salad (because it's weird to put kidney beans on salad) – Brother Plantree snuck up on him and whispered, "Dave!" Dave jumped and scattered kidney beans through the pineapple, Ranch and Italian dressings, cottage cheese, and those teeny tiny corncobs.

"*Dave*," he whispered, "have you done what we talked about?"

Dave was still recovering from the adrenaline overload, so it took him a moment to figure out what he meant. "Oh, the datey thing? Sure, you bet. All the time."

"All the time?" Brother Plantree seemed surprised by the fact that Dave and the Referee were – oh my gosh! – still friends enough to spend time together.

"Yep." Dave nodded for clarity. "All the time."

"All the time. Wow."

"Well . . . thank you?"

Brother Plantree nodded. "Great. I thought we'd talk again, but I guess you've got me all figured out."

Dave wished that were true.

"But I'd like to speak with you all the same, Dave."

"Well, thanks." And this time Dave meant it. All those times Dave had crashed the Plantrees' and spent as much time chatting up father as daughter must have meant as much to Brother Plantree as it had to Dave. But first he had to finish cleaning up his mess. "We should, but first I need to get those beans out of that cheese." Good thing he'd wanted some curd anyway. But adding kidney beans to his cottage cheese and pineapple was an act of bravery Dave had not intended.

THE PLANTREES HAD to leave immediately after lunch, which meant no after-lunch chat and the second of two insane days of driving. Ref and Dave hugged them all goodbye in the Chuck-O-Rama parking lot and waved to them as they drove away.

"My dad talked to me," said Ref.

"He talked to me too."

"Oh? What about?"

Dave tried to think of the best way to sum it all up. "Stuff," he said.

Ref smiled a smile that could only be called coy. She stepped up closer and took his arm. "I'm cold," she said.

"Oh, right! Sheesh. You're only wearing a skirt. Come on, let's get in the car." Dave opened her door, then went around to the other side and let himself in. "Let's let it warm up while we make some plans."

"What sort of plans?" And there was that coyness again.

"What does Ryan still need?"

"Oh. That. I have the list at my apartment. But let's get on that tomorrow."

"Oh, good, because, frankly, I had to work till eleven last night and still had to study for those tests this morning. I have got to get to bed."

"Oh." Ref turned away from him and looked out her window at the SUV parked next to them. "Sure."

"Where do you want me to drop you off?"

"My place."

"You sure?"

"Yeah."

"You okay?"

"I'm fine."

Dave nodded and tested the heater; they were bathed in a hot wind. "Great."

Ref reached over and turned off the fan. "Let's just go," she said. "I'm tired too."

A WRITER'S DOZEN THOUGHTS ON TEMPERATURE
by D. Them

1. *Sometimes it's cold.*
2. *Sometimes it's hot.*
3. *Sometimes it's just right.*
4. *Sometimes it's not.*
5. *If I'm cold, I want the heater on.*
6. *My amount of wakefulness does not appreciably affect my sense of temperature. I don't think.*
7. *If you're cold, and have access to heat, wouldn't you use it?*
8. *It's a little cold in my apartment now.*
9. *So I'm going to turn on the heater.*
10. *No, I'm not. How about a sweater?*
11. *Sweater it is.*

I hereby declare a writer's dozen to be eleven.

TWENTY-TWO

Rhodes Scholar Plus Ref

DAVE WATCHED REF – SITTING ON the couch and apparently suffering – through all sixteen versions of the opening theme Curses was playing on his keyboard, newly christened Captain Babycakes. "Take it away . . . Captain!" Curses said between versions. If Dave had been honest, he might have admitted he was suffering too. It was not Curses's best work, and the kid didn't seem focused. Everything sounded rushed. When he finished the sixteenth, he looked at his watch and said, "Talk amongst yourselves, what you liked, didn't like. Tell me later. Got to run," and ran through the front door, pausing only long enough to grab his bulky, Texan-in-Utah coat.

"Where's he going?"

Dave shrugged. "Probably to see Isabel." He stood up and kicked the door the rest of the way closed. "Strange name for a Mormon girl." He plopped down.

"Why?"

"The Isabel in the Book of Mormon."

"So you'll judge all Isabels by one little harlot? I think it's pretty. Tell me about her. Is she nice?"

"Yeah. She works at the hospital down –" Dave waved his finger around, trying to find the right direction "– there." He pointed. "They sort of caught each other. Peter hurt her the same night he almost broke Curses's nose."

"Peter's always bothered me."

"I know." Dave leaned back and looked over at Ref. They had spent most of the afternoon preparing for the morrow's shopping and being persnickety at each other. Dave checked his watch. Eighteen hours left till the battle of their lives.

🏮

EIGHTEEN HOURS LATER, Dave, holding the shield of price comparisons, and Ref, wielding the sword of plastic money, entered the mall. Yesterday, after they had called all over town to find out prices on socks, handkerchiefs, scarves, overcoats, cardigans, et cetera, Dave had made a chart so they could easily scan for the best price. It was a beautiful chart. Additionally, Ref had recently read in the *Reader's Digest* that most store managers are willing and authorized to haggle, so the plan was to find a manager who would beat everyone else's prices on every item in order to score Ref purchasing the entire list at their business.

Dave felt like screaming and pounding his chest and crying out, "Give me bargains or give me death!" but managed to restrain himself. For Ref's sake.

Dave's confidence was heightened by BYU women's lacrosse trouncing New Mexico earlier that morning sixteen to one. Ref had had six of those goals herself, after all. Rock and roll. Hail the conquering hero. Oh-oh, here she comes. Watch out boy, she'll chew you up.

They entered the first store and knocked on the counter in menswear. Dave had intended to wear a tie for the occasion, but Ref had told him that he had better change out of his polo shirt if he did, and that had seemed like entirely too much bother. A lady with a sweater-vest full of safety and straight pins and reeking of something likely advertised as enchanting/sexy came to the desk and looked them over. "Yeeesss?"

"Hi," said Ref. "We'd like to speak with the manager or a commissioned member of the sales force."

Dave watched the two women lock eyes. He was glad he was carrying the shield of price comparisons. It took a while, but Ref won and the woman sauntered off.

"Watch, Dave," Ref said. "Tough but polite, kind but unbending. Friendly but nary a please." Then she stood up straight to meet the approaching suit and his sweatervested valet. Dave matched Ref's pose and, looking at the man's duds, wished he had switched shirts after all. Dave tried to remember how dressy a look Ref had gone for, but couldn't. So he turned his head just enough to check her out. Okay, sort of Oxfordish: lightly plaid long skirt; white collared shirt with pullover sweater. She looked really nice, actually. Dave made a note to tell her this.

But Ref had already engaged the suit in conversation. "This is a list of the items we need," she said. "And this," she grabbed Dave's neatly typed chart from him, making him suddenly feel like nothing so much as a polo-clad file cabinet, "is a sheet comparing prices on these items in businesses across town. If you can beat or match each lowest price, we'll buy them all here. Otherwise, we're very busy and need to be going."

The man took Dave's list and frowned as he looked it over.

"You'll notice you don't currently have the lowest price on anything," Ref said, and the bepinned woman sniffed.

"Yes . . ." said the man.

"But you know even better than I do the kind of markups you employ. We've come to you because we believe you carry quality stuff, can offer us the prices we want if you so choose, and would rather take our three hundred or so dollars than have us give them to someone else."

The man nodded. "I won't make any promises," he said, "but I'll see what we can do." He handed the list to the obnoxious thing in the sweater-vest. "Get everything on this list. Go with them – that is, help them find everything they need – then bring them to my office.

"Thanks for coming in," he told them. "I'll see you soon."

▦

"THAT WAS SO awesome!" Dave said, for – what, the fiftieth time? – as they waited in line at one of those the-biggest-box-you-can-stuff-shipped-to-the-MTC-today-for-five-bucks places. "You are so cool, Ref! I didn't really believe it would work. And at the first store too! Stick it to those retail bandits! And did I tell you how great you look? 'Cause you do. That whole . . . *look* really works for you. Intellichic."

"Thanks, Dave." Ref looked up from taping the brown paper around the suitcase so it would look like a box and gave him a refined version of that coyish new smile she had come up with.

"I'm serious. Rhodes scholar plus Ref equals really quite dashing. Plus, the way you one-twoed those capitalists." Dave made like Sugar Ray Leonard and danced about, throwing punches. "Never saw anything like it. Made me tingly."

Here Dave stopped because he realized Ref was blushing and the clerks were staring. "Hey," he said, "it's just a compliment."

"Well, it's a very nice compliment."

"Well, thank you."

"Well, you're welcome."

"Well."

"Well."

"Well."

"May I help you?" asked the clerk.

"Yes," said Ref. "We'd like to send this box to the MTC."

TWENTY-THREE

Peter Doesn't Date

IT HAD NOT BEEN A good night for Peter. It may have started out promising, with a hot new date planned, but Peter's father had called just before he went to pick her up.

Dave had answered the phone. "Hello?"

"Hello, who is this? I want to talk to Peter Stanley."

"I'll see if I can find him for you." Dave had covered up the phone and yelled for Peter.

"Who is it?"

"It's your dad."

"Tell him I'm out on a date."

"Mr. Stanley?"

"What."

"Peter's already left for the evening. Hot date, you know."

"Don't take that tone with me. Tell Peter I know perfectly well he's there and lying does not bode well."

"Um, okay then." Dave had covered the receiver with his hand. "He claims to know you're still here, Peter."

Peter had sworn in his quiet, trying-to-be-good way and come in to get the phone, reeking of the latest New York-approved man-fumes.

"Hi, Dad! Caught me on my way out. If I hadn't come back for my wallet you would have missed me altogether. Ha ha!"

Dave had watched from the table as he read the day's *Universe* and dunked graham crackers into his Sailor Moon milk glass.

"Yes, sir," Peter had said. "No, sir. I understand. I understand, sir. But

Dad! . . . Yes, sir. Pure, one hundred percent dating expenses, sir. Yes! I wouldn't lie, Dad! It's true! Yeah, it's expensive! Of course it is! Yes, sir. Thank you for understanding, sir. Goodbye to you too, sir."

Peter had hung up the phone, then glared at Dave, who was suddenly re-engrossed in the paper's Scripture of the Day.

"I'm going on my date." Peter had walked out the door and slammed it so hard, milk had sloshed out of Dave's glass.

▥

WHEN PETER RETURNED home from his date, Dave and Curses were sitting on the couch arguing over whether it would be funnier to sing, "On a date with the Beast / My hair rises like yeast," or "On a date with the Beast / Let's go hide in the meest" at the end of a song they were writing for *Byuck* to celebrate Peter's dating exploits indirectly.

Before Peter could get fully through the door, he glared at the couch-sitters and snarled, "What are you looking at?"

Curses touched the side of his nose. "Well," he said, "I heard a sound and thought perhaps someone was opening the door. I merely looked in that direction to ascertain whether or not that was the case. Seems it was."

"Smartass." It was always easy to tell when Peter had been on a date by his choice of vocabulary.

"Do you talk like that on your dates?" asked Dave.

"Of course not! I am the ultimate gentleman. I even open their freakin' doors!"

"What a gentleman!" said Dave.

"Oh my, yes." Curses looked up at Peter. "So, who was the unfortunate young woman? No one I know, I hope. I hope you haven't lost me another friend."

Dave tried to shut Curses up with his eyes, but Curses had a bit more to say.

"Because if you have, I challenge you to a duel, right now. Ten paces and everything. It's time someone put a bullet through *your* heart for a change."

"I forgive you," Peter said in a sudden, uncharacteristic burst of magnanimity, "because you do not know the pain I suffer. Every date I go on, I feel it may be the last time I start anew. Perhaps this one is the one the Lord has selected for me. The girl I can grow old with. The girl who will hear what I say and follow my will as the priesthood. Perhaps this one is the one. But when I administer the test – if I even get to it – I discover that this is yet another tinkling daughter of Zion, mincing as she goes."

"What are you talking about?" Dave had a feeling they were about to discover something huge and unpleasant.

"The test – you know, where you ask them questions and make requests to see how obedient they are? Don't tell me you guys don't do a test!"

Curses had been tensing as Peter had spoken and now he leapt up and let that tension out. "No! Never! Of course not, you freak! What is wrong with you? And even if I was that messed up, I certainly wouldn't do it on the first date! What the heck? You are so sick!"

Dave looked from roommate to roommate. He had heard of apartment fisticuffs before, and it looked like some were on their way. Now that Curses had finally lost it, what was to stop Peter's temper from showing up full force? Dave was about to jump up and either put a stop to it or get the worst of the pummeling when he realized Peter was laughing.

"Ah, Curses! Dad told me I'd meet people like you at BYU, so confused by the world's ideas of women that you wouldn't have any idea what to do with them. But the test aside, let me teach you what I've figured out on my own about getting married. I tell you, it's a surefire method."

Curses stormed out of the room, kicking doors open and slamming them behind   him. Peter shrugged, placed a hand on Dave's shoulder, and pumped up the volume so Curses could still hear every word he said. "Now, first, what's the only way to obligate a girl to marry you? Sin, obviously. But committing sin isn't the right thing to do, especially at BYU where it can get you kicked out of school. But there's a principle at work here. If sex gets you married, then we can deduce the rest.

"In order to get a second date, you really need to get a kiss during the first one. Otherwise, she won't feel obligated. If she doesn't feel obligated – or at least a little guilty – it's just like trying to get her on the first date all over again. That kiss is all-important.

"And of course, as your relationship progresses – no, wait. In *order* for your relationship to progress, you need a few more physical tokens all the time. Engagement, of course, requires a few things that are technically against the 'For the Strength of Youth' pamphlet, but c'mon! We're not youth anymore! We're adults! We're supposed to get married without sinning. And that's how you do it."

Dave had never heard Peter say so much at one time before, and now that he was starting to really understand Peter, he wasn't sure he had enough charity to keep trying not to dislike him.

Peter nodded and wiped his incisors with his tongue. "So the whole idea is to temper religion with lust, planning it so consummation happens wedding night rather than before. It's a matter of timing your control with your temple date."

"That's the sickest thing I've ever heard!" Curses shouted from his room.

"Ah, don't mind him, Dave. The truth's hard if you're not prepared to receive it. We learned that as missionaries, huh?"

Peter removed his hand from Dave's shoulder and stretched. "Well, it was a lousy night what with my dad – you know what he was complaining about this time? He was mad 'cause my credit card bills have been high! Like he can't afford it. I told him it's just money for dates, but he's being all skeptical. Does he want me to get married, or what? Moron. How am I supposed to get the kisses necessary to move on towards eternal fulfillment without spending lots of money? Kisses are expensive at BYU. Anyway, talking to you I feel a lot better now. Thanks. I'm going to bed."

Dave watched him leave the room.

"Peter doesn't date," he said to the now quiet apartment. "He destroys."

Title (the bottom of the world?)

Jameson lifted his face and spit the dirt from his mouth. The impact had been painful, but it didn't feel like he had broken anything. He carefully stood up and brushed himself off as best he could.

Giving up on hygiene, Jameson peered into the darkness. The light from above filtered through the dust and cast a dingy glow about him. He looked up and immediately disregarded any hope of climbing out the way he had come. He couldn't see very far down any of the three passages that led off from where he now stood. He looked up again, bid the sun farewell and picked a direction.

*

Jameson had kept his right hand on the wall since he had begun walking so that, if necessary, he could find his way back. But when he stumbled into a freezing stream of water he forgot his precautions and dropped to his knees, burying both hands and his face in the water. He drank and drank, then crawled out refreshed to lie on the bank.

When he awoke, he realized he was lost. The stream still gurgled at his feet, but he couldn't remember which direction he had come from. "When I fell into it, was downstream to my right or my left?" He couldn't remember.

He decided to abandon the wall and follow the water instead of the path. After all, at least then he would have a source of water. But should he follow it upstream or down? Which way would be more likely to lead to the surface?

Rain comes from the surface, right? A stream could empty into the ocean two hundred feet below the surface, but rain must come from the sky. So he turned upstream, praying for the best.

*

Jameson had heard that being underground could turn you blind. Or drive you mad. Or both. He supposed he would find out soon enough.

The ceilings grew lower and the walls grew tighter until Jameson was struggling to squeeze ever deeper and upward.

Popping through a particularly tight spot, Jameson found himself under a small waterfall. He reached up and found some rocks to hold onto and pulled himself up. Trying to balance on the precarious ledge, Jameson realized he was perched on the edge of an underground lake, the overflow trickling down behind him and turning into the stream he had followed. Where to now? Walls towered above him on each side. Thrown rocks revealed the lake's breadth to be farther than Jameson could throw. He wanted to cry.

And then – was it the madness? Or was this what blindness was like? Jameson saw, off in the distance, phosphorescent blurs bobbing about. As they grew larger, he began to hear splashes. Finally, he realized what they were: mermaids.

They drew up next to him, their pale features and scales glowing, their blank eyes gazing to his side, unseeing. Then they spoke.

"Please, please, please."

"Please go."

More were arriving all the time, their silver bell voices chiming together, begging him to go.

Then the message changed.

"He is coming. He is coming."

"He will be angry."

"He is coming."

They begged him again to leave.

"We don't want to hurt you."

"We don't want to hurt you."

"Please go. Please."

"Please."

And then it was too late. A monstrous creature rose from the sea, his blackened and scarred visage oilily reflecting the quiet glow of the mermaids. He spoke in a familiar voice – the voice of a thousand remembered villains combined with the crackling fires of hell.

"YOU HAVE NOT DONE AS I SAID."

He reached down and plucked some mermaids from the sea, his leviathan size becoming apparent as he stuffed them into his mouth.

"I WILL TEACH YOU TO DISOBEY."

Jameson watched, horrified, unable to move or speak.

Then the blind beast turned to him and smiled, the lightly glowing scales of devoured mermaids illuminating his rotting hole of a mouth. It reached for him, lifted him up, and bit off his head, chewing slowly.

TWENTY-FOUR

Several Notches

Ref's ward met in the same building as Dave's and Curses's, but let out an hour earlier; however, since lacrosse was taking its only miss-school trip of the season Monday and Tuesday, Ref decided to hang out and read her scriptures, then walk home with them and Isabel before going home to finish packing.

"I can't believe they let you leave school like that!" gasped Curses in an apoplexy of counterfeit shock. "Universities are for learning!"

Ref piffed away his concern. "You should talk to a baseball player. They're never here. How did your substituting go?"

"That wasn't this week, but fine."

"He did a *great* job," said Isabel.

Dave couldn't help but notice that as Curses and Isabel walked side-by-side, their knuckles occasionally brushed. He had witnessed the dawning of Awareness, but when had *this* happened? Dave tried to figure out how many nights Curses had been out the past week.

"Dave, come up with us." Ref gestured at him and he stepped up between her and Curses.

Dave took a couple longer steps, exposing his leopard-print socks to fuller effect. "This makes for an awfully full sidewalk," he said.

Ref laughed and punched him in the arm – not so hard it hurt, but hard enough to still qualify as a punch. It was sort of a . . . *friendly* punch that didn't hurt. Dave felt his quality of life jump up several notches. In acceptance and, hopefully, reinforcement of this new plateau of safety, he gave Ref a friendly little punch of her own.

"Hey," he noticed, "you're back in Cambridge mode."

Ref smiled and looked away. Dave turned to Curses and Isabel. "Are you guys going back to the apartment?"

"No," said Curses. "We're going over to Isabel's."

"Figures. You're going there, Ref's going home to pack, and X is a figment. So that leaves me home alone with Peter." Dave suddenly realized this sounded like a desperate attempt to gain an invite. "Not that I mind! No! It's good, in fact! I'm almost a week behind in my Isaiah reading, so that's what I'm going to do. Seek ye out the words of Isaiah, after all."

The walk home took about twenty minutes; Dave didn't follow Curses and Isabel to Draftwood, but walked Ref home instead. They walked up the stairs and she opened her apartment door and stepped inside, and Dave suddenly felt like he was at the end of a date. It was a weird feeling, but there was Ref, one shoulder hidden behind the front door, expecting a parting word. Dave felt like he had to tell her he would call her.

"Well, I'll, ah, call you, I guess. When you get back. Oh. But not Wednesday. Or Thursday. I'm working late both nights. Calling Hawaii, I guess. Anyway, Friday. We'll do something." Dave felt like an idiot.

"Sounds fun."

Oh, sure, Ref, thought Dave, point out the idiot charade I've stuck myself into. But he gave a little wave and clown-stepped his way over to the stairs. And headed home to make some instant mashed potatoes. A double batch. Peter would be expecting Dave to feed him.

Das Potatoes
by david them

"Honestly, officer! I had no idea his bowl of potatoes was poisoned and mine wasn't! No idea! Oh, if only I had known . . . !"

The officer turned and furrowed his brow at me. "Detective," he said.

"Huh?"

"I'm a detective."

"Oh, sorry."

The detective stood and walked around the cement room. He paused and looked into the wall-length mirror and raised his eyebrows at his backswept, almost-black hair. "No idea . . ." he said.

"That's right, officer."

He looked at my reflection in the mirror.

"I mean, 'detective.'"

"Now, son, the Lime-A-Way has your fingerprints on it."

"Well, sure, I had, uh, just, uh, cleaned the kitchen sink, uh, Saturday."

"Sure you did."

"So . . . Lime-A-Way is poisonous, huh? Who knew? Me, I like limes. And I know this girl who squeezes limes in her Coke. Says it's really delicious."

He turned and held out a hand, stopping me.

"You like potatoes?" he said.

"Sure," I said.

"You recognize this potato?"

He held one out at me.

"I don't know."

"Liar!"

Author's note: What, is this supposed to make me feel better?

TWENTY-FIVE

Adorably Lost in Thought

IT WASN'T THAT DAVE DIDN'T like telephones. It wasn't that he didn't like noxious fumes either – he figured each had its place. And Dave decided this week was not for telephones. "One week telephone-free! No more subjection to its every ring and call! Except when I'm at work," he had declared in the middle of his Monday dinner, consisting of more mashed potatoes and some canned beans he had prepared and once again ended up sharing with Peter.

So when the phone rang Thursday evening, even though Dave was nearest the phone as he sat on the living room couch, he made no move to answer it. Instead, he made a very conscious decision to remain oblivious.

It was Peter, then, who stormed into the kitchen to answer the phone. "Dave," he growled in his best cross between psycho killer and grizzly bear. "Hello," he said in a cheerful tone coated in saccharine.

"Dave," said Peter in a marvelous imitation of good humor, "is not talking on the phone this week." Peter had finally given up trying to shove the phone onto Dave just that afternoon. "No, but next time it'll be because I've grounded him from it. You're so funny! And I like that contagious ear thing too, but actually Dave's just a jerk." Peter paused to listen. "Hang on." Peter poked his head around the wall so Dave could see it. "It's that girl, Llew, that Curses was talking about."

"Do take a message."

"'Do take a message.' What is wrong with you, man? It's a chick!"

"Well then, tell Llew I love her deeply but I'm phone-free this week, and it feels great. Besides, I said I wouldn't and thus my good name's at stake."

"Freak." Peter's head disappeared. "Dave says he loves you but can't be bothered –"

"Hey!"

"What are you doing tomorrow night, Llew? Really! Well, could you make time at seven? Sweet. So where do you live? Um-hum. Okay, got it. Cool, see you then." Peter hung up the phone and was startled to see Dave staring at him.

"Peter," said Dave, "I'm taking you up on that offer to double date."

▥

"DAVE! FINALLY!" SAID Ref as she opened her front door the next afternoon.

"Hi. Wow. I feel like the prodigal son." Dave squinted at Ref. "Why are you so happy to see me? I don't owe you any money. Do I?"

Ref laughed and let him inside. They sat on her apartment's frighteningly red couch – Dave wondered how many innocents had perished to give it its color. Dave could hear roommates bustling about unseen in the kitchen and he realized for about the tenth time this semester – at least the fiftieth this school year – that he didn't know any of them. This was an entire regiment of the female population to which he had easy access but had completely neglected. Which reminded him that he had not been on any dates yet this semester. Well, unless you included Ref, he amended. Which in turn reminded him why he was here.

"Say, Ref, what are you doing in a couple hours?"

"Nothing planned, why?"

"Well, Peter and I have a plan to take dates to some country club his dad owns, well, sort of owns. Anyway, no golfing in December, I mean January, well, December too, I'm sure, but anyway, the restaurant's open and – well, I don't actually know all of Peter's plans, but would you mind coming?"

"You know, Dave, I know we planned on doing something tonight, but you were supposed to call first – what if I'd had a lot of homework or something? You shouldn't have planned something so elaborate without at least calling first."

"Well," he said, "it's Peter who's done all the planning, not me. What he might really have in mind, I shudder to think. Oh! And speaking of shuddering, I should tell you this: I was never, as you might imagine, anxious to double with Peter, but he got sneaky and asked out my friend Llew. So we'll be on a mission of Save Llew's Life."

"Oh," said Ref. "What did you have in mind before you had to save Llew's life?"

"What do you mean?"

"For tonight? For us? You said we'd do something."

"Oh. Yeah. That's right." Dave considered options and decided that Ref, being his best friend, would therefore be naturally understanding, and that, therefore, honesty would be the best policy, said, "I forgot all about that."

Ref cocked her head and looked away. In absolute silence, Dave realized, as the noise from the kitchen had stopped. "Forgot?"

Dave shrugged. "Yep."

"Speaking of forgot," said Ref, "I forgot I do have plans tonight after all. Other places. With other people." She stood up. "And I have to get ready."

"You look nice," said Dave, assessing her jeans and collared shirt and sweater.

"No, Dave, I don't think that I do."

She turned and left. Dave could hear her roommates accompany her down the hall. He looked around. He opened the door, stepped outside, and closed it behind him.

Now two hours from date time without a date.

He sleepwalked across the street to his apartment and stumbled upstairs, inside, to the couch. Two hours, nay, an hour and fifty minutes. Ref was out. Who else? Dave wasn't sure when Curses would be home, and he doubted he and Isabel would want to double with Peter anyway – although they would certainly protect Llew. So who else?

Then it hit him: one of Llew's roommates. They were a fun bunch, if a little odd, and putting two of them together might manage to scare Peter off. Llew by herself tended to meld personalities with whomever she was with (always acting), but placed with one of her roommates, she could not help but be her gloriously weird self. Perfect. Now to call Llew and –

Dave remembered he wasn't using the phone. His good name depended on it. "Foolish oath!" he cried, shaking his fist at the ceiling in imitation of someone – Spartacus, maybe. Dave scrambled through his brain, looking for options: One: Call. Benefits: Save friend Marie Llewelyn's life. Bad because: Breaking of stupid promise to no one. Justification: Llew's more important than a stupid oath or my so-called "good name." Two: Don't call. Benefits: I can say I didn't use the phone for one whole week.

Dave stopped there. "This is ridiculous," he said, and went to use the phone.

LLEW HAD ONE roommate Dave had never met and, as fate would have it, she was the only roommate who could accept Dave's last-minute invite. Her name was Daphne, and as Peter pulled in front of the house that she, Llew, and three others shared, Dave was blown away by an unknown vision of beauty standing in the window.

"Is that Llew?" Peter asked, between squirts of Binaca.

"No. That must be Daphne," Dave gasped.

Like all of Llew's roommates, the girl in the window – now gone, presumably to tell Llew their delightful evening had arrived – was apparently an oddball, because her attire suggested nothing so much as Jane of Dick and Jane fame. But she pulled it off with such aplomb, such grace and beauty –

Dave realized his mouth was hanging open and closed it. "I'll go get them," he said, and jumped out of the car. He jogged up the sidewalk and hopped the steps. The front door opened as he reached for the doorbell, and there was Llew done up in perky goth, her smattering of freckles just visible under the pale foundation, and Jane, all grown up and looking like an angel of love.

Dave had completely managed to forget the atrocity Peter drove until he was opening the front door for Llew. Peter drove his rich daddy's cast-off two-year-old Lexus. Immaculate, beautiful, always well waxed, leather interior. Dave couldn't imagine why Peter would want to drive such an obscenity. Dave was embarrassed just being seen near it. But it was too late now, and after helping Llew in he opened the back door for Daphne the dream. He closed the door and ran around and got in the other side.

"And we're off!" said Peter with a jocularity Dave found strangleworthy.

Charity, he reminded himself. And with his heart reset to lovingness, he turned to Daphne. "Hi," he said. "You must be Daphne."

"Must I?" She pushed out her lips in an adorably lost-in-thought pout. "I suppose I must." She smiled and stuck out her hand. Dave took it and offered a friendly shake as his mind crackled, trying to commit to long-term memory every soft square milli-inch of hand.

"A delight, Daphne," he said. "Do people often tell you that, after her of the Scooby variety, you are the first Daphne they have ever met?" This simple statement was accompanied by an even simpler thought: I, Dave, am an idiot.

Daphne laughed. "Not so much," she said.

Good job, Them, you debonair dog, you, thought Dave. And what a brilliant, erudite reply on her part! What a woman! Then Dave stopped thinking entirely as, in his peripheral vision, the erudite Daphne crossed her legs.

PETER'S IDEA OF a date, as usual, was to spend a lot of money. Or at the very least to seem as if he were spending a lot of money. Tonight's plan: Gourmet Golf. Peter drove to the country club his dad owned twenty-five percent of (Peter's dad seemed to own twenty-five percent of a lot of things) and flashed his plastic money around. Peter made a big show of paying for everything and telling Dave with a wink that they'd "Do the math later," but Dave knew darn well that Peter could invite the whole ward and still only be charged the ten-dollar owner's fee. And Peter's dad would even pay for that! So Dave decided to stick it to the man and order lobster. Maybe it would make him feel better about all the potatoes and beans and macaroni and spaghetti and bread and such that Peter had eaten. And besides, Dave had never had lobster before. It was okay for a giant bug. He doggy-bagged most of it for Curses, who claimed to like seafood. But Curses also claimed to like Filipino sausages. Curses, Dave suddenly realized, was weird.

Behind the clubhouse was a five-hole miniature golf course designed to keep golfers' kids busy during White Ball Worship services. It had been closed for months, but Peter could do whatever he wanted.

It hadn't snowed since before Christmas, but it was plenty chilly, so they gave up after three holes. But that was enough time for Peter to wrap his arms around Llew to show her proper putting technique and to hold her close while she shivered and Dave and Daphne made their shots.

Dave didn't know what to say about it. And he was torn between his good side worrying about Llew and his natural man drooling over Daphne. It felt evil, but she had this half-smile that felt like love and pity at the same time. Then her laugh was clear and bright. And when he would say "clear and bright" to Curses later on, that was precisely what he meant. Her laugh was like cool spring sunshine, blowing kisses all around. Dave was smitten. And he liked it. He felt ashamed.

And then he would remember Llew, laughing off to one side at whatever idiot thing Peter the lech had come up with. Dave could still remember how he'd liked Peter at first, but that seemed a long time ago. As Peter and Llew walked back to the car, swinging hands, Dave had a sinking feeling Date Number Two was inevitable, even without Peter getting his liplock in.

Daphne must have seen Dave's worry, because she grabbed him by the elbow and whispered, "What's wrong?" Her eyebrows scrunched together like delightfully worried caterpillars over the ironic beauty of her expressive face –

Dave forced his eyes shut, then turned to look back at the other couple in the parking lot. "Peter's a cad," he said. "I don't trust him."

"You're worried for Llew?"

"Yeah." Dave looked back at the angelic creature next to him as a slight breeze grabbed a strand of perfect hair and flung it carelessly onto her perfectly formed face. "But she obviously thinks he's great," he said.

"No she doesn't."

"What?"

"She just likes going out. It's not so important who the guy is."

"But –"

"Don't worry, whatever he has in mind, she won't let him do it."

"But –"

"Hey!" yelled Peter. "You two lovebirds coming?" Llew was in the car and giggled as Peter winked at her and closed the door. Dave and Daphne ran over, Daphne taking the lead, giving Dave a blessed view of marble-carved calves and their graceful doe-like gait.

"What is *wrong* with me?" he thought. "I'm not that kind of guy." Then, though he tried not to, Dave smiled.

▥

"IT'S WEIRD HOW she goes by her last name. That's so manly," Peter said as they got out of the Lexus and headed up to their apartment. "But the freaky-chick look works pretty good on her. A little more makeup, a haircut, and a lower neckline and we just might push her over the line to beautiful someday. I wonder if they have plastic surgery for freckles."

Dave bit his tongue and decided to play along. "Oh yeah, totally. So . . . what? You like her? Going out again? Get first-date-far-enough?"

"No way, dude," said Peter. "She's your friend and anything I say might get back to her. No telling if you'd pick my side or hers. Too risky." Peter unlocked the front door. "Though why you'd pick some girl over the guy you have to live with and who, I might add, buys you lobster, I can't imagine."

They walked in on Curses and Isabel, chatting on the couch. Isabel stood to leave.

"Hang on, Izzy. Don't worry. I'm not going to touch you." Peter laughed and Curses glowered. "Besides. I know you both want to hear all about Dave's hot date."

"What? We can't talk about your date, but mine's fair game?"

Peter shrugged. "Sure, I'm not friends with the funky-dress girl. It's totally different."

"Than what?" Curses asked.

"Than Llew," said Dave.

Curses's leg fell off his knee. "Oh no. You mean he – tonight – ?" He looked at Dave.

Dave nodded and Peter smiled. "Thanks for the tip," he said. "She was pretty hot stuff."

Curses tried to say something, but Dave shook his head.

"Don't worry about it," Dave said. But as he said it, he knew he didn't mean it at all.

TWENTY-SIX

A Pheromone Thing

DAVE WORKED FIVE HOURS SATURDAY morning and spent that time calling former AOL subscribers and asking why, exactly, they now despised their pals over at AOL. Three times, after hearing a young female voice say, "Hello?" Dave almost said, "Hi, Daphne!" but each time he was able to transform it into "Hi, dere" in the nick of time.

So when he got home, having already given up on the whole telephone goal thing, he called her.

"Hi, this is Dave Them. Is Daphne there?"

"Daphne? Daphne. Dave and Daphne. No. She isn't," said Anna.

He tried an hour later: "Hi, this is Dave Them. Is Daphne there?"

"Dave Thumb? Oh, Llew's friend. Hello, Dave. Haven't seen you in a long time. Daphne's not here. If she's who you want to talk to, call when she is here," said Lina in her vaguely Scandinavian accent.

That evening: "Hi, this is Dave Them –"

"Dave! Oh, Dave!" said Llew. "Well, if it isn't good to hear your voice! It's been almost twenty-four hours, you know."

"How time flies."

"Indeed, indeed. Listen, do you think BYU would let us do *A Streetcar Named Desire*?"

"I don't know. I've never seen it. Sure. It's a classic. 'Stella!'"

"Are you sure? You know, 'Stella!'"

"Oh, I know. But I've still never seen it."

"Has BYU ever done it before?"

"I don't know, Llew. Don't you have an advisor or somebody?"

"He's in character this week. Have you tried getting useful information from a Caliban?"

"I've read that play. You have to get him drunk first."

"Thank you, Dave. That is incredibly helpful."

"You're ever so welcome. Is Daphne there?"

"*Stella!* Sorry, what?"

"My ears, Llew. Consider my ears. Is Daphne there?"

"Daphne? Hmm. Well, yes, that's an interesting question. Daphne. Wasn't last night fun, Dave?"

"It was."

Llew sighed. "Do you think your roommate will ask me out again? You can think about it. He may not. I don't know. It doesn't matter; I don't go out that much anyway. It's a funny thing. Anyway, I thought it was nice."

"Listen, Llew . . ." Dave didn't want her to go out with Peter again, but he didn't want to pop her optimism either. If that's what it was. "I –"

"Oh, that's right – I never answered your question, did I? She's not here. Sorry!" Llew laughed like . . . like a fairy, like Tinker Bell. *Tinkertink!*

"Oh. Okay, thanks. Look, Llew, just wanted to tell you –"

"Oh, don't worry about *that*, Dave! We've always been good friends, but I think we both know that's all it could ever be, so no big deal. Maybe it's a pheromone thing, I don't know. You've always smelled like my brother."

"Oh."

"His name's Steven. He's an engineer. We don't know what happened to him." She tinkertinked again. "Bye!"

"Bye," Dave said to the dead line. Smelled like her brother? How many girls' brothers did he smell like? He frowned, considering the unhappy implications.

He hung up the phone but left his hand on it awhile before stepping aside. He glared at it, then conceded defeat. "I'll call Daphne tomorrow. After church." He shuffled back and forth on his feet but maintained eye contact with the phone. "I do *not* smell like *her* brother." Then he walked to his room to conquer some paper.

Something

by david them

Dr. Heckyll had pulled many late nights on this project, and now, at one in the morning, this cold starless night, his furnace in an unfortunate state of disrepair, he held in his hand what might well be the formula he was looking for. The vaguely blue phosphorescent liquid filled the midsized beaker to the neck. Dr. Heckyll sniffed it. It had an unpleasant bouquet, but oh, if it might work!

Dr. Heckyll had been cursed with an unfortunate malady that made him smell familial to the female half of his species. This frightful disorder had gone unrecognized most of his life, and not until kissing his first girlfriend did he even have the slightest reason to suspect. After what had been a sparkling moment of joy for him, she remarked, "Ha! It's like *kissing* my brother, too!" It had been downhill with women from there.

After publishing his doctoral dissertation on biochemical processes and likely roles of olfactory agents in the sex lives of lemurs, Dr. Heckyll had turned his attention to personal matters. Just one month earlier he had made a radical breakthrough, and now, after thirty nearly sleepless days, he was ready to test his beta cure.

He laughed at his cleverness. "Now I shall be alpha male!" he cackled, then clasped his free hand over his mouth. He didn't want to turn into a mad scientist over something so silly as pheromones. Especially not when there were grad students just down the hall.

Dr. Heckyll walked over to a battered old armchair that sat in one corner of his otherwise hermetic lab. He sat down and took three deep breaths, then, down the hatch. He immediately passed out.

When he came to, his graduate assistants, Molly and Jo, were standing over him. Molly was dabbing his brow with a cold rag and they were both saying, "Doctor?"

Dr. Heckyll shook his head and tried to keep his eyes open. "Molly? Jo?"

Jo answered. "Are you all right doctor? It's after noon."

Molly frowned. "And you seem . . . different somehow."

Dr. Heckyll was awake now and on the verge of panic. "Do I – do I look all right?"

Molly nodded. "It's not the way you look . . ." she said.

Dr. Heckyll nodded and smiled. He had overheard Molly and Jo on a number of occasions talking about how he was like a big brother, but there was no ethical way to test the success of his new experiment on them. But now that he thought of it, he realized he had not planned for a testing method. Other than trying to date again, he supposed.

"Um, the chimp samples came back negative for their markers," said Jo.

Dr. Heckyll nodded and stood up. "Good," he said. "I need to go for a walk."

*

Sitting in his lab that night idly concocting another batch of his debrothering brew, Dr. Heckyll realized there was no easy way to ascertain whether his experiment had worked. He supposed he could get volunteers to smell his dirty shirts from before and after, but getting permission for such testing would raise unpleasant questions.

When he finished another beakerful of the blue, Dr. Heckyll corked it and took it with him as he locked up the lab and walked across campus to his car.

He was distracted by a young couple kissing on a bench in the middle of campus. He sat on the grass and watched for a moment, then uncorked the beaker and swallowed it down.

*

He was awakened by a strange mix of noise and smell and pressure. He opened his eyes, but could not immediately determine what he was seeing. He felt the grass poking his chest through his shirt, but above him – that noise, all that noise. Then he understood: women!

Dr. Heckyll began struggling, fighting to escape from the mound of girls. He could hear them screaming at each other and clawing at him and each other, crying and grasping his arms, legs, clothes. He tried to push himself into a kneeling position but that only opened up more of his body to attack. Cries of "Mine!" and "Oh!" and "Darling!" assaulted him. One of the sleeves of his shirt tore off and suddenly he felt nails in his calf and teeth on his ear. The blood only excited them more. The attack intensified and grew more brutal.

"Oh what have I done!" cried Dr. Heckyll, and, in what would prove to be his last words, "Was it really so bad to be a brother?"

TWENTY-SEVEN

Petrarch Was Right

IT WAS, DAVE REFLECTED AS he hit Save and opened up his Isaiah essay, really so bad to be a brother. There is nothing in the purpose of life about being a brother. A child, yes; a spouse, yes; a parent, yes. But a sibling? No. It's nice, sure, but not nice enough to warrant a mention in the familial purposes of life. It was a bonus. A swell addendum. But superfluous.

Dave's Isaiah essay was on how beautiful are the feet, an obvious absurdity – one of those paradoxes religions ponder to grow closer to infinity, like the sound of one hand clapping.

"Dave," said Dave to himself as he sat in front of his computer in the otherwise abandoned apartment, "not only are you not focusing on the task at hand, but you are wavering on the precipice – the very precipice! – of blasphemy."

"Blasphemy?" objected Dave. "No! Never blasphemy!"

"Well that's what it's sounding like."

"Pish-posh. Nothing wrong with a bit of paradox. What, you think religion such a weak structure it can't handle something that seems paradoxical to the mortal mind?"

Dave typed this argument into the computer, then nodded. "Good idea for an essay, probably even for this class. But not *this* assignment." Dave closed the document and opened a new one. He opened up his Bible for consultation of the verses in question. Dave knew whom they referred to and what they were about, and he even knew how to stretch out those two simple ideas into a thousand words. But he'd long since lost interest in blabbing for word count. If David Them was going to write a paper, then gosh darn it, he was going to write something the likes of which had never been seen before. Ecclesiastes says there's nothing new under the sun, but David Them's writing life was one disputation of that scripture after another. Or it would be if he could find something new under the sun to write about beautiful feet, an obvious oxymoron. ("There you go again!" cried Dave.)

The problem, Dave finally admitted, was that he was still thinking about Daphne, even though he smelled like her roommate's brother. "A striking disadvantage, that!" observed Dave to himself in a Dickensian accent – or in an accent he imagined Dickens might have had. Or at least might have employed from time to time.

"Why am I talking to myself?"

"The apartment's too quiet."

"Ah. You're right."

"Of course."

Dave opened his CD-ROM drive and thumbed through his CDs. Chicago, Billy Joel, Depeche Mode, Hall & Oats, Oingo Boingo. Finally he pulled Billy's *Innocent Man* out of its jewel case and popped it into the machine. He cranked it up and sang along with the first track, then turned it down and returned to his keyboard.

"Daphne," he typed, "is quite beautiful. And does not smell like my sister." Dave thought. "Or my brother, for that matter."

Dave leaned back and reread the first two sentences, grunted, came back to type some more.

"Although, come to think of it, I only met her yesterday. Which raises the question: Where has she been all my life? and Do I believe in love at first sight?

"The first question is easy: living her life. It might just as well be asked, where have I been all her life? This new phrasing points out that the first question was offensively narcissistic.

"The second question is interesting, but the answer is still no. I'm not so stupid as to suspect I'm in love. But I have to believe this could become love. No, let's be honest. I *am* so stupid as to believe I'm in love, even though I'm smart enough to know how stupid that makes me."

Dave turned down the music more and drummed the arrow keys. Then he put the cursor back at the end and hit Enter.

"Though here's a question: when you do finally find yourself in love – *getting-married* love – how do you know it *wasn't* love at first sight and it just took you ten months together to figure that out?"

The front door crashed open. Dave's fingers jumped to Ctrl-S, typed

"Daffy," and hit Enter to complete the save. Then he hid his tracks with Ctrl-WWWWWWWW and Ctrl-N. He typed, "How Beautiful Are the Feet," and pulled his Bible onto his lap. He heard some shuffling in the kitchen, then the front door slamming shut and feet stomping down the hallway. "Hello?" yelled Peter.

Dave weighed the pros and cons of answering. He needn't have. His bedroom door swung open.

"Oh. Dave," said Peter. "Why didn't you answer?"

"Hi, Peter."

"What are you doing?"

"Homework."

"Why?"

"It has to be done."

"Do it tomorrow. I want you to take me over to your friend's house. I'm not sure I'll remember which one it was."

"Llew's? Is she expecting you? I don't think she –" But Dave wasn't sure of that. Daphne had said Llew wasn't interested in Peter per se, but Llew had sure seemed interested when he'd talked to her earlier. But then, you never could be sure of anything with Llew. She had moods like some people had hair colors – always different, and you could never be sure which was real. Dave looked back on the computer screen and frowned. He shut down the computer, turned off the speakers and stood to leave with Peter. Again. Second day in a row. Hooboy.

"LET ME DO the talking," said Peter as Dave stood on the porch, wondering why he was here. Was he still protecting Llew? Was he wooing Daphne?

Miranda opened the door. She had a thin red stroke of paint under one eye that made her look like she'd just come in from a knife fight. "Hi, Dave," she said. "This must be your roommate."

"Oh must I?" oozed Peter. "Is your cheek hurt, baby? Should I kiss it better?" Peter laughed. "Just kidding. But seriously, I'm sure it's nothing a little lovin' couldn't fix." He laughed again. Dave looked at him in amazement. He wasn't sure who these lines were supposed to work on, but Peter had sure picked the wrong set of girls to try them on. Miranda had never even turned to look at Peter.

"Would you like to come in, Dave?" she asked. "You can bring *him* if you must."

"Ooh, icy!" whispered Peter as he slipped by Dave to enter first.

Lina and Daphne were sitting on the couch, facing the large front room window and the early stages of what might become a killer sunset through the thin, nearly transparent curtain. Miranda stepped around them to an easel on a drop cloth in the far corner of the room. The painting was angled almost away from Dave's view, but he had Daphne to look at anyway – although he was embarrassed to realize he'd rather look at a girl than a painting. He wondered if he'd be able to find the lemon-lime corduroy recliners in front of the window without looking away from her.

"Hi, Dave," said Lina in her accent that didn't sound like an accent because every word was individually normal and yet, somehow, wasn't. At least not strung together, though Dave wasn't sure why not.

Daphne waggled her fingers in a cute little wave and smiled. She was wearing so much rouge and mascara she looked like a porcelain doll. Her hair seemed darker than last night, though that may have been because of Lina's long straight shocking blonde hair next to it.

"Hello, ladies," said Peter, sweeping his arm before him in an embarrassing pantomime of a regal bow. "I am Peter. I suppose you've heard of me?"

"Yes," said Lina. And it sounded like yes, it really did, and yet . . . somehow . . .

Dave tried to clear his mind. "And I'm Dave," he said. "A pleasure to meet you." He felt dizzy.

Lina and Daphne smiled, but Miranda only turned and frowned for a few seconds before nodding and turning back. Dave looked, and from his vantage point, it seemed like she was painting bright red on bright red with a thin, thin brush. He wanted to go and look in order to escape the friendly spark in Daphne's open and loving eyes, so angelically cast in his direction, but that was also the reason he would not move, could not move, was rooted till forever and forever again.

Dave then realized Petrarch was right and Shakespeare was wrong. My love is *way* better than a rose!

"Dear ladies, hark!" said Peter, which was enough to break Dave's rapture and make him turn and stare. "Dear ladies," recommenced Peter, "is your lovely roommate here?"

"I am the lovely roommate," said Lina without a hint of smile.

Even Peter seemed thrown by this. "Well, yes, I can . . . I can see that . . . Where – um, what's your name?"

"My name is Lina. I'm from Scandinavia. Have you ever heard of it?"

"Well, yeah. I'm not stupid."

"I did not ask if you were. Do you know where Scandinavia is?"

"Of course."

"You are so smart. What is its capital?"

Peter opened his mouth and left it there. "The capital of *Scandinavia*?" he finally asked, and Dave remembered why he had stopped coming here almost a year ago – Lina could be pretty unnerving. Dave looked at Daphne again and she smiled and rolled her eyes and Dave fell in love for the, what, sixth? seventh? time since coming through the front door?

"Why don't you sit down if you're going to hang around?" asked Miranda without turning around. "You're in the light." Dave watched her squeeze more vermilion from a tube onto her pallet, and then, with a pallet knife, she scooped it onto the wall, in an arch over the easel.

"Miranda owns this house," said Dave to Peter, who was now staring gape-jawed in Miranda's direction.

"You *do*?" asked Peter.

"Yes."

"And she is a very reasonable landlord," said Lina.

Daphne giggled.

Eight times, amended Dave.

"Um, is –" Peter paused – "'Llew' here?"

"I'll get her," said Daphne, and she jumped up, her dark brunette locks bouncing in what Dave could only describe as girlish *joie de vivre*.

Dave watched her go, sat in one of the corduroy recliners, and turned to Lina. "Where's Anna?"

"She is dead to me."

Dave waited as Peter took the other chair, but Lina didn't elaborate. "Why?" he asked.

Lina raised one eyebrow three Scandinavian inches.

"Why is she dead to you?"

"She and her pagan god mathematics are going to make two equal three. Should such a thing come to be, God would cease to be God and I too would cease. Thus I have first made her dead to me. I suggest you do the same, Dave. If that's really your name."

Dave turned to Peter. "Anna's a math major."

"So . . ." Peter struggled to put things together. "She's doing her home-work?"

"Yes," said Lina. And it still didn't sound quite right. But Dave figured that probably only added to Peter's uneasiness, and anything that made Peter uneasy was good. Or at least couldn't hurt. Especially when it came at the hands of a woman. Especially a blonde woman. Peter had a declared preference for blondes, and it had occurred to Dave earlier in the week that if no blonde girl spoke to him at church that Sunday, it would be a full month since one had. Nice.

Speaking of blondes, Llew floated into the room in a witchy black dress, arms outstretched, with Daphne following, *her* hands behind her back, almost skipping, certainly smiling, vaguely four years old. Dave wondered if his attraction was the latent paternal instinct. "Dave, you smell just like my father!" he imagined her saying, and shuddered.

Llew passed back and forth in front of the couch a couple times, then withered into it, apparently dead.

"And how is Lady Macbeth this afternoon?" asked Miranda without turning around.

"A little . . . a little . . . overdramatic," said Llew.

Daphne laughed and sat between Llew and Lina. "She said that so you wouldn't be able to," she said, poking Lina, who replied, "I feel no need to state the obvious." Daphne then placed her hands on her knees, leaned back, then forward, tilted her head and raised her eyebrows. Dave gave up on counting how many times he had fallen in love. He was starting to feel a little self-conscious about it. He turned and looked at Peter, hopefully redirecting Daphne's gaze as well.

Peter looked either thoughtful or terrified – since Dave had never seen either expression on his face before, he couldn't be sure – but he guessed ole Petey was trying to decide if Llew was worth it. One of the founding premises of his Philosophy of the Female, Dave knew from having replayed the lecture several thousand times, was that women are essentially moldable and desire to be sculpted, Stepford-style, according to their man's whims. The only trick for the man would be finding an appropriately sexy woman to mold. Peter was probably trying to decide if Llew was worth the bother.

Dave suddenly, and more than ever before in his whole life, wanted to punch Peter in the nose. Repeatedly.

Peter finally smiled and asked Llew how she was. She said fine, if you disregarded the murders weighing on her soul. Peter laughed and said he never knew anything to relieve a filthy conscience like a spot of fresh air (Dave figured he would know) and would she care for a bit of a walk? Llew said that would be fine, by my troth, and to let her grab her sandals and a coat. She left and returned and they went out the front door. Dave turned and looked out the window just in time to see them turn onto the sidewalk and for Peter to take her arm. Lina sighed and stood up.

"Off I go," she said, and also walked out the front door.

It's her long *o*! – no – *is* it her long *o*? Dave shook his head. Which brought Daphne into view, still smiling, still well rouged. Dave blushed. Curious, he touched his cheeks. Hot. He searched for an opening line. "So," he tried, "where's Lina going?"

Miranda answered. "We take care of our own."

"Of course." Dave took a breath, mustered his courage, and looked Daphne right in the eyes. Time to get serious. "So, Daphne, how are you?"

Daphne rolled her eyes back and shrugged. It was the cutest thing Dave had ever seen. "Do it again," he wanted to say, clutching his hands between his knees. "Oh please."

"Have a good Saturday?" he asked, and she nodded, hair bouncing.

Dave nodded too and tried to think of another question when a piercing, vaguely un-English scream made him and Daphne jump to their feet and leap with Miranda to the window. They pulled the curtain away and pressed their cheeks against it to see Lina, a little south, screaming. And a little farther down, under a small barren tree, Llew pulling away from Peter to deliver a mighty slap. Peter then roared unintelligibly back at Lina. Llew ran back to Lina and grabbed onto her, and together they hurried back to the house through the front door and straight into the back rooms. Peter stormed to his Lexus, set off the alarm, beeped it off, got in, and squealed off.

The house was silent.

Miranda took a breath, then whispered, "I think you'd better go, Dave." She touched his shoulder gently.

He nodded.

"I'm sorry," he whispered. "I don't know why I let him come."

Daphne followed him to the door. Before closing it behind him, she said, "It wasn't your fault."

Dave watched the door close.

And realized he was going to have to walk home.

TWENTY-EIGHT

An Excellent Opportunity

FROM THE GIRLS' HOUSE ON Ninth East to campus was about five blocks, then the whole diagonal length of campus, where the sun set, past the stadium and clear over to Draftwood Apartments. Dave figured it was at least three miles home and probably lots more. And he was mad almost the whole way. By the time he opened the apartment door, he was emotionally exhausted. And so the sight of Peter pacing in the front room with his rust-sweaty hair smashed against his forehead barely affected Dave's blood pressure.

"Have you been pacing this whole time?"

Peter stormed over to Dave and stopped inches from his nose. Peter snarled, suggested Dave take a brimstone vacation, then paced off.

"You – you –" Dave said. "You –"

The door opened and Curses walked in. "Hi, Dave. Is Pe – Oh. Hi, Peter." His voice dropped. "Good thing Isabel went home."

Peter stomped across the room and pointed his finger in Curses's face, then yelled, "The same goes for you, Curses! The same goes for you!"

"The same what?"

Peter suggested the same unpleasant locale to Curses.

"You –" said Dave.

"I had a *plan*, Dave," screamed Peter, and he kicked the couch. "I had a *great* plan!"

Peter leaned over, grabbed the edge of the hot-chocolate table, and flipped it clear over to the far wall. Dave and Curses took a couple involuntary steps backward, into the kitchen. Dave wondered if he was in danger. Peter backed into the glass balcony door and pounded on it with his fist. It rattled in its slides. "We went out –" POUND – "we were talking –" POUND – "it was going great –" POUND – "Then, just when I sensed she was ready –" POUND – "for a bit of progress –" POUND – "I kissed her." Peter suddenly sighed. "It was a good kiss, too. I even pushed her up against a tree all romantic-like. It was a you-*will*-have-to-stick-with-me kiss." Then Peter started up with the screaming and yelling again. "It was a great plan, Dave! A *great* plan! And it would have worked! It would have *worked* if that blonde chick hadn't started screaming!" Peter looked like he needed something to pummel. Dave realized he was actually a little scared. "She was ready for the kiss! She wanted it!"

The phone rang. It was over on the couch, the side nearest Peter. Peter snatched it up. "You," he said, pointing at Dave, "*you* are *never* talking to her *again*."

He pushed the button and said "Hello?" in a sick, sick cheerful voice. Peter listened a second, then said, "No, baby, I didn't forget. I just had to find my car keys. Meet me in the parking lot? Okay, five minutes." He hung up the phone. "It's a new girl," he said. "Beth, I think. Just moved into the apartments Thursday. See you guys later." He threw the phone back on the couch and walked towards Dave and Curses and out the front door.

Silence.

"He kissed Llew?" asked Curses finally. "He *pushed* her against a *tree*?" Now Curses was yelling. "He just *met* her yesterday!"

"Out on Ninth East."

"He kissed her on *Ninth East*?" And now Curses was the one pacing. "What is *wrong* with that guy?"

"She's a nice girl," said Dave.

"They're all nice girls, Dave. Isabel is the nicest girl I've ever known. Ever! And Peter tried to pull it on her, too! She's the nicest, but – He is the vilest, foulest, most evil person I've ever met!" Curses waved his arms and let out a series of angry but meaningless syllables. "You want to talk about it being better that one man should perish, then let's talk about Peter! I wish God would do something about him, strike him down. God needs to take him out of commission. Before he hurts another nice girl. God needs to smite Peter Stanley. Now."

"Curses –" Dave didn't necessarily disagree with him, but he knew it wasn't right, what Curses was saying, what Curses was *doing*.

"He'd be doing everyone a favor," said Curses. "Man and woman."

"God –" started Dave, but he knew He didn't need little David Them to defend Him.

The sound of squealing tires interrupted them. Dave walked to the balcony door and looked out. "It's Peter," he said.

Curses came too, and together they watched Peter speed back and forth in the parking lot, doing donuts and wrenching his emergency brake into spins over the asphalt as some girl laughed and clapped on the sidewalk. Dave had seen him do this before, in stadium parking, but there was a lot less room in the apartment parking lot, even with most of the cars gone for Saturday night.

"Idiot," said Curses.

Dave shrugged his agreement. If there was anyone in the world he hated, it was Peter Stanley, but what Dave felt was regret and stupidity, not anger.

"This is an excellent opportunity," said Curses, and the Lexus bounced over a curb and slammed passenger-side first into the basketball pole, spinning halfway around it, backboard falling onto the windshield, spiderwebbing it, then clattering down the hood and onto the asphalt.

"Oh . . ." said Curses, but Dave was already out the door.

▥

PETER WAS LYING against the passenger-side door, several rivulets of blood creeping down his forehead and ears. The clapper girl was crying and calling out Peter's name and trying to open the smashed passenger door. Dave ran around to the other side and opened the driver's side and slid in. He turned off the engine and tapped Peter's leg.

"Peter! Peter, can you hear me?" Dave didn't dare shake him, in case his neck was injured, but didn't want him to die from shock either. He wished earning that First Aid Boy Scout merit badge hadn't been so long ago.

"Dave, get out."

A crowd had gathered – probably everyone still at home – and Isabel was standing at the driver's side door with a little duffle bag.

"Isabel?"

"Dave, I'm a nurse."

It took Dave a moment to see a connection, but then he scrambled out of the car and let Isabel in. He watched her check his pulse and other stuff he couldn't have done, talking to Peter the whole time, telling him he looked good, that he would make it. She stayed with him until an ambulance sirened up and the EMTs got out their stretcher. Dave stepped aside to let them do their job and looked up at his apartment. Curses stood in the balcony window, staring, eyes wide, staring.

Isabel came and stood next to Dave. "He should have worn his seat belt."

Dave nodded.

"He'll be okay. Probably a concussion. Nothing too serious."

Dave nodded. Curses was watching the ambulance close its doors, pull away.

"Are you okay, Dave?" Isabel took hold of his elbow. "Dave?"

"He was a terrible person."

"I know."

Dave looked up at Curses, who had leaned his forehead against the glass of the balcony window.

"It's not your fault," Isabel said.

Dave knew this. He knew it wasn't *his* fault. He looked at Curses, whose forehead was still against the glass, but who had fallen to his knees.

"It's nobody's fault," she said.

Dave nodded.

"Accidents happen."

Dave slowly shook his head.

PETER STANLEY

David Them will be privileged to live with I, Peter Stanley, during one year of his college education. Stanley is two years older than David and will strive to set a proper example to him as David acclimatizes to BYU's unique dating and marriage culture. Stanley himself patiently seeks the perfect girl, and encourages his naive roommates to do the same. Without Stanley and the lessons only he can teach, where will young David be tomorrow?

November 25
Provo, UT

TWENTY-NINE

Bloodshot and Bugsy

CURSES HAD PACED HIMSELF TO sleep two nights in a row. Dave had gone to school, then called Daphne (not home), gone to work, then called Daphne (not home), then sat and done his homework both days waiting – hoping – for Curses to speak.

Finally, he did.

He sat next to Dave on the couch. Dave set aside his deciphering of the Parson's Tale and waited.

"Dave," said Curses.

Dave waited.

"Dave," said Curses again. "Dave."

Dave waited.

"Ask and ye shall receive, Dave. Cause and effect, you know what I'm saying? We're judged by the intents of our hearts, Dave. So what's in mine? What's my heart been effecting?" Curses waved his hands at either heaven or fluttering demons. "It's a sin to steal agency; people have to make choices. You cut off the head of Laban. Are you the hero or the villain? Or are you just some guy who happened to be there? Do you fight? Give up? Mourn? Rejoice?" Curses hit his head with the butt of his hand once, twice, three times. "Should we be Moroni or Anti-Nephi-Lehi, Dave? Deborah or Esther? Sandwich or spoon? Right or wrong? Happy or hokey? Holy *smokes*, I need to shut up."

Dave let the echoes fill the room and waited for Curses to try again. Curses muttered something that might have been God's in his heaven all's right with the world, then slouched couchward into a close-lipped quiet.

The door knocked, but Dave hesitated.

"Come in," barked Curses.

The door opened and Isabel stepped in, passing the door from hand to hand as she closed it.

"Hi, Dave," she said. Dave smiled. "Curses?" she asked. He looked up. "You haven't called me in two days." He nodded and Dave noticed how bloodshot and bugsy his eyes were. "Is everything okay?"

Dave stood. "Excuse me," he said, and walked back to their room, making sympathetic eye contact with Isabel on the way out.

As he sat on his bed, Dave realized he had left his homework on the hot-chocolate table. He turned on his computer. "Something light," he thought to himself. "Something light and cheerful."

Something Light and Cheerful
by david them

There were these bunnies, see? And they were happy. And they lived their lives rubbing noses and eating wild carrots and miner's lettuce and raising little bunny families. And then a wolf ate them all.

No, they got away. They moved to a new hill, where the plants were greener and the wolves fewer. And then Daddy Bunny hopped into a steel trap and was cut in two.

No. There were no traps on the new hill. They were happy. Everything was great. Everything was just as a bunny could want it. Until their burrow was flooded out in a sudden rainstorm and all the babies died.

No, no one died. They frolicked in the rain. It was lovely and cool and a great deal of fun until the lightning struck.

Strike that. No lightning.

Just bunnies. Having a great time. Living their lives. Happy. Like us. Only happier.

THIRTY

The Girl for Me

PETER HAD, IN FACT, SUSTAINED a concussion – and a couple broken ribs and something minor but unpronounceable involving his lungs. He also convinced the hospital to let him stay until his father came to take him home. When Dave showed up to visit, Peter flashed thumbs up and said, "Well, Dave, I've been conscious for six hours now, so I'd say it's about time for a nap!" He laughed, though it obviously hurt him to do so.

"When's your dad coming?"

The life fell from Peter; his face collapsed and whatever thumbs-up energy he'd had was gone. "Today." He looked away. "I'm going home."

"What about school?"

"I'll start back in the fall."

"Oh." Dave didn't know what to say. "When's he coming?"

"My dad? I don't know. Whenever it fits his schedule." Peter fumbled at his nightstand for a cup of water. He took a sip, then rested cup and hand on his chest. "Where's Curses?"

"He's outside. He wants to talk to you, but wanted to know how you felt."

"Oh, fine. Never felt better."

"I'll tell him to come in." Dave stood up and walked to the door. He stuck his head out and said, "Curses." He gestured and came back and sat on the other side of Peter. Curses came in, tried to smile, and tiptoed to the chair Dave had been sitting in.

"Hey, Peter."

"Hey, Curses."

"Look, Peter," Curses touched his nose, then somehow bit and licked his lip at the same time. Dave tried it too. No success. "I owe you an apology."

"Why?"

"Because . . . you crashed."

"That was your fault?"

"I don't know. Anyway, I'm sorry."

"Oh," said Peter. "Whatever." But he seemed far away. Dave wondered if he should call a nurse. He started to stand when he abruptly felt an overwhelming sense of Presence. He turned to the door and froze.

Dave had never before understood what books meant when they said someone had a shock of red hair, but he knew the man standing in the doorway met that description. His hair on top was in David O. McKay waves, leaping like a frightened orange sea. The orange atop abandoned close-cut sides that mottled from a dark gray to near white.

His complexion was ruddy as well – another old phrase Dave had never understood before – but not ruddy in a friendly, Irish-pub sort of way, but ruddy in an I-just-beat-a-puppy-to-death sort of way. Dave wondered if he could escape without being introduced.

"Dad . . ." Peter said.

"Peter. Who are these people? Your friends, I suppose, come to visit. How nice. Have them leave. I have come to speak with Peter. Out. All of you."

Dave and Curses looked at each other. They had never really considered the two of them an "all of you" before, but they weren't about to argue the point. They were happy to leave.

They fled to the hallway as quickly as they could without wholly sacrificing their dignity, then stopped at the vinyl blue plaid chairs next to the elevator and looked at each other for a moment until Dave finally pressed the down button. They made their way to the parking lot and drove home. Back at Draftwood, Curses went off to talk with Isabel, and Dave returned to their own apartment. He shut the door behind him and realized he would probably never see Peter again. He wondered how he felt about that.

He walked into the kitchen, where the answering machine was blinking. Then the thought that it might be Daphne occurred to him and his heartbeat quickened.

The phone rang.

"Hello, Dave here."

"Hi, Dave. It's Daphne."

"*Hi*, Daphne! I was just thinking about calling you."

"Yeah . . . That's kind of why I called, actually."

"Oh?"

"Yeah, see, you've called me several times this week."

"That's true."

"But see – I mean, I like you, Dave, sure. You're kind of funny, I guess. But I'm not *interested*. Do you know what I mean?"

"I –"

"Friends. Say-hi-when-we-bump-on-the-street friends. Friends-through-Llew friends. Just friends. That's all."

"Oh."

"So, no offence, but you really don't need to call me so much."

"Oh." Dave tried to reorient himself in the kitchen, tried to establish the locations of the floor and ceiling, where the walls were. "Friends, right. Well, I thought that's what we were, Daphne – friends."

"Oh, good! Thanks, Dave. I was worried."

"Worried . . . Oh! How's Llew?"

"Llew's fine. She's had better kisses on stage. And you sort of warned us, so it wasn't that bad, I suppose."

"She's okay?"

"Yes." Dave watched his feet and planned his next move. "Good. Well," Dave said, aiming for nonchalant, "Peter wrecked his car and is going home till fall, so you won't be seeing him again."

"Really? Is he okay?"

"Mostly. But you won't have to worry about seeing him anyway."

"Okay."

"So if, say, I was to come over, he wouldn't be with me."

"Okay."

"So can I co –"

"No, Dave. Unless you're coming to see Llew. We're friends through Llew, same as we've always been."

"Right. Absolutely."

"Thanks, Dave. Enjoy the rest of your day."

"Thanks." Dave listened to her hang up but held onto the phone awhile, just to be safe. He pressed the off button and placed the receiver back on the hook to charge. The answering machine light was still blinking. He pushed the button.

"Hi, apartment three fifty-six, this message is for Dave. Dave! It's Julie! I need to talk to you. I accidentally got a boyfriend over the weekend and I don't know how to shake him. I really need your advice – I don't want to hurt his feelings or anything. Give me a call as soon as you can. Love you!" Beeeep. There. Are. No. Further. Messages.

"I don't doubt that," sighed Dave. Then he turned to the hall and almost soiled his pants at the sight of X coming out of the room he shared with Peter and walking right at him. "Oh! X!" Dave scrambled for an appropriate thing to say – like X's name. "Um, hi."

"Hi there, roomie. No need to 'oh heck' me. Which cupboard's mine?"

Dave pointed out the cupboard on the far right. X walked to it and opened it up. It was bare except for a rusted can of beef stew that Dave guessed had been there since, oh, 1985. Food storage, college-style.

"Try Peter's," said Dave gesturing to the next cupboard over. "He's gone home for the semester."

X opened it and found a host of energy drinks and ramen. He took out a package of shrimp ramen and paused. Dave pointed out the appropriate cupboard, and X pulled out a pot and filled it with water.

"Why'd he go?" said X.

"What?"

"Peter. Why'd he go home?"

"Oh. He was showing off for some girl and wrapped his car around a pole."

"Huh. Didn't strike me as the type."

"How long have you two been roommates?"

"Oh, I only moved in two months ago."

Two months! How many Xs had come and gone? And why hadn't he ever seen them move? Dave looked at X and tried to decide if he'd ever seen him before. The water started boiling, and X broke his ramen block in half and dropped it in. Then tried to fish out his MSG packet. Then held his fingers under cold tap water.

"It's backwards," Dave said.

"Oh, thanks." X moved the handle to the traditional position of hot and sighed.

Dave looked at him relax under the cool water. "You're engaged, right?"

"Yeah."

"How did –" Dave felt stupid asking the question.

"How did I propose? Oh, man! It was *good*. First I ordered a gross of roses –"

"No, no. I mean, how did you know she was the one?"

"The girl for me?"

"Yeah."

X shrugged, then reached over with his good hand and shook the pot in a sorry excuse for stirring. "Well, first, she was my best friend."

Friends. Dave had wanted to be Daphne's friend. But she just wanted to be acquaintances. Essentially.

"And then, one day, I knew."

Dave nodded and leaned against the wall. What a stupid theory. Friends! Dave lowered his eyebrows and suddenly and unexpectedly but whole-heartedly decided that love was a silly fantasy, a stupid idea. For the birds. Tweet tweet.

X opened the MSG with his teeth, spit out half and poured the rest into his pot o' ramen, keeping his other hand in the sink the whole time, cooling.

Friends. Oh! That reminded Dave. He hadn't talked to Ref since Friday, and she had seemed mad about something.

"Yeah, well, thanks," he told X. "Enjoy your ramen." He grabbed the phone and headed for his room.

▦

"HELLO?" REF WAS the one to answer the phone. Perfect.

"Martha Plantree!"

"Who is this?"

"Agent Jones, Pragmati. I understand you maintain contact with known creative interlopers Curses Olai and David, er, Thumb."

Ref sighed. "I suppose that's true. What can I turn them in for?"

"Well, ma'am, it's a Tuesday. If you'd care to just stay home and be bored, do your homework and so forth, that would help us more than you can imagine. But don't try imagining. That's disallowed."

"Disallowed."

"Yes, ma'am. Also disallowed: juggling. Especially with fish. Living or sun-dried."

Ref laughed. "Okay, okay. How are you, Dave?"

"Fine, how are you?"

"I'm okay."

"How's Ryan?"

"Oh! Gosh, that's right. He's good, he is, but he just wrote me and asked about gym socks and I found them under our couch."

"Your couch?"

"I know – I have no idea how they got there. I thought we went straight from shopping to sending, but he asked and the next day, that's where they were. I got them right here."

"Weird."

"I know. Sock fairies, I suppose."

"Socks." Dave fumbled under his desk and pulled out a manila envelope. "You know, Ref, it'd be cheaper to just mail them USPS. I've got an envelope. Want to go down to the post office tonight?"

"Now?"

"Sure. The lobby'll be open and we can get stamps from the machine and mail it. Piece of cake. He might even get them tomorrow."

Ref paused before answering. "Well, all I've got is boredom and homework scheduled . . ."

Dave laughed. "I promise not to tell the Pragmati. You'll join me?"

"Sure. I'll meet you at your car."

Dave hung up the phone and grabbed his coat and keys. He walked to the front door and was halfway out when he stopped and looked around. X was nowhere to be seen, a dirty pot lying on the kitchen table the only evidence he had ever existed.

THIRTY-ONE

Dark Secret

LUCKILY, REF HAD THOUGHT TO bring tape, but by the time they got enough on to hold the envelope closed and to reinforce the corners, the weight had risen enough they had to buy another string of penny stamps starring a colorful kestral. "Now we have a whole hawk flock," Ref said.

"It's a good thing it has all that tape protecting it," Dave said after brutally shoving the envelope down the mail slot. "Shall we go?"

Dave unlocked Ref's door and opened it. When he got in the other side, Ref had pulled his *Oxford Shakespeare* from the backseat and was flipping through it.

"You've got a lot of bookmarks in here."

"Yeah, well, I write a lot of papers."

"They're all postcards."

Dave rolled his eyes. "They're my dark secret. They say everybody has one."

"They're all from your mom."

"They sure are."

"'What do you get when you cross St. George with Nome, Alaska? A cold night in hell.' That doesn't even make sense. 'Dave, lavender is a soothing aroma. Lavender shampoos are inexpensive. Girls will relax in your presence.' Is that advice?"

"Supposedly." Dave started the car and left the parking lot.

"Have you been following it?"

Dave grunted.

"Because you should. I could be totally relaxed right now, but because you didn't listen to your mother I'm all frazzled."

"Yeah, I can tell."

Ref replaced the card in *King Lear* and pulled out a Santa Cruz Mystery Spot card from *Romeo and Juliet*. "'A Utahn walked into a bar. (That's the whole joke.) Here's another one: A Utahn walked into a bar. It swatted him. Dave, you told me on your mission about one in ten first discussions led to a second. Perhaps it's the same with first dates? Love, Mom.'"

Dave tried to decide how embarrassed he should be as he put on his blinker and got into the left hand turn lane. "My mother is ... very helpful."

Ref laughed. "No she's not!" She pulled out another one. "Oh, this is a good one. 'Dave, in the old days when people never left their two-horse hometowns, people just married their childhood friends. Maybe you should try that.'" Ref turned and batted her eyes. "Well, Dave? How 'bout it?" She stuck her tongue out at him.

"My mother has, from time to time, *ideas*."

"Hoo. Mine too."

"Your dad too," added Dave.

"Not yours?"

"Well, yeah. He thinks that's why I came to BYU."

Ref rolled her eyes in a big, theatrical movement that involved every muscle from the shoulders up. "That's why *everyone's* parents think they came to BYU."

"Yes." Dave nodded. "Even Peter's. Byuck on."

They drove in silence until they turned off University Parkway. "Shall I take you home?" Dave asked.

"Yeah, I should probably study for my sports nutrition test tomorrow."

Dave pulled in and found an empty spot of red curb near Ref's stairwell.

"Thanks, Dave."

"You're welcome."

"I – Before I go, I owe you an apology."

"What? Why for?"

"I was kind of rude when you asked me to go out with you and Llew and stuff."

"Well, you said you had other plans."

"I lied."

"Then why – ?"

"I just couldn't, Dave. It's kind of hard to explain. I –" Ref blew out her breath.

"You ... ?"

"The strangest thing happened a little while ago." Ref looked out her window. "I had . . . ideas of my own, I guess. You, me." She turned back and smiled. "Silly, huh?"

"Ideas?" A rusted gear broke loose in Dave's mind. "You mean – ?"

"Yeah. I know." Ref cracked open her door. "It's kind of embarrassing now. Anyway, sorry I didn't go with you."

"That's fine, but when did – ? when was – ?"

"After Christmas. I don't know why. But it's over now, so we're back to normal. You're my best friend, Dave. My soul brother." She laughed. "Can you dig it?"

"Consider it dug."

"Dug it is. Anyway, thanks for taking me to the post office."

"You're still welcome."

Ref got out and headed for the stairwell. Dave watched her go. The engine kept running and Bryan Adams kept singing about the summer of '69 and Dave's hands remained in the 10:00/2:00 position. Then he took his foot off the brake and headed for home.

a jameson story
by d them

Ever since Sparklin Omamy Appearance Transmogrifier hit the market, it had been impossible to be certain who you had or had not seen. Jameson's vet looked like his mother at twenty-two; his mother looked like his grocer at sixteen, and his niece looked like him at four. Once you strapped an AT around your waist, you could be anyone. It was quite unsettling.

Jameson had elected not to purchase an AT for himself, affordable though the Sparklin Omamy was. He was happy with how he looked for one thing, he didn't mind his friends and family being able to recognize him for another, and, for a third thing, he just wasn't sure it was right.

There were other problems with ATs as well. Just the previous night, Jameson had gone to kiss his girlfriend and her lips were three quarters of an inch farther away than he had expected. Ever take a step that was a bigger drop than you expected? Yeah, it was like that.

Jameson saw a Special Report on the rash of crimes committed by AT users. Then Sparklin Omamy released a statement that tried to prove that law enforcement was using ATs more successfully than criminals were. The next night, a new incarnation of *Mission: Impossible* appeared on the tube, featuring Sparklin Omamy products several times every episode.

Jameson turned it off.

He stood and frowned at his television.

He had liked the world better when every person had but one identity, an identity that was theirs and that they were responsible for. An identity you could count on. When people lived their lives as God had made them. When you could kiss a face and know where the lips would be.

It was time for action. First, he found a display mockup of an AT that had been thrown away. Then he put together a costume of black spandex with a purple velvet belt and shoulder pads. That night, at the stroke of twelve, with the Sparklin Omamy logo of his fake AT prominently displayed on his waist, he hit the streets.

His first target was a young couple making out on a park bench. He slipped in and smashed their ATs before they knew any better, and when they opened their eyes, the two fat middle-aged white guys – one scrubby, one clean shaven – both screamed.

The rest of that first night, Jameson raided two clubs, a state party, and an upscale sandwich shop.

The morning papers screamed of his exploits. And each night he performed more and more daring raids. Each morning the papers ran descriptions of his costume and maps of where he had struck, but never any mention of his face, which they of course knew was fake and different every time.

After one particularly brazen performance Jameson snuck up to the police and listened in.

"Did you get any footage with that cutter they gave us?"

"Yeah, but Sparklin Omamy lied. He looks the same through the cutter as he did just looking at him."

"Maybe he's developed some sort of anti-cutter cloaking technology."

"Great Scott! Do you suppose? Evil *and* a genius?!"

They shuddered. And Jameson crept off under the cover of night.

In this land of deception, deprived of identity, a hero was needed. A hero who would show humanity for what it was and reveal the truth of things. That hero had been found.

Jameson was that hero.

THIRTY-TWO

A Valid Point

"WHAT HAPPENED WITH DAPHNE?" ASKED Curses, and Dave realized he had forgotten all about her. A blessing! Hallelujah!

"She preemptively dumped me," said Dave. He finished spellchecking his paper and turned to look at Curses, who was playing his favorite card game, samurai solitaire, on his bed. "I was ripped up about it at first, but it didn't last."

Curses nodded but didn't look up. Dave watched him play, then it hit him this was the first time Curses had been home this time of day in weeks. Maybe months.

"What about you and Isabel?"

Curses was only five cards away from "scoping" the samurai, and Dave watched him finish, then shuffle the discard pile. He drew five more cards and looked up at Dave. "All we ever talk about is Peter." He found spots for the five cards quickly and picked up five more.

"How many samurais have you scoped?"

"Seven."

"Is that pretty good?"

"Eh. I've done better. I'm trying to beat fifteen, but it's not looking good."

Dave didn't understand the game, and Curses wouldn't teach him. He tried to say it was something only blue-blooded Texans could do, but Dave had countered that it should be called gunslinger solitaire then. Curses had said Dave was a California brain vacuum and Dave had not known how to reply. That was nine months ago, but Dave had watched Curses yell "Scope!"

156   THERIC JEPSON

and point at his cards often enough that he had some idea how to make conversation about it.

"Are you still feeling guilty?"

"No . . ." Curses stared at the queen of hearts like it was Bigfoot. "Ah, crap. I thought I played you." Curses threw her across the room and gathered up the cards. "What I am still is angry. I don't know if I love Isabel or not, but I like her enough to be mad at Peter for what he did. It's all we talk about."

Dave didn't know what Peter "did" exactly, but he supposed it was time Curses got over it. "Is Isabel still mad?"

"No." Curses started dealing the cards.

"You're missing one." Dave pointed at the queen, lying face up by the dresser.

"Oh yeah." Curses tossed the deck to the foot of the bed and stretched. "Dave, man, I gotta go, do something. I'm going crazy. Are you done with your homework?"

"Only just."

"How's the laundromat sound?"

"What?"

"I have a need to wax turtle and be Michelangelo," Curses said.

"What are you talking about?"

"Teenage Mutant Ninja Turtles, man."

"Oh, the game at the laundromat. Got it. But wait – isn't Michelangelo orange? I'm feeling orange tonight."

"I'm not interested in how you feel. I am always Michelangelo. And as Michelangelo, I am mighty. You'll drive?"

"Yeah. I'm the only one of us with a car." Dave waited for what he thought was coming, but it didn't. "Are you going to invite Isabel?"

Curses bit both lips and looked something Dave had never seen on him before: nervous. Curses's head moved sort of up and sort of down, but you couldn't really call it nodding. "Yeah. Yeah, I'd better." He sighed. Then, suddenly happy: "After all – it's a four-player game!"

"Okay good. I'll see if . . . Ref is busy."

#

DAVE AND CURSES were leaning against double-loader washing machines and taking turns checking the time as Ref climbed the ranks of the greatest *TMNT* players of all time. Isabel sat on the floor with an ice cream sandwich from the sixties-era vending machine. Dave was feeling like one himself, but had run out of quarters trying to keep up with Ref. A cheer came from the three six-year-olds who had been watching almost since Ref had started. It was her third quarter.

"What kind of men are we, anyway?" asked Curses rhetorically. Dave didn't even bother to shrug. Isabel patted Curses's foot in a show of sympathy. "I've never beaten her at anything," Curses added. "And I put a roll into that machine every day for three months last year."

"Really?" said Dave. "What a waste of money. Think of all the laundry you could have done."

"Not a waste – not if I could have posted a better score than ole Martha there. Not if I had beaten her trash."

Dave nodded. Curses made a valid point.

"If you two whiney young men over there would care to come and look," said Ref amidst a sudden burst of prepubescent cheers, "you can come see whether or not Curses won."

"Ha ha," said Curses. He helped Isabel up and they walked over.

Dave followed them. "It's not as bad as I'd thought," he said. "She only just barely tripled your score."

"No, no. Not even," corrected Ref. "I'm still thirty-five short of *that*."

"See?" said Curses. "Math too."

Isabel laughed and laid her head on his shoulder. "Poor Curses," she said.

"Poor Curses," said he.

"Poor Curses," said Dave and Ref, and they all four laughed together. "I feel like our half-hour sitcom just ended," said Dave as they walked to the door and, just to be postmodern, all laughed again.

They stopped for hot chocolate at an all-night diner, and after they ordered (Dave: with marshmallows, Ref: with whipped cream, Isabel: with hazelnut-flavored cream, Curses: straight up), Dave excused himself to use the bathroom. Leaving the bathroom, he was surprised to see Isabel pacing the little two-door hallway.

"Isabel?"

"Dave, I need to ask you something."

"Shoot."

"What's Curses think of me?"

"Well, he likes you, if that's what you mean."

"No, no, no. This isn't junior high, Dave. I mean, is this it?"

Dave didn't like her asking him this. "Why don't you ask him?"

"I'd like to, but he's ... so unfocused."

"Oh." Dave looked at a faded watercolor of seashells that hung on the wall. "He told me all you guys can talk about is Peter."

Isabel made direct eye contact and proceeded to use her superpowers to sear Dave's eyeballs. "That's all *he* can talk about."

"He's still mad at him."

"He needs to get over it, Dave. It's all he thinks about."

"Sorry."

Isabel sighed. "It's not your fault. I just don't know what to do." She turned from Dave and looked at her hands. She frowned. "I might as well wash my hands while I'm back here," she said, and walked into the restroom.

Dave returned to his seat and Ref scooted over for him.

"Did you see Isabel?" asked Curses.

"Mm. That I did. Had to wash her hands. She's a nurse, you know."

"I've heard."

"Cleanliness," said Dave in his best Toastmaster voice, "may well be a virtue, but chocolate is both a virtue and a vice."

"Hear, hear," said Ref.

"Let's diversify."

And the three of them clinked mugs.

FEB 22, 1:47 (SO I GUESS IT'S REALLY FEB 23. HOO BOY.)

Well, it's late and I stinkin' stinkin' have school tomorrow, so just the highlights of today, which means the last few hours basically. Curses was grumpy (re: Peter of course), so we got Isabel and the Referee and headed for the Wash Hut, which only seemed like a good idea, because Ref then proceeded to thrash us up one side and down the other at Teenage Mutant Ninja Turtles. So to keep the evening from being a total bust we hit Sandy's for hot chocolate. Which was extremely good. Except when Isabel cornered me by the bathrooms and, I think, asked if Curses wanted to marry her. I'm not sure.

Hmm. Isabel Olai. That's kind of fun to say.

Welcome back to the apartment for a few minutes, then I left to walk Ref home. On the way she gave me one of Mom's postcards back. She'd been looking at them when we mailed Ryan's socks and I guess she accidentally kept one. The childhood friend one. I don't know if you've read it, kids. Your grandmother, I tell you.

She gave it back to me and we talked about parents, crazy parents, and muy loco parents and how they're all about marrying their kids off, and I happened to mention how her dad made me promise to take her out and then, all of a sudden, just like that, she was all put off.

Ref: When did he say that?

Me: Over Christmas.

Ref: He made you promise to take me on a date?

Me: Yes.

Ref: Well then, why haven't you?

Me: What are you talking about? We hang out all the time!

Ref: Sure, but we've never dated.

Me: Yeah, well, but can you imagine us at a candlelit Italian restaurant? Do you think that's a good idea?

Ref: Why not?

Why not. Why not! Sheez. Telling her why not would be almost as bad as going on the date – especially after what she said a couple days ago (look it up). But she made me promise to call her up and "do it right." And then, to top it all off, she punched me just before she went into her apartment. And we'd been doing so well in that respect.

THIRTY-THREE

To Pretend to Dance

DAVE COULDN'T REMEMBER THE LAST time he had been so stressed. He couldn't get his *Othello* paper going and it was due tomorrow. He also had a test in Shakespeare tomorrow and an interview for a teaching assistant position. Plus, he still hadn't called Ref and knew he had to soon. On top of all that, Curses was in the front room composing on his keyboard a loud and extremely repetitive song. Mostly, all he was saying was "Don't Mess with Texas," and Dave knew that already. Oh boy did he know that. At least he wasn't cooking his sausages – that smell would have been the last straw. Although what, precisely, would result after breaking the camel's back, Dave wasn't sure. Best for Curses not to find out.

Now: Iago. His hypocrisy seemed like a good topic. And it was a definite theme throughout Shakespeare. The Keanu Reeves character in *Much Ado* – what was his name? Don John? And Prince Hal. Ooooh, that Prince Hal! Dave clenched his fists. What a . . . Dave searched for a word that was true but that he wasn't ashamed to think. Phony. What a phony. Pompous jerk. Problem was, Dave's professor had fallen for that cock-and-bull Saint Crispin's Day speech and thought he was a hero, and Dave didn't want to get into *that* argument again. Especially not when there was a grade on the line.

But what about Brutus? The tragic hero, the right-hearted traitor. Is the friend who kills you – because even though he loves you he thinks it's the right thing to do – a hypocrite? Dave often thought Dante had been too hard on him.

He wished he'd thought of this when they'd read *Julius Caesar* –

contrasting Brutus and Cassias via their respective hypocrisies would have made a better paper than Brutus and Iago, but oh well. The last minute makes everyone beggars. Dave started typing and the paper came quickly. It only had to be three pages, so after finishing the rough draft, adding the quotes and formatting, it was actually too long. A bit of editing . . . voila! A new record.

Dave stood up from his chair and pointed a stern finger at his Shakespeare anthology. "I've bested you again Willie Shakes, you old fool, every part about you blasted with antiquity, you foul and pestilent congregation of vapours! Will you never learn?"

Putting a highfaluting author back in his place should count as studying, Dave told himself as he left the room and headed north to where the Olai factor was almost deafening.

"*Don't mess with Texas,*" Curses was singing. "*Don't mess! Don't mess! Don't mess!*"

Dave entered the living room and messed with Texas by unplugging the keyboard. "Shouldn't you be at Isabel's or something?"

Curses shrugged. "She's covering someone else's shift. She's been trying to pick up as many hours as she can lately."

"Why?"

Curses shrugged again. "She needs the money? Maybe it's her good old-fashioned Protestant work ethic. Speaking of, why aren't you at work?"

"The dialer's down again. It's amazing I ever make enough money to pay the rent. But you're one to talk. Where's *your* Protestant work ethic?"

"I'm not Protestant. I'm Mormon."

"I –" Dave walked to the couch and sat down.

"What's up, byucky boy?"

"Oh yeah. Speaking of *Byuck*," Dave waved a hand in a frenzy of false freneticism, "I'm, um, going to write something tonight."

"Great. But what's wrong?" Curses leaned lightly against Captain Babycakes and folded his arms. And waited.

Which was good, because it took Dave a second to realize what was wrong, although once it hit him, wow, obvious.

"Ref," said Dave, but then started over. "I'm going to be taking Ref out on a date. You know, asking, going, paying, et cetera. A real date date. The sort of date that's actually a date, you know?"

"Uh huh."

"Well?" Dave opened his hands like he wanted alms. "Don't you see the problem?"

"I guess not."

"Curses, I've never even danced with her since we were fourteen and the only way we felt less stupid at stake dances was to pretend to dance, and the best way we could think of to do that was to go out on the floor together. You see what I mean?"

"Of *course* you're mean – I've always known that – but I'm not sure what you're getting at. The best way to pretend to dance was to really dance?"

"That's not the point. We're talking a *date* here, Curses! A *date* date!"

"Why are you doing this, if you're so concerned about it?"

Dave groaned and fell back in the sofa and told the story in twenty-nine seconds flat. "But it's a terrible idea. She's my *friend*, Curses. Sheez, it'd be like dating *you*."

"Um," said Curses, "there's actually a rather important distinction between me and Ref."

"Yeah, yeah. But the principle's the same."

"I'm really not sure it is. Haven't you heard what they say? 'Marry your best friend.'"

"Yeah, but Curses, don't you think you're being a bit presumptuous?"

Curses leaned over and plugged in the keyboard. *"Don't mess with Texas!"* he played. *"Don't mess with my Lone Star Home."* He lifted his hands and looked back at Dave. "Since when is the Texan your best friend?" he asked.

Byuck at Night

(The audience should be provided with night vision goggles [those who are still awake] or at least encouraged to bring their own so they may see this unlit scene in the darkened theater.)

JAMESON.
It's a moonless night . . .

CHORUS.
Moonless Night!

JAMESON.
The stars aren't coming out . . .

CHORUS.
Not coming out!

JAMESON.
I can finally sing and dance alone, 'thout fear of being seen.

CHORUS.
Being seen!

(Jameson dances wildly across the stage, singing primeval syllables throughout. Suddenly a female form appears, dancing also. She is silent; they avoid each other and Jameson is never aware. As the song winds to a close the female form disappears. Jameson stops.)

JAMESON.
That was beautiful. That was good. That was special. It felt meaningful. It felt like love. I felt like I wasn't alone.

CHORUS.
You weren't alone!

JAMESON.
This is why I came to BYU.

CHORUS.
Cha cha cha!

THIRTY-FOUR

Perfectly Symmetrical

DAVE HAD PICKED UP THE phone almost twenty times and had gotten as many as five numbers in before hanging up. He wouldn't call himself *nervous*, no. But it felt a lot like nervous. And they weren't butterflies he was feeling either. Just miniature moths. Souped up on amphetamines. And wearing lead boots. Dave had no idea why he felt this way.

1. He had a plan. Ottavio's and a movie.

2. The girl was just Ref. He called Ref all the time. And to do about as much.

3. He had gotten the teaching assistant position so, even though he would be making less per hour, and there were fewer planned hours, there were still more *guaranteed* hours, and he would probably be making more. So Ottavio's and a movie was no big financial deal. So long as it didn't become a habit.

4. Being nervous about a date is always stupid when you're twenty-three years old.

Dave picked up the phone and got to five numbers again before hanging up. So he tried a different tactic. Instead of dialing a seven-digit number, he dialed eleven, then a one, then ten more numbers, then another eleven.

"Hello?"

"Hi! Julie! Just who I wanted to talk to. How's the love life?"

"Oh, so you're finally calling me back. Great. Hi, Dave." Dave could hear her roll her eyes.

"Hi, Julie."

"Hi."

"Hi."

"Hi."

"Hi."

"What do you want?"

What Dave wanted was advice without Julie having any idea who he was talking about.

"Dave?"

"How's the boyfriend?"

"Oh, he's gone. It wasn't that tough. Just didn't return his phone calls, avoided him at school. Then called him and told him to shove off. Nicely."

Dave wasn't sure Julie was the best person to get advice from. "Aren't you a little young to have a boyfriend?"

"Well, yeah. Duh. I'm only fourteen."

When Dave was fourteen, he'd been terrified of girls. Especially girls like his sister.

Julie sighed at him. Aggressively. "I told you it wasn't my idea. I don't know why he thought that."

"Oh. Well, good." Julie was too young. What did she know about peculiar dating situations? Just because she *looked* twenty and sometimes *acted* twenty didn't mean she *was* twenty.

"Yeah, he just started telling people I was his girlfriend and calling me all the time."

"Just like that?"

"Um, yeah."

"Um, right."

Julie sighed and made a sucking noise, then got defensive. "Well, is that the only reason you called? I've got homework."

Dave thought about saying yes and just calling Ref, but he doubted that would work. It hadn't worked yet.

"Well?"

"Yeah ..." Dave tried to frame the question in his mind. Couldn't just start talking. "What if – say there's this girl and you're pretty good friends – See, I have to ask out this – Now, for instance, what if you found yourself –"

"Would you like to talk to Mom about this?"

"No. Thanks."

"Then what's your question?"

"Never mind."

"Okay, bye."

"Bye." Dave threw the phone against the arm of the couch. "Thanks a lot," he said.

####

DAVE SAT ON the couch holding the telephone and the remote. Since sitting down an hour ago, after hanging up with Julie, Dave had turned the phone on six times. The television seven. This had passed ridiculous and was waxing otherworldly. Ooh! *The Waxed Otherworld*. Good fifties sci-fi horror, there. "They Came to Wax the Earth!" Scary.

Anyway, Ref. Reasons to call her: He said he would. She's expecting it. It's been almost a week. It'll be fun. Reasons not to:

This is where Dave had gotten stuck each time he'd started listing. He either didn't know the reasons or, for some reason, he was determined to keep them secret from himself. He turned on the telephone. He turned off the telephone. He turned on the telephone. Take that, television. The dial tone filled the apartment and his head.

BEEP BEEP BEEP *If you would like to make a call, please hang up and –*

Dave hung up, but he didn't try again. The phone rang. "Hello?"

"Hi, Dave, it's Isabel. Is Curses there?"

"Curses? No, I figured he was with you."

"He was."

"Ah. Should I have him call you?"

"Yes. I mean no."

"No?"

"No," and she hung up.

Dave turned on the TV.

####

WHEN CURSES CAME in, Dave was still sitting on the couch, though he was reading now, an old copy of the *Daily Universe* from under the couch.

"Dave! You wanna play questions?"

Dave paused to reorient his brain. "You mean like in *Rosencrantz & Guildenstern*?"

Curses tapped his chin. "The one by Tom Stoppard?"

Dave shrugged. "What other one is there?"

"Are you implying there is another one?"

"Are you implying there isn't?"

"Are we talking about our dimension only?"

"What other dimension might be eligible for consideration?"

"Why not all dimensions?"

"Are you dissatisfied with our dimension?"

"You find it perfectly satisfactory?"

"Is there a problem with being satisfied?"

"Can't I like being dissatisfied?"

"Can't you at least try being positive?"

"Isn't questioning the opposite of positivity?"

"Why can't questioning lead to positive things?"

"Must everything be positive with you?"

"Don't you believe *some* dimension at least must be positive?"

"Can we move to some other topic than dimensions?"

"What do you want to talk about?"

"Well, what's happening in your life?"

"What does it look like?"

"It looks like you're just sitting on the couch."

"Haha! Point for me!" Dave jumped up, crumpled the newspaper, and threw it at Curses.

Curses batted it away and laughed. "Dang. You won," he said, and they sat down. "So, what's up?"

"I did the last of Peter's dishes – a plate under the sink with dried-on rice and beans on it – *my* rice and beans – couldn't call Ref, and fielded a call from your girlfriend."

"Isabel?"

"You got another one?"

"What did she say?"

"Just wanted to know if you were here."

"I wasn't?"

"Curses, I already won."

"She's not really my girlfriend."

"Well, it's hard to tell."

"I know." Curses pulled out some small paper circles out of his pants pocket. "I raided the holepunch at my sister's house yesterday."

"What are you going to do with it all? Besides spill all over the carpet, I mean."

"Circles are perfectly symmetrical. In every direction. I appreciate that. If I were a returning war hero, I wouldn't want a tickertape parade. I'd want a holepunch parade." Curses didn't seem to be talking to Dave; he was just sitting there, talking. "A parade . . ."

"How are you and Isabel?"

"Me and Isabel?" Curses dribbled a few of the circles into his hair. "Don't you mean me and Peter? Or rather, me and Peter and Isabel?"

"Peter's gone, Curses."

"As a physical phenomenon." Curses put the rest of the holes in a pile on the couch and turned to face Dave. "I feel poisoned, Dave. He poisoned me."

"What do you mean?"

"I mean I can't get over it. And Isabel's losing patience with me."

"Have you been praying about it?"

"I've been trying." Curses sank back into the couch, and his pile slid toward him. "I'm going to use Fast Sunday for it. Make a real go."

"What about Isabel? How is she?"

"She's fine. She's great. Peachy keen. She's over it. She's *so* over it. She's a true Christian."

Dave didn't know how to interpret Curses's tone.

"I'm twenty-two and a bitter old man, Dave." Curses sighed. "It's not that what Peter did was so bad, though it *was* – take Llew for instance: what's the difference between that kiss and rape, save as a matter of degree? – but that I'm so . . . so . . ."

Curses pulled on his hair and slapped his face a couple times. "So enough from the bitter old man, huh?" He nodded in apparent agreement with himself and scooped up most of the confetti. "I need to byuck or something." He tossed the confetti all over the hot-chocolate table.

Dave cleared his throat. "How to Get Over It?"

"Perfect."

How to Get Over It

a public service message
© 2001

When in the course of human events, one entity is wronged by another, it is incumbent upon the wronged party to Get Over It. A number of methods have been proposed and used successfully in Getting Over It, all of which can best be described by archetype. In other words, in order to best demonstrate how one (that means you, you poor, dear, damaged soul) can Get Over It, we are providing various scriptural precedents, and then butchering them.

Method #1: The Joseph Method.

Joseph, who later would use the stage name "Joseph of Egypt" (and, much, much later, "Joseph of the Amazing Technicolor Dreamcoat"), was sold into slavery by his brothers – to a bunch of hairy Ishmaelites no less. Years later, when Joseph next met his brothers, it is apparent that he had Gotten Over It. Except for the whole planting-stolen-goods-in-their-backpack thing, he was really very good to them. He gave them food and a house and collectible Pez dispensers for the kiddies. (Some translations interpret the Pez dispensers as "corn," but why would kids want corn?)

Now how, precisely, was Joseph able to Get Over It in regard to such a vile offence? Joseph explained to his brothers that, in his case, "it was not you that sent me hither [i.e., sold me into slavery and left me to suffer and sweat and rot in prison and then become second only to Pharaoh, no, that was no thanks to you], but God. God sent me before you to preserve you a posterity in the earth . . ."

The Joseph Method is ideal when, after some prayer and meditation, you discover that there was a great purpose in that hit-and-run in the Macy's parking lot, or in your roommate's insatiable appetite for feta cheese (*your* feta cheese), but the Joseph method should only be applied, we feel, when God's hand was actually involved. We do not consider it prudent to blame all your problems on Him. That would be wrong.

Method #2: The Naaman Method

Naaman, if you will recall, was a Syrian (of all things), and a highfalutin' Syrian at that. A highfalutin' Syrian with leprosy, that is. But he had heard about a prophet in Israel, a worker of miracles, and decided to come and get himself a miracle. When he arrived, the prophet didn't even bother to come out and see the highfalutin' Syrian with leprosy, but just sent out a messenger. And then – get this – the best this "prophet" could come up with was "Go and wash in the River Jordan seven times." Needless to say, Naaman was gravely insulted. First slighted, then insulted. He left in a huff.

Fortunately, Naaman traveled about with a servant not so highfalutin' as himself who said, in essence. "Golly gee whiz, Naaman, sir, but it wouldn't *kill* you." So Naaman did it, was cleaned, and praised God.

The Naaman Method, then, is to realize you're blowing this whole thing out of proportion so just Get Over It already!

Method #3: The Rehoboam Method

Calling the Rehoboam Method "The Rehoboam Method" is something of a misnomer, because Rehoboam was actually the wronger in this story. He became king and then immediately wronged the people of Israel by saying things like "I will chastise you with scorpions" when they hadn't even done anything that required chastising with lollipops. Rehoboam was, to be technical, a "punk."

What is instructive in this story is how the people of Israel Got Over It. The Bible simply reads that "all Israel went to their tents." In other words, get out of the situation, go home, do your own thing, and, thus, Get Over It. A nice little method, that.

Method #4: The Samson Method

Boy, you think Joseph had it bad, at least he didn't have his locks ravished by a bunch of Philistines like Samson did. So Samson asked God for one more moment of strength and brought down the building, killing everybody.

The Samson Method is just that: kill everybody. Its drawbacks are too numerous to mention within the scope of this brief monograph.

Method #5: The Jeremiah Method

Jeremiah spent a great deal of time in prison and on more than one occasion had people trying to kill him as well, which is bad enough to be sure, but once, King Jehoiakim took the prophecies which Jeremiah and his sidekick Baruch had carefully prepared for the king's benefit and "cut [them] with the penknife, and cast [them] into the fire that was on the hearth, until all the roll was consumed in the fire that was on the hearth."

Now, Jeremiah had not only spent a lot of time working on these prophecies – really, he was doing that jerk Jehoiakim a favor. But on top of all that, these were *prophecies* he'd burnt up! Jeremiah had every right to be angry. But instead, he just shrugged his shoulders, dictated them to Baruch again, and "added . . . unto them many . . . words."

So the Jeremiah Method is this: Lose yourself in the work of the Lord. Which is actually good advice, come to think of it.

THIRTY-FIVE

Varying the Proportions

CURSES HAD TAKEN THEIR ESSAY into Peter's room so he could use his Internet connection to post it on dorkytexan.com or whatever his website was called and, presumably, to decide which method of Getting Over It might work best for him. He had decided he'd already tried the Rehoboam Method, that the Samson Method wouldn't help in his case, and that the Joseph Method was probably just not applicable. That left the Naaman and Jeremiah methods. Hoo.

All of which meant that Dave was back to being alone on the couch. Alone, that is, except for the potential person implicit in his holding of the telephone. It was pushing ten now, and although that was hardly too late to call college folk, it did serve well as one more excuse to procrastinate.

And then, like the centipede forgetting her legs, Dave dialed and heard a phone from across the street ringing in his ear.

"Hello?"

"Is Ref there?"

A pause. "Oh, yeah. Sure. Hang on."

About forty-five seconds of shuffling sounds.

"Hello?"

"Hi, Ref. It's Dave."

"Oh, *hi*, Dave."

"Hi."

Silence.

Dave noticed one of his fingers was painfully wrapped up in a belt loop. He tried to pull it out. "Anyway," he said, "are you busy Friday night?"

"I don't know, why?"

I don't know, why? Give me a break. "*Because*, Martha dear, I'd like to take you out on a date date Friday night. Yea, even to dinner and a movie."

"Wow, dinner *and* a movie? Hard to say no to that."

"Try yes then."

"Yehyehyehyehyeh. Nope. Too hard. How about okay?"

"Okay."

"What time?"

"Six? Seven?"

"What time, Dave?"

"Six. No, six thirty."

"Six thirty?"

"Yes."

"Six thirty it is then. Ciao."

Ciao? Oh, Ref, please.

▥

FRIDAY, SIX THIRTY, and Dave had, after the manner of Dave, forgotten his wallet. So after picking up Ref, they swung back by his apartment to pick it up. Ref came up with him in case it took a while. It sometimes did, with Dave.

When they entered the apartment Ref took off her coat and set it on the couch. She was wearing an argyle sweater vest over a white collared shirt, neck open, sleeves turned up, with plain slacks and black shoes. But there was something about her ... "What?" Ref asked, and he realized he had been staring.

"Nothing, sorry," he said. But before heading to his bedroom, he looked one more time. Makeup, he realized. She was wearing makeup. Not much, but Dave was taken aback to realize how it brought her eyes and lips out of his everyday life and gave them a new, rather startling emphasis. He shook his head and found the hall.

His wallet was, miraculously, in the first place he looked – laundry bag – and so Ref was putting her coat back on less than 120 seconds after taking it off. The phone rang with Dave standing right next to it and before he could register an internal complaint about the tyranny of the telephone he had picked it up. "Hello?"

"Hi, is Curses there?" The voice, male, was rushed, hurried. Stressed.

"No, he isn't."

"Do you know when he'll be back?"

"No, sorry."

"Do you know where he is? Can I reach him?"

"No idea, sorry. He might be with Isabel. Do you have her cell number?"

"No, do you?"

Dave looked around at the pieces of paper on the wall and corkboard. "No, I guess not."

"Crap. Crap. Crap. Who's this?"

"Dave."

"Oh, hi, Dave. It's Marty, Curses's brother-in-law."

"Hi, Marty." Dave had never met Marty before.

"Dave, look, please, it's an emergency. Lorraine's in the hospital for an emergency appendectomy and somehow, in the shuffle, I guess Lorene got left at home. I'm up in Layton right now – I'm leaving as soon as I hang up, but it'll be a while before I can get down to Provo. Could you possibly go over to our house and watch Lorene?"

"I . . . gosh."

"Do you know where we live?"

"No."

"Okay, grab a pencil and paper."

Dave ran down to his room and wrote down the address, directions, where the spare key was, then said goodbye and hung up. "Boy," he said.

▥

DAVE COULDN'T SHUT up all the way to Marty and Lorraine's about how bad he felt, but the balance between guilt for no more dinner and a movie, and feeling like they were doing the right thing was confusing him and so he went on and on and on. Ref told him it was all right twenty times. Maybe thirty. Maybe more.

They pulled up in front of a yard full of bare rose bushes – giving them the sense they were about to mount an offense on Sleeping Beauty's briar-encapsulated suburban home. They found the key easily enough, but decided to knock first. After a moment the door swung open and little Lorene stood in her nightgown, looking out. As Dave opened his mouth, he realized he was about to sound like the evil stranger every little kid has been warned and warned about. "Hi, Lorene. Your daddy sent us."

"Hi," said Lorene. "My mom's having a baby." And she turned and walked away, leaving the door open. Dave and Ref looked at each other, shrugged, went inside and shut the door.

They followed the sound of the TV through the darkened hallway and found Lorene watching *Powerpuff Girls*.

"How are you doing, Lorene?" asked Ref.

Lorene didn't turn around. "Fine," she said. "There's a baby in her tummy."

Ref frowned. "So, you do know she's at the hospital, right?"

Lorene stayed fixed on Blossom and Buttercup fighting over a dangerous-looking ray gun. "Duh. Where do you think babies come from?"

Dave giggled. Then he saw Ref, whose look was changing from a plea for help to a why-don't-you-help-me, with a you-jerk implied. "Sorry," he said. He took a step closer to Lorene and crouched down by her side. "That's not why she's in the hospital, honey."

"Uh-*huh*!" Lorene jumped up and ran on her little girl legs over to a bookshelf near the table. She stood on tiptoes, reached above her head and pulled a slip of paper off the shelf. Then she walked back, smirked, and handed it to Dave.

It looked like a receipt, except it was nothing like a receipt, with these huge black squares with squiggles in them blocking up the strip of thermal paper. Ref came over to look.

"It's an ultrasound," she said.

At one end of the strip of paper was written in blue ballpoint, "Baby Dallin."

"Baby Dallin," said Dave.

"Baby *Dallin*," said Lorene, a tad over-triumphantly, Dave thought.

Ref took the ultrasound printoff from Dave. "These were taken less than two weeks ago," she said, pointing out a date to Dave. She looked at him. "Will the baby be okay?"

"The baby's fine," said Lorene, apparently to Fuzzy Lumpkins.

Dave nodded. "She's probably right. Appendectomies happen all the time. Even to pregnant people, probably."

Ref sat down by Lorene. "How big is your mommy?"

"She's a giant."

"No, I mean, how pregnant is she?"

Lorene considered this. "Like a horse, maybe," she said. Then she stood up and turned off the TV just as Mojo Jojo was about to finally take the girls down. "I'm hungry."

AS DAVE AND Ref watched Lorene eat macaroni and cheese and corn puffs, they wondered if they had been suckered.

"Do you think they really feed her that?"

Dave shrugged. "She *is* Curses's niece. When's your bedtime, Lorene?"

"A hunnerd o'clock."

Dave smiled. "That's a big time."

"Yes," said Lorene. "It's Barbie time."

Dave laughed and turned to Ref. "Mac and cheese? It's not Ottavio's, but pasta, cheese – what could be more Italian?" So he split the rest of it between two bowls, and after some foraging, they sat down with their faux-Italian cuisine.

Dave winked. "I guess this is how you learn about people," he said. "I've known you all my life, and I never would have guessed you for a ketchup-on-the-mac person."

"Yeah? Well, celery seed? That's just weird. Weirdly exotic maybe, but weird."

"It's good. I'm glad they had some. You should try it."

"If you try mine."

Dave considered. "Well," he said, "if that's what it takes."

They reached into each other's bowls, forked some up, and chewed, swallowed.

"Well?" asked Ref.

"Not as bad as I thought. But I still won't ever do it to my own. And I have to wonder what your dietetics professors would think."

"Dietetics is not home economics."

"I know. What about mine?"

Ref hesitated. "Weirdly exotic? Oddly vegetably? Might've been better if you'd thrown them in just before draining the water. They're pretty hard." She shrugged. Then they were both startled by a loud and large burp coming from a little, little girl.

"You should try mine," she said. "It's got corn puffies."

<hr>

LORENE WAS UP five to two in a best-of-ninety arm-wrestling contest with Dave. Dave was lying on the floor, his right arm ready for the next attempt. Ref was lying perpendicular to him, ready to referee the match. Lorene was standing, arms raised, thanking the fans. "Thank you, thank you," she said. "Ahhhhh. Ahhhhh." She turned to Dave and pointed at him. "You're going down, homey!" she squeaked.

Dave and Ref laughed. No, Dave laughed; Ref rolled on her back and guffawed. "Don't get ahead of yourself," said Dave. "I'm a slow starter, and you've got forty wins to go."

Lorene scoffed. "I beat my daddy all the time and he's way strongerer than you."

In fact, Dave was so not a challenge that she got tired of him and she and Ref took up pattycake, Dave as the accompanying percussionist, slapping his thighs and face in time with them, when the phone rang. "Rock on," he said. "I'll get it."

"Hello, Smiths."

"Dave?"

"Yes."

"This is Marty."

Dave took a moment to shift from silly to serious. "How's Lorraine?" he asked.

"Good. Surgery went well, but because of the baby and all, they want her to stay overnight. She asked if I'd stay with her."

How'll I get Ref home? Dave thought in reply.

"But don't worry. I got ahold of Curses and Isabel. They're down in Nephi for some reason with a flat tire and no spare. They've found someone to come fix it, but it'll be a couple hours. Do you mind staying with Lorene a little longer?"

"No, that's okay. We're having fun."

"Thanks. I appreciate it."

Marty hung up and Dave returned in time to see Lorene yawn and crawl into Ref's lap.

"S'unner clock," she mumbled.

"That was sudden," said Dave.

Ref started to stand up with Lorene, but she jumped up and ran away, screaming. She reached the door and turned back. "Brush teeth! Brush teeth!" she yelled.

After brush teeth and go potty and brush hair and feed fish, Dave and Ref listened to Lorene ask God to bless Mommy and Baby Dallin. Then she crawled into bed and Ref tucked her in as Dave slipped away to the bathroom. When he returned to the living room, Ref was going through cabinets.

"What are you doing?"

"Well, we've had dinner. I'd say it's time for a movie. The night is still young." She turned to look at Dave. "What are *you* doing?"

Dave looked at his hands and felt himself blush. "Um, it's, uh, lotion. Cucumbers and cream. It, ah, it smells good?"

Ref laughed at him. "Okay, they've got some good Woody Allen. *Annie Hall*, that's good. *Bananas*, weird but funny. I like the opening scene where they kill that guy. *Sleepers*, too weird. *Manhattan Murder Mystery*, the best. Red Skelton sketches which would be easy to turn off if Curses shows up. A bunch of old war movies, bluh. A bunch of Meg Ryan romantic comedies, one or two good ones. Wow! *Hard Day's Night*! Nice. And a whole bunch of Little Rascals and other little kid stuff. Oh. *My Neighbor Totoro*. Good movie."

"Very good."

"Want to watch it?"

"No, let's do Woody Allen."

"*Manhattan Murder Mystery*?"

"Sure. It's good?"

"Very. It's like *Rear Window* only funny. And it has a car chase. A low-speed car chase, but a car chase is a car chase, right?" She pulled it out and popped it in and sat with Dave on the couch. He took the remote and started the movie while she dug in her purse and pulled out a sandwich bag full of baby carrots and chocolate chips. "Get the lights, Dave."

He did.

"Too dark. Turn on the kitchen light."

He did.

"Perfect. Okay, you can sit down now."

He sat next to her. "This is your movie snack?" he asked.

"Yes. It's good. Semi-sweets and carrots, a match made in culinary heaven. You have no idea until you've tried."

"When did you try?"

"In college."

As the movie progressed, the tension heightened, the suspense intensified, the laughs came more freely, Woody panicked more readily, and Dave's respect for Ref's genius increased. Normally not a big fan of semi-sweet chocolate, Dave had to admit that the mild sweetness and moistness of the carrot element was the perfect complement to the bitter sweetness of the chocolate. He tried them together and in alternating mouthfuls. He tried varying the proportions of chocolate to carrots and carrots to chocolate. He wondered why See's didn't sell chocolate-covered carrot slices and if the market was big enough for him to start his own Them Chocolate Co., then celebrated his business acumen with another fistful. Ref observed it was a darn good thing she'd brought three bags.

Then carrots and chocolate scattered everywhere as the movie scared them three feet into the air. They landed on the couch laughing, and Ref punched Dave in the shoulder, claiming he had scared her. Dave wasn't about to put up with any more of her punching, so he hit her back and counterclaimed that it was she who'd scared him. Still laughing, Ref punched back and Dave pushed her away and she leapt for him and he struggled against her and they fell to the floor and they laughed and pushed and tussled, roughhousing under the television set where Woody Allen was trying to break down a door.

Suddenly exhausted, they collapsed on the floor and just laughed, on their sides, facing each other. Ref told Dave he had a piece of carrot between his teeth and Dave tried to get it with his tongue and Ref said he should just let her get it and she stuck her only long fingernail between his front teeth and then it was stuck under her fingernail and they laughed again, but not so hard, and they looked into each other's faces and suddenly something seemed different. And Dave wondered if Ref wasn't a couple of inches closer than she had been and am I losing my balance? and then they heard the front door opening and jumped up quickly and returned to the couch and their movie.

"Hey, Dave, Ref," said Curses. "Thanks for watching Lorene. Isabel dropped me off, so you can go home now."

"Oh. Hey, Curses. Thanks," said Dave as he stood up from the couch and stretched, then turned to help Ref up, but stopped before he finished raising his hand, so she stood on her own.

Curses walked into the kitchen and opened the fridge. "Was she okay?"

Dave nodded. "She was really good. We left some dishes for you, though."

"She was fun," said Ref. "We had a really good time."

"Well, anyway," said Curses. "Thanks." He sighed. "I'll see y'all to-morrow."

"Wow, Curses," said Ref, turning back. "I've never heard you sound so Texan."

"Well, I'm in a Lone Star state of mind." He smiled. It was a little wry, but it was a smile.

Ref picked up her purse, and Dave tried to remember where he had put his wallet and car keys before being Lorene's horsey. Then they picked up the scattered carrots and chocolate chips, said goodbye to Curses, and headed out.

"Would you like me to walk you up?" asked Dave as they entered Ref's parking lot.

"No," she said. "Thank you. I don't want you getting towed." She opened the door and put one foot into the stiff air. "I'm seeing you tomorrow, right?"

"Yeah," said Dave. "But even if not, it would be the day after. You know, like usual. Just can't get enough and so forth."

Ref smiled and got out, shut the door and ran off.

Dave rested his head on the steering wheel. He reached for the CD player and punched through for the loudest song. Turned it all the way up. And drove home.

THIRTY-SIX

They're Both Foxes

THE NEXT DAY WAS SATURDAY morning, and when Curses came home, though he spoke of being glad his sister and her baby were okay, he was sullen and walked in and out of doors all morning. Finally, he came into the front room wearing white jeans and white socks and a white t-shirt and offered Dave, grading eighty freshman compositions, this fact:

"Isabel is moving to Minnesota."

"What? She is? When? Why?" Dave set down his pen and straightened up.

"She got a job. At a hospital." Curses sighed, hands in pockets, and leaned back on his heels. "So I guess that's it."

"I'm sorry."

"Yeah. Me too. I think if the timing had been better I really could have loved her, you know? And it hurts to give that up, that chase, that possibility."

"Yeah."

"Anyway, as you can see, I'm wearing all white, representing that I am going to – as best I can – forgo the mourning process. I intend to return from dating and girlfriending to fence-building and byucking as my hobbies of choice."

"Oh. Okay, hang on." Dave leaned over the arm of his couch and rifled through his backpack, finally pulling out a little steno pad. "Here. Scenes I've written, mostly this week."

Curses took it and flipped through reading lines here and there. He looked to be rereading a small section over and over again.

"What?" asked Dave.

"Jameson and this girl, this Little Miss Accidental No-Name, fall off a bench and accidentally kiss on the way down?"

"It's a comedy."

"And then what happens?"

"I'm not sure. Something comedic?"

There was a knock on the door and Curses turned to answer it. It was Ref. She looked at Curses. "Well, Curses," she said, "you're right. We're long before Labor Day."

"Hey, Ref," said Dave. "Your phone's always busy."

Ref laughed. "Yours too. Maybe it's the timing."

"Must be."

"May I come in?"

Curses stood aside and Ref walked in, shedding her coat in a heap by the TV, and squeezed between the couch arm and Dave. She picked up one of the freshman papers. "Ew," she said and set it back down.

Curses closed the door, then immediately opened it again. "Ah! Breakfast!" he said, and ran off, returning with his wallet. He gave the pizza guy a twenty, took the pizza, and shut the door. "It's important to tip pizza guys generously," he said. "You never know when you'll be one. You guys want any?" Curses sat on the other side of Dave; Dave picked up the papers and put them in a stack under the hot-chocolate table.

"No thanks," said Ref. "I just ate. Last home game today. You guys coming?"

"Yes," said Curses. "My Saturday is overwhelmingly free. All I need's a white coat." Curses grabbed a napkin and started coaxing out his first slice of pie.

"And Dave?" said Ref, poking his arm and blinking.

"Of course. I haven't missed one yet."

"Do you mind byucky conversation, Miss Plantree?" asked Curses.

"No. Why?"

"Because," said Curses, the cheese dripping pepperoni back into the box, "what if, instead of people peopling *Byuck*, animals people it? Talking animals?"

"What?" Dave and Ref looked at each other, then quickly looked away.

"Yeah, and see, we can have all that species-based symbolism, creating dramatic irony. I mean – even if you didn't already know the story, you'd know Robin Hood and Maid Marian'll end up together because they're both foxes."

"Because they're both foxes," said Ref.

"Yes! Because they're both foxes," said Curses. "And Mickey and Minnie, Donald and Daisy, Pluto and Fifi –"

"Not Eric and Ariel in *The Little Mermaid*," Ref pointed out.

"Well, sort of," Dave disagreed.

"But not really," Ref insisted.

"Well, sort of," Dave agreed.

"So, we have our protagonist be, say, a monkey –"

"A rooster," Dave interrupted.

"– a rooster –"

"An aardvark," Dave suggested.

"No," said Curses. "How about a –"

"A rabbit," said Ref.

"Rabbit?" asked Curses.

"Bunny!" cried Dave.

"That is," said Ref, "a hare."

Curses nodded. "Okay, a hare. And when he meets a girl hare, the entire audience will know that she's The One because they've been trained by so many Disney movies growing up."

"Disney," said Dave, "as Pragmati."

"Mm," said Curses. "Well, be that as it may, we have dramatic irony."

Ref frowned. "Why do we need dramatic irony? Doesn't that spoil the story?"

"It's literary."

Dave shook his head. "What it is," he said, "is weird."

"No," said Curses, "it's speciesist. Specist. Something. But you know what? I'm comfortable with that. And you know why? Because I grew up in San Antonio, Dave, and in San Antonio, people don't marry horses or dogs, love them though we do. No, the best you can hope for in San Antonio is good friends, because in San Antonio, people marry only people, horses marry only horses, dogs marry only dogs. And I like to think I'm people." Curses shrugged and cleared his throat. "I guess it's just what I'm comfortable with. It's what I grew up on. So there you are. Call it specist – speciesist – if you will, but I think most of our audience will feel the same."

"Wow," said Ref. "San Antonio sounds like quite the place."

"Do you know where San Antonio is, Miss Plantree?"

"Um, Texas?"

"That's right, Miss Plantree. Texas. Don't Mess with Texas, Miss Plantree. Don't Mess." Then Curses remembered the pizza in his hand and took his first bite.

"Eat your pizza, Curses," said Dave. "Eat your pizza."

IT WAS COLD and windy, and scarce dry snowflakes flew over the field and through the stands. Dave and Curses had their hands between their knees and were shivering as the Cougars warmed up on the field. "I can't believe I lost my gloves again," said Curses for about the sixth time this winter.

"I can't believe you lost *my* gloves," said Dave.

"Yeah, me neither. So is Ref the leading scorer yet?"

"No." Dave pointed out a bleach-blonde Indian girl with (though you couldn't tell from the stands) an English accent. "Sarabhai is. She took it back from Ref two home games ago."

"So number fifteen is the one to watch?"

"And Ref too. Also number nineteen, Holmburg. They're the three homes – that's where the points come from. But for sheer entertainment-slash-athleticism, watch BYU's defense. There – numbers thirteen and seventeen – Coulter and Smith, A. – they are a coupla tough broads, let me tell you, point and coverpoint. Plus, since it's the last game of the season and she hasn't been kicked out of a game for almost a month, expect Smith to kick some Cowgirl trash."

"I don't know how I feel about that," said Curses. "I know it's just Wyoming, but it feels so un-Texan to speak of kicking Cowgirl trash. I'm not sure I can condone it."

Dave acted shocked. "What kind of Cougar are you!"

"A Texan Cougar. With cold hands."

As per plan, the same second the game started, Dave and Curses broke out their chemical hand warmers.

"Why didn't we do this earlier?" whined the Texan Cougar.

"Because we wanted them to last the whole game. Sheez, listen to you. You'd think it never snows in San Antonio."

"This isn't snow, this is white sand! Frozen white sand! Have you got any in your eye yet? Wait a second ... What did you sa – ?"

But Dave was on his feet, cheering. BYU had wasted no time in kicking Cowgirl trash and getting on the scoreboard, and it was his own number 23, little Miss Plantree, with the point.

"What happened?" asked Curses. "I missed it."

Dave laughed at him and pointed at a now empty patch of grass.

Plantree Plays Perfect Game (with a P)
by roving reporter Dav. Them

Cougar Martha "Referee" Plantree scored an amazing nine points in today's game against the Wyoming Cowgirls – not only a personal best, but better also than any player in one of those silly NCAA-recognized teams this year. Alas, alas, she was still one point away from being the Coug's leading overall scorer of the season, but Sarabhai's four points (down from five her previous two outings, yet still impressively high) proved necessary to BYU's win, with their defense weakened by both Smith and Coulter sustaining ankle injuries in the first ten minutes of the game. Barbaric Cowgirls!

Anyway, Plantree. This reporter has attended every home game, and has never seen any player – Plantree or otherwise – play with such grace, such aplomb, such – dare I say it? – beauty. Gazelle-like in form, her lithe little legs leaping over downed Cowgirls. Her third goal, a behind-the-back marvel the likes of which I've never seen, was one for the ages.

And her identical fifth and sixth goals – what a hoot! Totally fake out the goalie with a feint to the left, then *IN!* Wow.

The only sad thing is that BYU does not "officially" recognize women's lacrosse and so this fine team cannot aim for a national title – or even play a full season. Stupid BYU. And if it weren't so obvious that a certain player is one of my best friends, I might just send this in and make my case in the *Universe*. As if they would publish anything with such startling, Themian intelligence.

THIRTY-SEVEN

Human Puddle

"Ah, Curses! Didn't you learn *anything* from the angst guy?"

"Oh, come on, David!" Curses cackled (yes, cackled). "This'll be fun!"

"Maybe. But what do we tell this guy if he's actually good and we still don't need a musician in five minutes? We don't have a script, you know."

"Ah, that never stopped anybody."

"Hello?" called Ref from outside their door.

Curses opened it and Ref stood there, holding brownies.

"Ah! Brownies! Do come in." Curses stood aside and saluted. "We haven't had any of these since Peter. Word must finally be getting out."

"Have you heard from him? Is he okay?"

Curses shrugged and shut the door. Dave walked over and Ref handed him the brownies so she could take off her coat. The paper plate was warm, but her fingers were cold. Dave was startled, though, by how . . . nice they felt. Nice? They'd been friends for so long now, it was hard to believe they might not have ever touched hands before, and yet he could never remember having done so. And it seemed like he would. When he'd bumped Curses's hand earlier – they'd both been reaching for the remote – that had just been . . . hand-like. But Ref's hand was different; it was . . . nice. It was –

"Dave?"

Dave blinked.

"You can have a brownie, you know."

Dave saw Ref standing in front of him. Very close, in fact. Right there. In front of him. Cheeks . . . flushed. From the cold.

"Okay," said Dave. He took one out from under the plastic wrap and nearly broke its gooey mass in half as he tried to lift it to his mouth and hold the plate simultaneously. He ended up with a spot of chocolate on his nose. "Mmf. Good," he said.

Ref smiled and took the brownies away – that was another new smile, Dave was sure – and went for the couch. Curses sat beside her and helped himself to a brownie. So it was up to Dave to answer the door when someone attempted to pound it down, apparently with jousting equipment. And it was also left to Dave to then help a rather scrambled-looking person into the apartment – scrambled in hair and clothes, and a little shorter than Dave's chin. Dave helped him lug in an amp, three big speakers, and a leaden guitar case.

"Hi," said Curses. "You must be Crabby."

Crabby smiled and stuck out his hand, then opened his mouth, releasing force sufficient to knock down the walls of Jericho. "Right! Crabtree! Harron Crabtree! Glad to meet you!" he yelled. Loudly.

"Oh, *Crabtree*," said Curses, as he walked over to shake his hand. "I thought you said 'Crabby' on the phone."

Harron laughed. "Beauty! I'm glad! Like you already!" he yelled.

Dave stepped over the hot-chocolate table and sat down by Ref. He took another brownie and smiled at Ref while Curses continued conversing. After a manner.

"I see you brought your equipment."

"Uh?"

"Your equipment – I see you brought it."

"Uh?"

Curses pointed, and shouted, "Your *equipment*! I *see* it!"

"Oh yeah! Cool, huh? I love it! I played some guitar before my mission! But then I didn't for a while after! Now I do again!"

Dave and Ref shared raised eyebrows and tried to surreptitiously cover their ears. "Wow!" Curses was yelling, with embarrassingly exaggerated gestures – like the kid was hard of gesture, as well.

Harron nodded. "Yeah! After that pipe bomb went off, I couldn't hear at all for a while, so I started playing guitar again! Wanna hear?"

Curses looked to Dave and Ref, but they just shrugged. This was Curses's show. So he turned back to Harron and said, "Yeah."

"Uh?"

"YES!"

"Great!" Harron dropped to his knees, pulled out his guitar and started plugging things in.

"Way to go, Curses," said Ref. "Another winner. Better than Garth maybe even."

"Garth!" said Dave, silently trying to snap a finger and failing. "That was his name." He tried to snap again. Nothing. Time to trade in for new fingers.

Harron jumped back to his feet and slung the guitar strap over his arm. He jumped up and down a little and smiled his rather scrambled smile. "Ready?" he yelled.

"Ready!" Curses yelled, and gave him a double thumbs-up.

And then Harron began to "play" the guitar. It would have been hard to believe he had ever so much as touched a guitar before except that no one without a bit of training could have possibly coaxed so much horrendous noise out of just one instrument. There were no discernible chords, progressions, nothing. On top of that, Dave doubted he had ever heard something so *loud* before. At least not since Pangaea separated. It occurred to Dave that they would have to let *Byuck* patrons with pacemakers leave the theater before Harron was allowed onstage. Or even backstage.

Then, Harron stopped. He was panting and collapsed onto one of his speakers. Dave, Ref and Curses were also drained. Dave felt like his muscles had been vibrated into useless goo and that he would now sit forever, a human puddle, a mess of English-major DNA good only for a housecat's liquid refreshment.

"Hello?" asked Ref. "Hello? Hello?" She hit her head. "Hello?" She turned her head on one side. "Hello? I can't hear me."

Curses turned to her, holding his head like it was an explosive medicine ball. "What?"

"I can't hear me."

Curses turned his head gently, but kept it in his hands – for safekeeping, Dave supposed. "What?"

"I said!" said Ref, "I can't hear me!"

"Oh . . . Me neither."

Harron took off his guitar and stood by, shaking his shoulders and looking up and down a bit. "Phew! How about that, eh? Wrote it myself. I admit I'm not one hundred percent sure about that coda, but, and I hate to brag, but I'm really quite the composer, eh? I'm a major artist in bud, I can feel it. Did you like how I incorporate elements of the fight song? Beauty."

Dave stood up, then paused a moment to monitor his blossoming headache. He stepped over the hot-chocolate table. "Could you hear that?"

Harron looked confused. "What? Hear? Hear what?"

"Your, ah, music! Your song!"

Harron laughed "No man, not really, but I can *feel* it! It rumbles through my bones, man! Like thunder! Like . . . eternity!"

"I see." Dave nodded. "Doesn't that make it hard to compose?"

"No, I'm not married!" He held up his left hand and pointed at the ring finger. "See? No ring!"

"What?" Dave shook his head. Ouch. "No, *how do you compose if you can't hear?*"

"All feel, man! All feel! You know, like Beethoven!" Harron closed his eyes and went crazy on the air piano.

Curses opened his mouth, but Ref beat him to it. "I knew Beethoven, and you, my friend, are no Beethoven."

Curses pouted. "That's my line," he said.

Harron finished his air concerto and crouched down to start disconnecting his equipment. "Wait – did you want to hear another one?"

"No!" three trembling people screamed.

Harron nodded. "Cool."

Curses went over to help Harron unplug. "Thanks, Harron!" he said. "We'll be calling you when we get some script down!"

"Liar," said Ref.

"Beauty, man! Talk to you later." Harron finished unplugging and packing, and somehow got everything on his person, with straps galore and electronics protruding dangerously. Ref and Dave stood and all three shook Crabtree's hand. Dave closed the door after him and locked it, then all three walked to the couch and, as if on cue, collapsed.

Dave sighed and said, "That was an exhausting interview." No response. "Wouldn't you say?"

Ref said, "Uh."

Dave said, "Take that notice off your website, Curses. I'm not kidding."

Curses said, "Uh."

Dave flopped his head over to look at Curses, who was staring at the corner of the hot-chocolate table. Then he swung it over to Ref who was staring at her knees from a lazy perspective under Dave's arm. She looked kind of cute with her neck up inside his elbow like that.

Dave's eyes flew open. He yelped and jumped up and fell over the hot-chocolate table.

Ref and Curses sat up to watch him. By the time Dave had successfully found a sitting position against the far wall and was rubbing his injured shins, Curses was slouched back into the couch, though still regarding him. Ref, however, was touching her neck and her expression was rapidly cycling though annoyance, shock, recognition, confusion, worry – the gamut – so rapidly Dave got dizzy just looking at her.

"I," said Dave, "am thirsty." He stood up. "Anyone want some water?"

"Yes," said Ref in a voice so small that if Dave hadn't been watching her face with his eyes wide he would never have heard her. "Me."

Curses looked at Dave, then at Ref, then at Dave, then at Ref, then at Dave again. And, slowly, his eyebrows began to relax. And his mouth began to smile. "Arrooo," he said. "Arroowoowooo."

iiiii

REF HAD LEFT without her water, and Dave was irritated at Curses for reasons he couldn't articulate. Curses was getting ready for a goodbye!-we're-just-friends-now! date with Isabel. He walked back to the front room, buttoning a clean shirt. Dave was sitting on the couch, suffering from emotional potluck.

"You know, Dave," said Curses, "I really, *really* was smitten with Isabel. Am, maybe. I didn't tell you this, but after I replaced you and Ref at Lorraine's, I cried pretty much all night. But it's okay now. It's best for her to move on with her life, to go to Minnesota, and I'm happy for her." Curses sighed as he did up his shirt's last button, then looked ceilingward. "She really was beautiful, though. And so good. I'll miss her."

Dave had listened carefully, and empathy was easy to come by – always is after an all-night-crying story, but when Curses finished talking, only two words remained: Smitten and Beautiful. And he thought of Ref.

"No," he said. "Oh no, oh no, oh no." But didn't it make sense? Falling to the floor and breathing each other's air. The way she looked in long skirts and sweaters. The electricity in her fingertips. The way she so casually fit under his arm . . . "No, no, no, no, no."

"What is it?"

Dave looked up at Curses and could feel the horror on his face. "Ref."

Curses nodded and started retying one of his shoes. "Yeah. I know. You didn't notice till just now?"

Dave dropped his head into his hands. He thought of a day early last fall when Ref had been over. She'd been sitting on the couch and Dave had been lying on the floor, reading the newspaper, when a distinct odor hit him. "What's that smell?" he'd asked. "It smells like . . . childhood summertimes and swimming pools."

"Good description, writer-boy," Ref had said, and Dave remembered feeling flattered. "Maybe if you would turn west, no, south, and look at me you could figure it out."

Dave had turned and seen Ref squeezing sunblock onto her forearm. "It's not sunny today," he'd said.

"UV rays know no limits. They disbelieve in clouds."

"Me too – no little black clouds in my worldview."

"Clouds," Ref had said, "make sunsets spectacular."

Dave had considered this as he'd watched Ref rub the sunblock into her arms and hands and then he'd taken the bottle off the hot-chocolate table and put some on himself; but from the perspective of today, it seemed like all he'd been considering were her arms. Like he'd been in love with her arms.

"Maybe it's been a long time," he told Curses. "A very long time." Dave was shocked at this discovery and depressed by his shallowness. His best friend, and he liked her because she looked nice. She was attractive. She was a beautiful girl. "What?"

"I said," said Curses, "maybe it's time you do something about it."

"What do you mean?"

"Ask her out, you nimrod."

"No," said Dave. "It would be a disaster. I've told you this before but I need to remind myself as well: I'll never – and that means ever – date anyone I'm primarily – let alone only – physically attracted to. That's my policy. It's a good policy. It's the only speck of possible righteousness I have left."

Curses untied his other shoe and checked the laces' lengths against each other. "Let me get this straight," he said. "You're telling me these feelings for Ref – your best friend since infancy – are merely physical?"

Dave leaned back on the couch. "They're not feelings, and they're not for Ref. At least, not the Refness of Ref. You know what I mean?"

"Let me ask you something, Dave: do you even have any idea what she looks like from the neck down?"

Dave was appalled. "I can't do that!" He spluttered some. "That's a terrible thing to do!"

"Try anyway."

Dave dropped his head. He might as well. This was par for the lechery course, after all – cataloging girls by physical attributes. Embrace your status as a sinner.

"Well," said Dave. "I guess I like it when she dresses sort of Ivy League, with –"

"No," said Curses. "Stop. I'm not talking clothes." Curses turned and looked right into Dave's eyes. "Tell me about her body."

Dave trembled. He felt like he was before the bar of God, awaiting announcement of punishment – he had just to admit his guilt. Maybe this was part of the repentance process for his lustfulness. "She's ... She's ..." Dave paused. "Well, she's an athlete, right? So she must have some sort of athletic build." He concentrated. "Muscles ..." He frowned. "Or something."

Curses smirked and finished tying the second shoe and stood up. "That the best you can do?"

Dave dropped his face into his hands. "Isn't it enough?"

"To prove my point, not yours."

"Oh? And what point is that?"

Curses placed a hand on Dave's shoulder. "My point is that you are not in the shallow depths of some silly hasty physical infatuation." Curses paused, removed his hand, stood up. "You need to talk with her."

"Yeah? About what? That her longtime friend's as shallow a lech as anyone she's ever met?"

"Do you really think you're Peter?" Curses looked away. "What do you think love is, Dave? You need to talk to her."

"I do. Practically every day."

Curses turned back. "Good point in my favor, but I mean *talk* talk."

"A talk talk, huh? And what, O Byucky God of Relationships, might that be?"

"Use your head, Dave." Curses turned to the door and threw on his coat. "Or no, don't. *Stop* using your stupid head and listen to your heart for a change. If between you, your heart, Ref, and her heart, you can't manage decent talk, then maybe I'm wrong, you're right, and you're just a crazy lust-hound. But call her."

Dave frowned. "I thought you were supposed to be the comic relief in my life. The funny friend."

"With a name like Curses?" Dave had no answer so Curses opened the door and stepped out. "You know, Dave. It's something good. I have to say goodbye to something good tonight – I wish I ... I just wish ..."

Dave looked up, but Curses had closed the door.

194   THERIC JEPSON

MARCH 10 (LATE)

Well, Curses had another guitar player over today and man this guy was LOUD. My ears are still bleeding haha not funny.

After he left, we were all worn out by the noise. We: me, Curses, Ref. So we sat on the couch.

Duh.

Anyway, somehow,

Jameson Misplaces His Mind

You would think a mind would be hard to misplace. Jameson certainly had thought so. Jameson, in fact, still thought so after misplacing his. Here's how it happened:

He wasn't in love with a girl, but accidentally touched her anyway and some hormonal reaction things happened that expelled his mind from his body. Or maybe he *did* love a girl, but that was wrong, so he was smitten. From on high, I mean.

Jameson did *not* love a girl. And he should have known better. He may have ruined one of the most important things in his life just because he couldn't control his own stupid self.

Jameson was a moron. To be frank, I rather doubt he had a mind to begin with.

Anyway, Curses is telling Isabel goodbye tonight. They UPSed her stuff yesterday, and she flies out early tomorrow.

Curses is sort of a know-it-all. He seems to think this tryst with Isabel makes him an expert on all matters intergenderational. Listen to him and you'd probably think I should fall in love all over the place and get married or something.

No.

He thinks I should marry Ref.

And why not?

Well, she's my friend.

"Exactly," he would say. What a wit.

Jameson had a friend. Jake. No, Jerk. Jake the Jerk. Yes. And what a jerk he was. Thinking he was man of the hour, king of the swamp. The know-all and end-all. Jameson came to him for advice regarding his missing mind, and what do you think the Jerk said? "Lose it some more," he said. "Lose it some more."

Some friend.

He's broken up because he screwed things up with Isabel so now he's filling my mind with crap like "Ref's a girl*" and "She's so* pretty*" and "You guys are such good friends" –*

What – does he think I don't know that?

The Jerk got a job telling futures, but all he did was rifle through people's wallets and make up wild tales of love and heartbreak and venereal disease and then give people absurd solutions to eternal human problems.

But Jameson didn't need platitudes. He needed to remember the difference between touching someone and loving someone.

And Jake the Jerk needed to learn the difference between having a friend and having a fling.

I'm going outside. I'm going for a walk. The air's still cold out there. Cold air's supposed to be good for you. Refreshing. Mind-cleaning. Perhaps mind-finding.

Cold showers have a rep too. Maybe it'll rain. Maybe I'll catch a cold. The flu. Pneumonia. That stuff puts people in hospitals, so it must be good.

But Ref would visit me. Because she's nice. Because she cares. Because she's a good friend.

I've got to go.

THIRTY-EIGHT

Better Find

A COLD WALK, A FRETFUL night, a distracted Sunday, an aimless drive, a better sleep, a warmer walk, two tests, a pop quiz, a cooler walk, laundry, and an argument with Curses over the proper syllables to emphasize in "byuckalicious" later, Dave had to admit he felt much better. His head had cleared. He hadn't talked to Ref. A funky coin-collecting magazine had arrived in the mail for some ancient resident named Bill Presly – Sixteen Bolivian Mickey Mouse Collectible Medallions for eleven dollars. Yes, Dave was more in charge of his life than he had been in weeks.

"I feel great," he reminded his reflection before brushing his teeth. He said it again after he had finished and was practicing Disarming Smile Number Three.

The phone rang and Curses picked it up.

"It's for you, Dave!"

Dave came up the hall to the phone. "Who is it?"

Curses shrugged. "A girl?"

Dave considered. His mom? His sister? Probably his sister. "Hello?"

"Dave?"

It was Ref.

"Hi, Dave. This is Ref. It's been a couple days since we've talked."

Dave frowned. This didn't sound like conversation. This sounded like reading a script.

"Anyway, the reason I'm calling is simple. You were at all my games –"

She seemed to require a reply.

"I was."

"And don't think I don't appreciate it. In fact, you've been my biggest fan since, well, high school at least. My best friend, my biggest fan, what a combination."

Don't you know it, thought Dave.

"Anyway, even though we're not 'official,' we did so well this year that BYU is hosting a women's lacrosse banquet and awards ceremony. As a player, I've been given two tickets, and I thought you might like to come. You know, um, free food and everything."

Dave's mouth was dry. He listened to the silence. He needed to think of something to say. "When is it?"

"Oh, yeah." Ref laughed. Sort of. "Next Friday. Seven thirty."

Dave felt a polluted sea of relief, regret, and cowardice wash over him. "Gosh, Ref, I don't know. I'd love to, I really would, but I'm supposed to help some freshmen prepare for a test Friday at seven."

"Can't you change it?"

The sound in her voice made Dave's stomach drop. "Well, I can try." And Dave suddenly remembered that not only was Ref his best friend, but he was hers too. Hubris. But he knew it, anyway. Hubris. How could he be *her* best friend? He was just some guy, after all.

A guy who wanted to go.

For some of the right reasons.

And about half the kids had said Thursday would be better anyway. He could just change it. It wasn't too late – it was only Monday. But Ref deserved an answer now. And he loved her.

No, stupid, listen to yourself. It's Daphne all over again. Stay away. You owe it to her.

"I'm sorry, Ref. I'll try, but you better find someone else. Just in case."

"Okay," she said on the edge of saying ...

"Bye."

Click.

THE MEMOIRS OF DAVID THEM
Thoughts on Referee Plantree

I've been thinking a lot about her lately; I've been trying to remember the first time I ever met her. We were young. We knew each other before kindergarten anyway; that was when our families both lived on the same block and so we played a lot. She was called Referee even then, and her older brother was Clipper – still is, actually. Then, I think it was first grade, her family moved into the house they live in now, a couple miles away.

But we remained best friends. Not as close, perhaps, in junior high, but I guess that's the way junior high goes. And I don't think it was really until high school that we understood why we weren't allowed to sleep over at each other's houses, I mean – why not? She's my best friend. Wow, we were young. I opted never to have a slumber party for my birthday since Ref couldn't have come. Although, come to think of it, she had one each year of junior high. There you go.

I went to all her sports meets and we even went to junior prom together, though we never thought to call it a date. And we both thought it was lame, so we didn't go back as seniors. We went to Denny's instead. Denny's and the dollar theater. We took our younger brothers with us, who were freshmen at the time. That was fun.

Then she left me for BYU. And I left for a mission. Then I came back. And before you knew it, we had seen each other maybe three or five times in four years. So when I decided to come to BYU, I wondered. I wondered what she would think. I wondered if she would care. Would we still be friends?

I remember back when her family moved, crying on my mom's lap. Even though she was still in Mrs. O'Keefe's class with me, I thought we couldn't be friends anymore. She lived so far away. But we were still friends.

But now I don't know if we can be anymore. I'm afraid I've ruined it. I'm afraid the only stage left in our lifelong relationship is regret. And I don't know how to change that. I don't know how to save what we had. But I don't want to lose it.

I don't know what to do.

THIRTY-NINE

Nice Quiet Place

DAVE SPENT THE FIRST PART of Tuesday trodding head down from class to class, utterly failing to enjoy the first day in months that not only could be called warm, but was warm. Instead he was berating himself for one failing or another (you like girls! you like unbowdlerized Grimms' fairy tales! you like shampoo commercials!) and watching his shoes strike sidewalk over and over and over again.

As he approached University Parkway on his way home, one of those shoes suddenly tripped over the other one and Dave flew face first into a signpost, barely getting his hands out in time to prevent a nice crease in his forehead. The impact bounced him back a couple steps, then he staggered on to the intersection, his mind void of thought.

As he stood there waiting for the light to change he realized, One, he was moping. Two, no one likes a moper. Three, he should knock it off. So he took his keys out of his pocket and threw them over University Parkway into the nearly deserted stadium parking lot. "Keys!" he cried. "Where are you going?" The light changed and he thanked the little green man for appearing – "Martian or leprechaun?" he politely inquired – then ran into the parking lot and kicked his keys as hard as he could. He chased his keys kick by kick to the low hill at the east end of the lot, then grabbed them and ran up the little incline to the stream that flowed there, already filling with spring runoff. It was actually a ditch, he supposed, but too pretty to be called that. He put the keys in his pocket, sat on the dirt, listened to the water, looked at the parking lot through the soon-to-green foliage, and prayed.

He started by mentioning the beautiful day, the good semester he was having, his new job and this nice quiet place to sit and clear his head and, he realized, pray aloud. Like Joseph Smith. Dave smiled. He thanked his Heavenly Father for his friends. He mentioned how good they were to him, then admitted maybe he wasn't such a good friend in return. He mentioned Ref. They reminisced about his many years with her, about the times he and she'd had. Then he admitted something he had never even admitted to himself. He searched for the right words. It wasn't that he was *Aware* of Ref, though that was suddenly true. And it wasn't that he *Loved* her either. But she was his friend and somehow . . . that wasn't enough. Dissatisfaction. Was that his problem? Ingratitude. Not exactly.

Dave leaned back on his hands and looked up at the sky through the trees. "I told her I couldn't go to her banquet with her," he prayed. "Why did I do that?" Why *had* he done that? Dave lowered his head and shook it. He brushed his hands on his pants and leaned over his knees. And kept talking.

Dave hadn't checked his watch when he'd started praying, and didn't when he finished either. It hadn't been an Enos-a-thon and it hadn't been earth-shattering. But he felt better. A lot better. He walked the rest of the way home smiling, and he kept talking to God in his mind because he felt He was still there, listening.

Dave felt like doing frabjous cartwheels down the sidewalk, or some other acrobatic act of derring-do. Pity he didn't know how.

FORTY

An Expiration Date

SOMEONE HAD DRAWN HOPSCOTCH SQUARES on the basketball court near where Peter had wrecked his car and Dave hopped through them on his way home. He really wasn't any closer to figuring out what was wrong with him, but at least he liked himself again. He could even understand why Ref might (might) like him. Not that he would go so far as to recommend himself. But the day's sunshine and doldrums having given way to just sunshine, Dave was glad to see the curtains were open when he opened the door. But the cherry on top had to be the music that greeted him: Billy Joel's "Tell Her About It."

"*Listen boy . . .*" Billy sang. Curses had brought his podunk stereo into the front room and was sitting on the couch, going through some three-by-five cards. "Cheaters," he explained, "for my speech on situational ethics."

Dave dropped his bag on the floor and joined Curses on the couch. "Curses," he said. "I'm glad to see my influence has finally begun to rub off on you."

"How so?"

"Billy Joel, man! *These* are the groovin' tunes."

"Oh, that." Curses nodded then returned to his cards. "Whatever."

Dave reached over to his bag and pulled out the much crumpled syllabus to his Introduction to Folklore class to try to decipher its ever more illegible wisdom, while Billy Joel sang about the importance of constant communication.

Which is the wisdom of syllabi, thought Dave as he smoothed the tattered green paper on his leg. Looks like something's due Friday.

He returned to his backpack and pulled out that class's purple spiral-bound notebook. No. Wait. Crap. This is the purple spiral-bound notebook for byucking. Where's the – ah! Here it is. Now let's see . . .

Dave looked for his pencil, finally finding it already sticking out of his mouth. He rifled through his notebooks and made some notes and discovered, to his delight, that the thing due Friday had been postponed till Wednesday because of some conference his professor was attending and that he had already finished it anyway. Go Dave!

"My Thursday night has been freed from its shackles!"

"If it were Friday, I'm sure Ref would be happy to hear that."

Dave looked at Curses, who yawned and fanned his mouth with the cards like he was trying to shoo in a fly.

"You think I should take her to her banquet thing then?"

Curses gave up on the imaginary fly and pointed at Dave with the cards. "You want to hear what I think should happen?"

"Yes?"

Curses dropped the cards and started ticking off some items on his fingers. "I think Arctic terns should be able to take a year off if they don't feel like flying twelve thousand five hundred miles one year. I think storks should have to choose whether they want to be harbingers of death or bringers of babies – no more of this both crap. I think blue-footed boobies should apply for a name change, loons should take voice lessons, and speaking of birds, I think you should take Ref to her banquet." Having ticked the final item off on his thumb, Curses leaned over to start picking up his cards.

The barrage had left Dave feeling . . . discombobulated? Close enough. Dave felt discombobulated. "Tell Her About It" played on in the background, but jouncy rhythms can feel a bit like a paintball in the thigh to the discombobulated.

"No offense, Curses, but Ref's my actual genuine number-one best friend. Even with that four-year hiatus when she was here and I was elsewhere, she was my best friend again as soon as we came back together. I'm not going to mess with that."

"Dave. Fence-building rhetoric aside, do you want to get married someday?"

"Well, yeah, I suppose."

"But I assume that since you don't want to date Ref, you don't want her to be the girl you marry either?"

"I –" Dave frowned. Did he agree with that statement?

"Because, if you won't take Ref to her banquet, I'm guessing you've eliminated her from your pool. That's pretty smart – eliminating the people you already like. Prevents you from marrying them for the wrong reasons."

Dave frowned.

"And I'm sure your wife will love having Ref come over all the time to hang out. That'll be great fun. Where'd I leave my highlighter?"

Dave watched Curses leave the room then leaned over the armrest and switched purple notebooks. Half of him wanted to force the other half to think about homework or byucking or Cheez Whiz or *anything*, but instead both halves kept mulling over what Curses had just said, and began listing facts. The first three put his mind on pause:

Ref is my best friend.

I want to keep her my best friend forever.

Once one of us gets married we can never be best friends again. That'll be it. Zip, zop, finitto.

Billy Joel admonished Dave that he was a big boy now, and Dave's mulling intensified.

"You don't mind, do you?" Curses was carrying Dave's Crayola Big Box. "I think I left my highlighter in Spain."

"Spain?"

"Why not?" He sat down and pulled out a crayon. "What the heck kind of color is Cerise?"

The door blasted open and Dave and Curses and ninety-six crayons all leapt skyward. "I'm gettin' married, boys!" cried X. "Two weeks from today!" He skipped inside and walked to the kitchen table to look through the shoebox for mail. "You know, I haven't gotten mail the entire time I've lived here. I wonder where it's all going?" He thumbed through the shoebox again, but Dave and Curses both knew it only contained ancient residents' mail, credit card applications, and some wedding invitations Dave hadn't bothered to open. "Huh." X shrugged, and walked back out the open door, closing it gently behind him.

"Was that a new X?" gasped Curses.

"How new is 'new'?"

"I don't know. Cerise-new?"

Dave fiddled with his notebook, drawing little images of spaceships in the crayon box's closest approximation of the puke-yellow bricks that defined half the buildings on campus. He stared at his ugly spaceships and wondered if they were a metaphor.

"Thanks for helping me pick up your crayons, Dave."

"Huh? Oh. Sorry. Here. Take this one. Found it in my lap."

"You're too kind. It's not like I have a speech tomorrow or anything."

"You'll do great."

"I know that. I can't believe you think that needs to be said. Do you not know I'm Curses Olai? I'm totally offended."

"I've been doing that a lot lately."

"Don't mope."

"Sorry," Dave said.

The song lyrics went on giving him advice for several more minutes. *Tell her about it!* Billy implored.

"I need to tell Ref I'm sorry, don't I?"

"What for now?"

"The banquet thing."

"Ah, the banquet thing."

"Wait. How did you even know about the banquet thing anyway?"

"She told me about it," Curses admitted.

"She did? What did she say?"

"Oh, just the normal stuff. That you suck and so forth. Nothing I didn't already know. Why didn't you just say yes?"

"It's hard."

"Hard? *She* asked *you*."

"Don't be dense. We go out, that may kill our friendship. We *don't* go out and *that* may kill our friendship. And even if neither of those things does it in, then once one of us gets married, *that*'ll kill it! I just – I just – I don't want to *ruin* anything! It's not like you can just change your mind and step backwards. Don't you know a kiss would change the world forever?"

"Whoa, whoa! Settle down, Ethel Barrymore! Auditions are over! You get the part!"

"Sorry."

Curses swept one arm in front of him. "How about an evolutionary example? Say there were, oh, I don't know, a bunch of dinosaurs. Then one day some of them start growing feathers. The other dinosaurs all make fun of them. I mean – not only do they look stupid – but talk about impractical! And in this tropical clime!

"Then one day a comet hits and the planet's covered in clouds of soot for six years and immediately after everything plunges Ice Age ho! And the only dinosaurs that make it are the ones with feathers.

"Things change, Dave. Things always change. The only question is whether you're an adapter or extinction-bound. That's science. You wanna die out?"

Dave shifted his weight and pulled a crayon from under his rear. He scribbled out his spaceships with a sudden blast of burnt sienna and leaned back into the couch. The problem was . . . the problem was that he and Ref had an expiration date. He'd never realized it before, but it was true. They did. One way or another, things were going to end.

Dave squeezed his eyes shut and tried to think of his patriarchal blessing. Regarding marriage, all it said was, "you will marry someone who will bring joy to your life," which, it suddenly occurred to him, must disqualify Ref, because it didn't say someone who *had* brought joy to your life or who *does* bring joy to your life but who *will* bring joy to your life.

Hang on. How could prior and/or present joy somehow prevent and/or preclude future joy? That was the stupidest thing ever. So Ref qualified after all.

Dave was surprised to feel his heart react.

Or tap dance, more like. Ta tata ta. He tapped his toes to "Tell Her About It." *Man* he loved this song. And –

Wait a second.

"Curses?"

Curses looked up over his cards.

"Curses, how many times have we heard this song?"

Curses shrugged. "Several."

"It's on repeat?"

Curses nodded.

"Oh . . . You – you're some kind of evil genius."

Curses nodded. "That's more like it."

▥

BILLY JOEL MAY have offered some really bad advice to Virginia and Captain Jack, but he had offered some pretty prescient advice to David Them. And as Dave closed the door behind him, he felt guilt at the thought that Ref was a trusting soul who had put her trust in him, and steely determination at the memory of Billy's stirring exhortation to tell her how he felt right now.

As Dave headed for the crosswalk, he began an emotional inventory and was surprised to discover that a) Ref really was his number-one very best friend, b) he was willing to marry her to keep her as such, c) it would probably take only two or three steps in that general direction before she went from being his best friend to being the person he cared most about in the world – and not just this world, but any world, any time. Which was terrifying and exhilarating, like shaving a tiger.

Usually he feared for his life crossing University Avenue. But today, even if a 1985 Ford truck swept past with as much inertia as a wayward comet, he imagined it would pass right through. Dave didn't know how to quantify what he was feeling, but he knew it felt good.

After all, Ref would bring joy to the rest of his life. Ref! That little girl in pink overalls. That gangly teenager with a killer volleyball spike.

That woman on the other side of the street.

Dave finished crossing University Avenue; he floated into Sierra de Provost and up the stairs, his shoes cushioned with an endorphin gel. He knocked. Ref opened the door. And although he had noticed she was pretty before, he had never realized how lovely she was, how stunningly beautiful. He almost couldn't speak.

"Ref," he managed. "I'm sorry. I don't know what I was thinking. Nothing could possibly make me happier than to accompany you to the lacrosse banquet thing. Nothing. I would quit my job it that's what it came to. I'll change the review tomorrow. I will. If you would let me take you and see you suitably honored for your role on the team, I would be honored – no! pleased – no! gratified. I would be really gratified."

Before Dave could smile at her and at how well his speech had turned out, he was deflated by a faraway sadness in her eyes. "Ah, Dave," she said. Every joint in Dave's body went rigor mortis on him. "Thanks, but don't worry about it. My old ... friend Ned called. He's going with me."

Dave had nothing to say.

Ref looked at an inside wall. "I'll talk to you later?" And she closed the door.

a jameson yarn
by david them

Jameson had never met Ted before, but that hardly mattered. He knew the slimy cowpoke when he saw him.

"You Ted?"

"What if I am?"

Jameson flung his poncho to one side, revealing his Colt .45, a pearl-handled beauty he had never before had to shoot. Before today, that is.

Ted squared off, his ten gnarly fingers bristling over his own revolvers. A two-gun man, Jameson noticed.

"You callin' me out, stranger?" Ted drawled.

Jameson snorted into the cool, dusty air of a Dodge City morning.

"So y'are callin' me out."

Jameson snorted again. "I'm not the stranger here, Ted. You should have known better than to take a man's woman."

Ted laughed. "Ah, so you're the good-for-nuthin', yeller-bellied drifter ole Maybelle tole me bout, eh? An you think a wild shot from that pearly o yourn'll maker want yuh back, eh? Well yer a fool."

Jameson knew he was a fool. He didn't need a rustler like Ted to tell him that. The only question now was what to do. Count off? Draw and fire? Fire first or take time to aim? And if to aim, where to aim? His head? His chest? The knees?

Too late! Jameson scrambled for his gun but was lying on his back before he could grip it. He felt warmth spreading out under his back and coolness descending into his body from above. Whatever the best place had been, Ted had found it.

FORTY-ONE

Accelerated Force

Hope, they say, springs eternal, and Dave's was of that variety. But, eternal or not, Hope had settled down in his heart somewhere between Vain Futility and Certain Blessings, uncertain where it belonged. Dave decided to skew his data toward the latter, and in this spirit he changed the review session to Thursday, sought out the banquet dress code, and picked out a suitable blue tie for the occasion.

Wednesday came and went and by that evening Dave had settled into his new role of lovesickfool.

"Lovesickfool? No way, Curses. That is an unfair characterization. I'm not even in love with her. I just suspect that could be an easy position to find myself in. She's just a friend. Like you."

"Not like me."

"For which I say prayers of thanks daily."

Dave and Curses were sitting on their respective beds and trying to fling paperclips onto the flypaper Curses had hung from the ceiling. Curses had one sock on and one sock off and was, between bouts of calling Dave things like lovesickfool, planning some chummy banter for the date he had in an hour.

"Ah ha! That's five! I am totally kicking your trash, Dave. What have you got, two? No, that's right, you have one. I'm kicking your trash. I laugh in your lovesick face. How many times, Dave, how many times have I got to tell you not to mess with Texas?"

"Bluh, Texas." Dave was still regretting he'd given the Wednesday night preview tickets for *Newts and Lutes* Llew had given him to Curses, and also that Curses had managed to find a date so quickly. It hadn't occurred to him that Ref having a date on Friday did not preclude him from asking her out on a Wednesday. Stupid!stupid!stupid! Dave had no idea how many times he had called himself stupid today. Forty-five? Eighty-five? A hundred?

More. Probably more? Certainly more.

Dave flung three paperclips at once; two flew left, one right. "Ah, fiddle."

"No, Dave, you can't say that. Because it's only if you play in Texas that you've got to have a fiddle in the band, and you're a California boy. And man, the *surf* isn't even up in your hometown."

"We had a soap opera named after us once."

"Woohoo, sounds cool. Was it, oh, half as popular as, say, *Dallas*?" Curses missed with his paper clip and paused to put on his second sock. "Seriously though, my being annoying aside, do you think it's weird that Isabel would call me from Minnesoder for the first time two hours before my first post-Isabel date?"

"Maybe. But I can't believe you're worrying about that."

"I'm not worrying about it. I'm just asking you if that is not weird."

Dave's latest paperclip grabbed tenuously for a flypaper grip and wobbled a moment before plunging floorward to join its brethren. "I'll tell you what would be weird, walking into that flypaper by dawn's early light."

"What are you trying to say, Dave? That flypaper's the national flag of Texas? 'Cause I'm taking issue if you are."

"For the last time, Curses, Texas is not a nation."

"Shows how much you know." Curses bounced off his bed and into his shoes. He'd claimed not to have untied them since his mission and Dave could think of no reason to doubt him. Their stretched and discolored suede and the ragged laces testified on his behalf. "Dave, I will see you later." And with a salute and a backwards step between their beds, he walked hair-first into the national flag of Texas.

THE NEXT MORNING Dave's first class was canceled. It was cold. It was dewy. He was tired from reading all night for his now-canceled class. He sat on an uncomfortable wooden bench inside the humanities building and picked up someone's discarded *Universe*, hoping for a news item to cheer him up.

Hmmm. The fact that at least *his* home hadn't been flooded out overnight and at least *his* university did not have a huge binge-drinking problem and at least *his* small third-world country wasn't overwhelmed by machete-wielding diamond-hungry terrorists failed to do the trick. Then the comics were duds. But the classifieds – ah! A surefire cheerer-upper. He checked the help-wanted section for jobs he would never ever have. Or at least never have again.

HELP NEEDED!!! MAKE MONEY!
FLEXIBLE HOURS!
GREAT FOR STUDNETS!
$8-$12/hr POTENTIAL! NO SALES!!

"Ha ha, studnets! Suckers!"

Dave ignored the curious glances and looked through more ads, feeling more and more grateful he wasn't selling pest control or washing dirty dishes or bleeding himself for money – and that he didn't think such a fate was likely.

Then there was the spate of *real* jobs and BYU positions, some one-shot deals – stadium concessions for a special event, translator needed for a conference on Malaysian literature, several like this:

Help needed waiting and bussing tables
this Friday for events in the Wilkinson.
Apply at 180 SASB by Thursday
at 5 for opportunity of a lifetime.

Dave wondered who would bother. Maybe two hours work at maybe six bucks an hour? And a lost Friday? Absurd. Dave set the paper back on the bench and took out his notebook. He flipped to the last polluted page and found this:

"Idea: Jameson gets locked in library overnight. And falls in love, of course!"

Dave closed the notebook back up and put it back in his backpack. Wow. Dave thought about this. Notebook back up back in backpack. That's a lot of backs. Anyway, Dave zipped up his *bag* and leaned against the unpleasantly yellow bricks, intending to take a nap. Taking a nap, however, required ignoring the paper sitting beside him. "Recycle me! Recycle me!" it cried. "The bin is right over there!"

Dave ignored it. He hadn't taken the paper from the display – it wasn't really his to recycle.

"A clean campus is everyone's responsibility."

"Shut up."

"Lazy bones."

Dave did not intend to take this from a stupid newspaper. Besides, hadn't he already recycled the newspaper? Instead of getting a new one, he had read someone's discarded one. Voila: recycling.

"Lazy bones! Lazy bones!"

And by the same token, if he put it in the recycle bin now, it would be taken out of circulation. But if he left it on the bench? Well, the day was still young. Besides, hadn't he picked up many an orphaned newspaper in the past and seen it recycled? So there you go.

"Harumph," said the paper.

"Fine." Dave had had enough. He couldn't concentrate on being tired. He picked up the paper and stomped over to the recycle bin. It was already Thursday and he was dead tired and had yet to find a way to break Ned's legs without creating suspicion before Friday, tomorrow. And besides, he still had to print out his rewrite for English 321 and read Isaiah 35 to 41 and . . . it seemed like there was something else. What was it? Oh. Just that dumb job thing in the paper for that dumb thing on Friday. Just the sort of stupid thing you need floating through your head when you're tired.

Dave sat down on the bench and checked the wall clock, but didn't read it, as the words "dumb thing on Friday" hit him with the accelerated force of an atom smasher. "Friday!" he yelled, and grabbed for the paper, but it was gone. He ran to the recycle bin, but couldn't reach the bottom. "New paper!" he wailed, and realized he was making a scene again.

He calmly and deliberately strolled out into the cold for another paper, then ran back inside to the bench and opened it to the back.

Help needed waiting and bussing tables
this Friday for events in the Wilkinson.
Apply at 180 SASB by Thursday
at 5 for opportunity of a lifetime.

Events. Plural. That must mean there is more than one. "Duh," Dave editorialized himself. He looked up at the wall clock again. A little over twenty minutes still before his next class. He grabbed his backpack and headed outside, making a beeline for . . . the SASB . . .

Hmm.

He grabbed the closing door, stepped back through and over to the courtesy phone, and called BYU-INFO for directions to the SASB.

FORTY-TWO

Better in Practice

FRIDAY ARRIVED. DAVE CHECKED IN at four to help set up chairs for the four events going on that evening, then had time to get something to eat before returning at six. The events were staggered – Multicultural Council at six thirty, Society for Creative Anachronism (College of Arrow's Flight barony) at seven, Women's Lacrosse at seven thirty, and a BYUSA Meet 'n' Greet for current officers and potential candidates at eight – so they wouldn't all need their food at the same time. The first and last were basically just having brownies and triangley pastries, and all the SCA required was lots of brown Jell-O molded into the shape of giant drumsticks, with some foul-smelling, frothy stuff to wash it down, so Lacrosse was having the only real meal. Dave had thought this would mean he would have more time to poison Ned and get the girl, but when he arrived at six he found out that what it actually meant was that the regular Dining Services staff intended to work that event themselves and leave the simple stuff to the neophytes. Dave was not much pleased by this turn of events.

"I am not much pleased by this turn of events."

"Well, *phyoo*, Dave, wasn't it? Dave. *Phyoo*. Look, be glad, be glad. We're making it easy for you."

Dave looked at his wan and waxy red-headed nemesis in a sissy blue apron matching Dave's own. "I didn't take this job because I wanted it to be easy. This may be my one day in Dining Services. C'mon, *challenge* me!"

Waxboy folded his arms. "*Phyoo*," he said. "Boy, I don't know. *Phyoo*." He shook his head and looked heavenward in a fine show of resignation. "Okay, I'll tell you what. At 7:50, if you still feel up to it, I'll let you man the punch bar. *Phyoo*. I hope you can handle it. See, this is how it works. After we're done serving, but before we stop bringing out rolls and filling glasses, you'll stand at a table in the corner of the room and, after we clear plates and everything, they'll have to come to you if they want more punch. And, boy, I have to warn you, they will want more. It's good punch. *Phyoo*. Do you know how to use a punch ladle?"

"It just so happens that I do."

"Oh, good. *Phyoo*. Okay. Do you think you think you could handle that detail?"

"I think I could."

"Okay. Well. *Phyoo*. Okay. I'll check in on you, so if you need relief or anything . . . *Phyoo*. Boy, I hope I know what I'm doing."

"Thanks." Dave smiled. "I won't let you down."

"Okay, good. Boy. Help Liz get those brownies out to 3211."

"Aye-aye!" Dave slapped a fist into his hand and hurried away.

ⅢⅢ

DAVE HAD NOT so much as walked past the Women's Lacrosse banquet room until Waxboy led him to his station a few minutes before eight. Waxboy nervously explained the ladle and the bowl and how full to fill the cups and how much ice a cup may have and how to pour from the ladle to minimize spillage and how many full cups to allow to build up and a good three dozen other last-minute hurried and crucial instructions before scurrying off.

"*Phyoo*," said Dave.

Considering the number of girls on the team (twenty-four) and considering how many could sit at a table (eight) he had expected only seven or eight tables – maybe a few more for visiting dignitaries. Engelbert Humperdinck, perhaps. Or the Pope. Dave liked to imagine the Pope was a big lacrosse fan. Go Irish! But in fact, there were about twenty tables, each mostly full. Some had an empty chair or two, but those could be bathroom runs. Dave scanned the room and finally found Ref sitting most of the way across it, past the small podium and over near a far exit. There were boys sitting on either side of her, and Dave wasn't sure which was the evil Ned. Also at the table were Coulter and Welch and a girl whose name Dave couldn't remember. She had gotten married in the off-season and had to drop out after a couple games when she found out she was pregnant. From where Dave was, and with her sitting down, she didn't seem to be showing, but when she laid her hand on the guy to Ref's right, Dave looked to Ref's left and knew he had Ned.

Ned was, of all the people at the table, most directly facing Dave, who, in turn, was now stirring the punch as if it needed constant discipline to prevent it from prancing about the room. Ned had brown curly hair. Brown and curly like, like, like *worms*! Dave scoffed. Disregarding Ned's ruggedly unhandsome jaw and Ned's charmingly unhandsome eyes and Ned's disarmingly unhandsome smile, Dave considered what he knew about him.

First, he had at least sort of been Ref's boyfriend in the dorm days, about four years ago.

Second, Ref decided waiting for him during his mission would be "stupid."

Third, he's surely been home from his mission at least a year by now.

Fourth, yet he hasn't gone out with Ref since the dorm days of freshman year.

Wait – was Dave sure of that fourth one? How could he know that Ref hadn't been covertly dating this Ned character all along? Would she have told him? After all, Dave was co-author of "To Build a Fence" and, judging by the e-mails still trickling in, an avowed woman-hater and marriage-despiser.

Or maybe she had just been keeping Dave along as a backup this whole time, waiting to see if Ned would make a move. Stupid Ned. Boy, if –

"Excuse me?"

Dave jumped. "Sorry?"

"Could I have some punch please?"

Dave looked down. His prefilled cups were all gone. "Oh, sorry." He filled the cup and handed it to her. He couldn't remember her name but . . . "Number twenty-one, right?"

"Yeah. How'd you know that?"

"Oh, I'm a fan. Seen all the home games. Loved it versus New Mexico when you lobbed that pass clear across the field to Sarabhai and she stuck it right in. That was an awesome play. ESPN highlights worthy."

"Hey, thanks." She nodded at him. "Do I know you?"

"No, I don't think so. In fact, don't tell anyone, but I'm even blanking on your name right now."

"It's Carrie."

"No, I mean your last name."

"Benson."

"Benson. Right." Dave snapped his fingers. "Benson. Anyway, that was your finest hour. At home anyway. Glad I was there to see it."

"Yeah . . . Are you sure I don't know you?"

"I don't think so."

"Huh. Okay. Anyway, thanks. It's good punch."

"The very best for you lacrossers."

"Oh. Thanks."

Benson walked back to her seat, and Dave started filling a new reserve of cups.

Smith, A. came up next with a cane and Dave asked about her ankle and she shrugged and said, "Fine." He asked if Coulter was on a cane too and she said no and took a cup and went to sit down. Dave finished filling the approved number of extra cups and was startled to see the feminine population of the two nearest tables staring at him with identical puzzled expressions. Smith, A. sat at one, Benson at the other. A girl from Benson's table stood and walked toward him. Dave couldn't remember her name or number, but he did remember she single-handedly botched the Cougar defense the only time he saw her play – the game in which Utah blew them out.

She picked up a cup and looked at him. "Hi," she said. "I'm number twenty-seven, Anita Coltraine."

"Hi, double zero, call me Dave."

"Hi, Dave. Did you see me play this season?"

Dave considered lying.

"Yes."

"What did you think?"

"Well . . ."

"Honestly now."

"Would you like a cup of punch for your date as well?"

"He's gotten me three already and four for himself. I'm actually not thirsty. Did you see me play or not?"

"Yes."

"And?"

"Um, I'm guessing you did better in practice?"

She smirked at him. "So you're for real then." She nodded curtly and returned to her table, where the girls conferred. Then Benson came back. Dave was blinking. He looked over at Ref. He didn't think she had seen him yet, but that seemed mostly because Ned was so irritatingly captivating. Right now, he was making her laugh, the slimy monkeyman.

"Dave, huh?"

216   THERIC JEPSON

Dave looked at Benson. "Yes?"

"Who do you know here?"

"Well, you're Carrie Benson, number twenty-one, and at your table I see number six, number twelve, and the Cruel Inquisitor. So I guess you could say I know all of you."

"What's your name, Dave?"

"It's Dave. Really."

"Your full name."

Dave wondered if there were any nearby caves that might offer him shelter. None came to mind. He swallowed. "David Matthew Them."

"*Them?*" Her eyes widened and her hands flew to her mouth and she gave an excited little jump and an excited not-so-little squeal. "You're Plantree's boy!" Dave nervously jitterbugged his eyes around the room and realized this was one time in his life when everyone in the room really *was* looking at him. Including Ref. And Ned. The latter seemed oblivious, but the former looked, well, surprised. Like if her right arm were to fall off she wouldn't notice. Dave tried to smile at her and she fell back in her chair. It took six or seven eternities, but finally most of the room returned to their own little conversations. Dave looked back at Benson, whose hands had left her mouth and were now on her hips. She looked stern. She was even tapping her foot. "Why aren't you here *with* her?" she demanded.

Dave opened his mouth, then reconsidered. He sloshed some punch with the ladle and nodded. "Frankly, Benson, because I'm stupid. That's the honest truth. I'm possibly in love with the girl and yet I turn her down when she invites me to one of the most important nights of her year. I am, in short, an idiot. I'd rather be telling her, but, well, she's sitting way over there." He pointed with the ladle and dripped on the tablecloth. He couldn't believe how good it felt to just *say* that. But by the time Dave finished having this thought, Benson had reseated herself and was urgently whispering to her tablemates.

And then Dave got to see a curious phenomenon. Girls told other girls at other tables, who told other girls at other tables. He could tell they were talking about him by the constant glances. He looked at Ref and wondered if she could see it too. He watched the rumor fly through some tables and die at others, where, apparently, no one cared. And as the news pigeoned and imped and jumped and crawled and rolled and leapt its way to number 23, Martha "Referee" Plantree, Dave felt his stomach knotting up, like the appendicitis he had had in fourth grade during *shh! be quiet!* reading time with Mr. Thorne.

Dave leaned against the punch table to steady himself. The rumor was two tables away from Ref on one side, three on the other. And his body was starting to melt.

FORTY-THREE

Everything's Clicking

"**D**AVE. *PHYOO*, BOY. HOW'S IT GOING?"

Dave didn't turn to look at him, but kept his eye on the rumor. "Fine. No problems." The rumor jumped sideways to another table. No closer, but still moving.

"*Phyoo*. Good. Look, you got a watch?"

Dave glanced at the clock to his left and pointed at it.

"Oh. Okay, good. Good. Look, *phyoo*, in fifteen minutes would you mind coming back to the kitchen? Staff meeting."

Dave turned to look at him. "Staff meeting? Now? Why? And why me? I'm only going to be staff for another couple hours! At most!"

Waxboy shrugged. "Staff meeting in fifteen minutes."

"All right. I hope these people can work the ladle without me."

"Oh. Gosh. *Phyoo*. I hadn't thought of that." It seemed impossible, but Waxboy paled even more and scurried off, tripping as he went. Dave watched him go, then snapped back and tried to find the rumor. He looked at face after face, but though it still felt like everyone was looking at him, he didn't think anyone was.

Panic.

Dave held his breath, and felt his heart slowly relax. Then he saw Ref walking toward him, carrying an empty cup.

Panic!

Dave felt himself shaking a little as she approached. She was wearing a long black dress he'd never seen before and, well, she looked good in it. She seemed to sashay as she weaved through the tables and chairs. Dave wondered why he had never seen her sashay before. She seemed good at it. Dave's stomach took a tour of his body as he watched her approach. He tried to fill another cup for the reserve, and dribbled punch over his fingers.

Ref reached the table and stopped. Dave wondered if he was supposed to speak first.

"Hi, Dave."

"Hi."

It sounded like his stomach had finished its tour in his throat.

She handed him her cup.

Dave nodded and managed not to spill, as Ref watched.

"What are you *doing* here, Dave?"

"Working."

"Yeah, but *why*."

Dave shrugged. He had figured it was obvious. "I couldn't bear to miss it. To miss you."

Dave realized that most of the room was watching again when Ref cocked her head to squint at him and about twenty people cocked right along with her. Not to mention all the people who had turned around in their chairs to watch. Dave licked his lips and wondered if this was really the best place for one of those talk talks.

"Yeah, well, that's not what it sounded like when I asked you."

"I know. I'm sorry. I was – I was just – really confused right then."

"And you're not now?"

"No. Well, not as much. I'd like to make it up to you." Dave thought about adding "I'd like to spend the rest of my life making it up to you," but, at the moment, he was wearing a blue apron. And holding a ladle. And was it even true?

"I'm not sure punch is going to cut it."

"I – yeah. Right. How's Ned?"

"Oh, he's fine. He's fun, you know? He's called me a few times the last couple months, and we were on the same intramural Ultimate Frisbee team as freshmen, so a sports banquet seemed reasonably appropriate."

Dave wanted her to say he, Dave, would have been more than reasonably appropriate, but she didn't. And he gave her plenty of time.

"I'm sorry about all that, Ref."

"All that what?"

"All that ... everything. I've been kind of a jerk."

Ref seemed to be waiting for him to say something else.

"I want to make it up to you."

Nothing.

"I *will* make it up to you."

Nothing.

Dave felt the panic rising, but then Billy Joel's words came back to him.

"Ref, look, I guess I said no because. Because I was afraid." Dave's eyes lowered, but he forced them back up to hers. "Ref, see, I like you. Well, of course, I mean, we're friends, right? Best friends. More than that. Maybe more than that. I hope more than that. What I mean is, I might have fallen, no, I mean, I am, when you said." Deep breath. "When you said you had, you know, *ideas*, it shocked me – but it made me think. And now maybe I have some ideas too. I think I do. Big ones. And so I wanted to try putting our ideas together. See what happens. Am I making sense?"

Ref took a step backwards and almost fell. Dave watched her stumble, then turn and head for her table. Dave himself felt hollow, gutted like a pumpkin, leaving only a face with no real emotion. He noticed she had left her cup on the table, and he softly touched its rim. Electricity.

Oh, *what* is going on? It's *just* a *cup*.

He noticed his wrist was shaking, banging the ladle against the side of the bowl, making soft lapping waves across its surface. He hung it onto the bowl edge and took Ref's cup. Ostensibly to throw it away. But he held it. He wanted to drink it down. Quickly. In a gulp. Before anyone could see.

But everyone was watching. He could feel it.

He moved the cup behind the punchbowl, out of sight.

Ref found her seat and plopped into it, then immediately laughed. Ned asked her a question and she pishposhed it away. They conversed a bit, then he stood up and headed for Dave.

Dave was feeling every known emotion, plus several he didn't know. His hands hung dead at his side, then spasmodically unclenched and clenched.

"Hi!" Ned stuck out his hand and reflexes held out Dave's. "I'm Ned Peterson, old friend of Ref's. You're Dave, right?"

Dave nodded.

"Yeah, I've heard all about you. Ref's been talking about you all night. Is it true you wrote that 'To Build a Fence' thing?"

"Co-wrote."

"Man, that was *hilarious*! So cool. And Ref mentioned you guys are working on a rock opera or something?"

"*Byuck*."

"Yeah, *Byuck!*" Ned laughed. "It took me a second to get it, but yeah, *Byuck*. That's hilarious too. True brilliance."

"You get it?"

"Totally. I'm still laughing."

"Wow." He got it. Ned. Ned got it. Why did he have to hate his one true fan?

"Anyways, I'm up here to get Ref's drink she forgot. You know, chivalry and all that."

It took Dave a moment to convince himself it would not be soul-scarring to give it up and a bit longer still to actually take it from its safe place and hand it to Ned, who took it from him in obvious ignorance of the cup's talismanic properties. Dave wanted to snatch it back. This man did not deserve it.

"Thanks, Dave. I hope to see you more often. I guess you hang with Ref a lot so I bet we probably will. Everything's clicking, you know what I mean?" Ned winked, and as Dave watched him walk away, he felt contempt burn through him. Why did he have to be such a cool guy? Waxboy grabbed Dave's sleeve and pulled him out for the meeting where, regrettably, he was informed that circumstances were such that they were going to have to let him go.

Laid off from a one-night job.

Dave had never felt so worthless.

He walked down to one of the primary entrances to Ref's banquet and listened to awards being given away through the door. It was hard to hear exactly what was said, but he knew he heard Martha Plantree's name at least two times. He sat with his elbows on his knees and imagined Ref and Ned on their happy night, a couple of clickers clicking away.

FORTY-FOUR

Something Profound

DAVE TRIED NOT TO THINK about them. Which was a laugh. Dave's brain had a strict policy of not not thinking except on the most arduous of final exams and so he stood up and left the student center, hoping to at least leave behind thinking about *her*.

"Well, you know how BYU love stories go," his brain started back up as he cut through the humanities building. "They'll be engaged by the end of the semester, most likely. Good for Ref. That Ned certainly is a strapping lad."

"A *strapping lad*? Are you serious? Whose side are you on, brain?"

"Side? Side? I'm on Ref's side. And if you really loved her, you'd be on her side too. Don't you want her to be happy?"

Sometimes, Dave really hated his brain.

"I hate you, brain."

"Spoken in a moment of true *agape*, I'm sure."

They went on like this down Campus Drive and across the street into stadium parking. And through stadium parking. Across Canyon and into Draftwood parking. Onto the hood of his car for a thirty- or forty- or fifty-minute funk. Up the stairs. Through the door. Back to his bedr –

"Ref called."

"Huh? What?"

Curses was sitting on the couch, his pink-striped feet on the hot-chocolate table, Captain Babycakes on his lap. "Ref called."

"What did she say? And why are you wearing my socks?"

"I don't know. And I'm not."

"You don't know what she said?"

"Look, Dave. One does not spend six monthly installments of forty-nine ninety-five on David Them's Patented Communication Method only to then go around answering phones. She left a message. Also? You're not the only one with pink-striped socks."

"Oh. Thanks."

Dave walked over to the blinking light and stabbed it, gently, like pagan sacrifice was something he really only did on Sundays.

"– wn to our offices for your chance at a free, two-night, three-day stay in Reno for only ei –"

"Not that one!" Curses yelled. "That's my girlfriend! Private! Private!"

Dave hit skip.

"Hi, Dave, [background giggles] this is [giggles] – hold on one second, will you? – knock that off! – this is Ref [giggles]. I just wanted [giggles] just wanted to ask you [giggles]. Sorry, maybe this isn't the best time. Just give me a call sometime this weekend, okay? We need to talk [giggles]."

Beeeep.

There. Are. No. Further. Messages.

"Sounds like you had a fun night."

Dave looked over at Curses. "No, sounds like she had a fun night."

"Good for her."

"Yeah."

Curses hit a dissonant chord on the Captain. "Now what?"

"Now I guess I go to bed."

Another dissonant chord. "That sounds nice. Perchance to dream?"

"I doubt I'll fall asleep."

"No reason you can't have nightmares."

Dissonant chord.

"I know."

Dave turned toward the front door and stared it down.

"I'll be right back."

▥

DAVE HURRIED ACROSS University Avenue and into Sierra de Provost's parking lot. The nearest light was out, and Dave was able to look up at million-year-old starlight. The dense swath surprised him, and he stopped dead on the asphalt, staring, his eyes picking away star after star, looking deeper, farther, as if for the generation where gods began to be . . .

Dave lowered his gaze and shook his head and directed his attention to the steps ahead.

On his last visit, Dave had taken the stairs in three giant leaps. Today he took them one at a time, each step earning his deliberate attention. He walked from the stairs to Ref's apartment and knocked.

And again.

And once more. A little harder this time.

The pinpoint of light in the peephole disappeared for a moment, then reappeared, followed by the moving of the deadbolt.

Ref opened the door, one hand in her fallen hair, her eyes worn. She slowly blinked at him once, twice, then: "Hey, Punch Boy."

"Hi."

"What's up?"

Dave took a moment to look at her before answering. Although she looked exhausted, she was still sharp in the black number she had worn to the banquet. With the nice addition of pink velour slippers.

"I got your phone call. I thought we could talk."

"Lovely. What was wrong with tomorrow?"

"Tomorrow? By tomorrow the stars will have set and the sun will have risen and you know better than anyone how many things I can screw up in that length of time. I'm sorry, I have to talk now."

"Right. Very poetic. So do you want to come i – No. Wait. My stuff's all over the couch and – Let's just sit outside. Is that all right?"

"Sure."

Ref checked to make sure the door was unlocked then closed it behind her. She walked ahead of Dave, her dress making quiet swishings. She stopped at the top of the stairs and her shoulders turned and she looked back at him, the blue light of night washing her in an ethereal glow. "Coming?"

"Yeah. Yeah, I am."

Ref sat down on the top step and Dave walked over to sit next to her.

He turned his head to spy at her profile. "It looked like you had a good time tonight."

"I did. I did. Ned's a great guy. I had sort of forgotten."

"He is a great guy. You'll do good with him."

They sat for a while, watching the occasional car pass on University, then Ref said, "Wait – what?"

"Ned. He's your boyfriend again, right?"

"Ned was never my boyfriend. Not really. I mean, he was fun and I liked him, but, you know. I can't imagine marrying him or anything. But we've always been friends." She frowned at her hands. "I'd forgotten how much I liked hanging out with him actually. And if you hadn't said no, I might never have let him take me out. So, uh . . . thanks."

Dave suppressed a sigh. "I'm glad you did. I only talked to him for a minute, but he seems like everything I would want for you. He's nice, he's got a byucky sense of humor and he's got more man-beauty than anyone at Draftwood can throw a stick at. You're really lucky, Ref. Ned's really lucky."

Ref laughed softly, then pulled back and whaled Dave in the arm.

"Ow!"

"You deserved it. Listen to you moping. And what was it with you and the punch, anyway?"

"Oh. That."

"Yeah. That."

Dave looked at his hands. The starlight wasn't doing the same things to his skin that it was to Ref's. "I – I just wanted to be there. With you."

"It was hard to tell."

"I know. I'm sorry."

Dave looked up into Ref's face.

She turned to meet his gaze. "Why did you come over? It's not getting any warmer."

"No."

"I should have brought out a blanket or something." She turned back out to the street and something in the angle of her face reminded Dave of something.

"Hey, Ref. Remember when we were juniors or seniors and you dragged me to a football game – I think we were playing Clovis – and it was freezing and so foggy we could barely see the game at all?"

"Yeah." She nodded, then turned to him with a deviant smile. "We totally got trounced. We only had a passing game that year and it was way too foggy for that."

"Right, I remember." Dave matched Ref's grin. "They should have called it for weather – I remember a couple of the Clovis High people got in wrecks on the way home."

"Yeah, somebody we knew."

"Janeil's cousin."

"That's right. I hated that guy."

"You did? I always thought – Anyway, it was so cold that night we went from our regular, shyer, one-blanket-per-person philosophy to a bolder two-blankets-per-two-people philosophy."

Ref laughed. "I remember that! It was so weird! Like we were a couple of school kids – which we were, I guess. Or like we were on the verge of a tremendous sin."

"Exactly. But it worked. We survived the night."

"Mm. But we never did it again, did we?"

"No. And there were much colder nights than that one."

Ref leaned back on her hands and shook out her hair. The tired was gone from her face now. "Why do you suppose that was, Dave?"

"I don't know. I've always been shy. Or stupid. Or both."

"Yeah, but that wasn't – that was – it was platonic – survival snuggling. If you will."

"Was it?"

Ref frowned. "Well. I."

"'Cause it wasn't for me. And that terrified me."

"Me neither." Ref sat back up and laced her fingers on top of her head. "And me too."

Dave thought about that game and he remembered now how hard he had tried to forget it. And he remembered falling off the couch at Lorraine's house. And he wondered at the hidden, ignored complexity of their relationship.

"Dave?"

"Yeah."

"I need to ask you something."

"Shoot."

"Pchooo." She smiled, but it didn't last. "Dave, what, exactly, did you tell people tonight? About me?"

"About you?"

"It's just – people told me funny things."

"Funny?"

"No. Not really." She rested her arms on her knees and leaned over. "Just rumors, I guess. But they all seemed to start with you."

"Yeah. I guess they did. I could even see the rumor moving through the room."

She looked up. "What? How do you mean?"

"It was the strangest thing. I said something to Benson and she told her table and then I saw them talking to another table who looked and stared at me, then they talked to some other table and they looked. All the way across the room. It was ... bizarre."

"It sounds bizarre." Ref turned her head and rested it on her arms so she was looking at him sideways. "So ... what did you say?"

"What did you hear that I said?"

She shrugged. "It's like telephone, you know? It was probably all wrong."

"Please."

Her shoulders shrugged. "It changed. Everything from you love me and you want to marry me, to you think I'm a jerk." She turned to the street again and sighed. "Besides, Dave, I'm not even sure what *you* told me anymore. I've run it through my head so many times I feel like my own game of telephone."

She sat up and stretched. "I'm freezing. Let me go grab a coat."

She stood up and Dave followed her into the apartment and watched her disappear down the hall before turning to look around. The walls were a near-white pink and covered with tasteful but cheaply framed prints of temples; in one corner stood a bookcase filled with what looked like sketchbooks or journals.

"I don't think I've ever been in here before."

"What?"

"I don't think I've ever been in here before!" Dave yelled down the hall.

Ref walked up the hall wearing a light jacket over her dress. "Yeah, well, that's no accident. My roommates have a lot of boys over and I didn't want you to be One Of The Boys That Comes Over. They seem to become community property."

She walked to the front door and patted her jacket pocket before turning the lock on the knob. "Let's go."

Ref took her velour slippers down the stairs at full speed and Dave hurried to catch up. She led him down a thin black path between two buildings and into an opening with a newly whitewashed gazebo catching all the starlight and floating like a blue buoy in a sea of night.

"Behold, Gazebo de Provost."

"Seriously?"

"Yeah. But that's nothing compared to the toll-painted sign over the laundry room."

"No –"

"Yes. Cleanliness de Provost."

"Wow. That. Is totally. Awesome."

"I know. I love this place. You've never had ramen till you've had Ramen de Provost."

"I can only imagine."

"That's right. You can only imagine. Come on."

Dave followed her into the gazebo and they sat down.

"I don't know where everybody is tonight – the whole complex seems deserted – but at least this way we don't have to share this space with the make-out crowd."

"And allelujah for that."

"Amen."

"You know," said Dave, "I always wanted to yell allelujah at a Bulldogs game."

"You should have."

"Maybe so."

"Of course you should have. Why not? You want to do something, you do it. Otherwise you'll never do it."

"Now you tell me. Let me write that down." Dave took a pen from his pocket and tried to write on the back of his hand. "This isn't, huh. Stupid pen – I can't get it to – There's something wrong with this pen . . ."

"There's nothing wrong with your pen, there's something wrong with your eyes. Gimme." Ref grabbed his hand and the pen and scribbled hard. Dave howled and tried to jerk his hand away but she held tight. "There, see? Now what do you want me to write?"

"That's not ink! That's blood!"

"Don't be a moron. What were you going to write down?"

"I – Shoot. You said something profound. What was it?"

"What *was* it? Well. That's the last time I waste profundity on you."

"Sorry."

"Take your hand back." He did. "And your pen." He did.

"Sheez, Ref. Thanks a lot – you really uglified my hand this time. Like that Halloween."

"Face painting."

"During recess –"

"Yeah." Ref laughed. "That was pretty bad."

"Pretty bad? The whole school hated you!"

"Me? You were the one who gave Melinda that purple scar!"

They laughed. And Dave kept laughing so he could keep listening to Ref laugh.

"Do you remember – ?" she said, and they were off. She started with the time they painted their own faces for a Bulldogs game; football led to basketball and from there to women's lacrosse and how robbed they were of that Utah game. That led to professional tennis and British celebrities, the wackiness of parents, what they missed most (and least) about California, and the movies they liked in high school. They laughed at people who have big trucks but never take them off pavement and considered the responsibility of Saints to be an example of the word. They reminded each other of the tension-filled mudpie-eating contest they had staged the summer before second grade and how its outcome nearly tore them apart though now they couldn't remember who'd won. They wondered why neither Fresno nor Provo seemed to have decent thunderstorms and whether fog was safer winter weather than snow and ice. They doubted whether the Darwin fish was supposed to be insulting or just funny. They mocked each other's mussed-up hair. They complemented each other's mussed-up hair. They threatened to pull each other's mussed-up hair. And then they were silent.

Dave's mind ran backward. He started here, in the gazebo, and ended with the e-mail he had sent Ref a year previous, telling her was coming to BYU, worrying over whether she would reply.

He turned his head now to look at her, saw her perfect nose pointing to heaven.

"I can see the stars through the slats," she said. "There are so many tonight. No one's apartment lights are on. It's dark – just us and the stars."

Just us and the stars. Dave followed her gaze into heaven, then followed it back to her face. Just us and the stars. He followed the curve of her ear back, into her mussed hair, down her back, her arm, onto her hand, lying next to his, two hands between them on the bench.

"Ref," he said, but went no further.

She waited awhile before asking, "What?"

"I –" Dave saw starlight catch the fine hairs on the back of her hand. He'd never noticed them before. He let his eyes travel back up her jacket-clad arm to her face, her profile, soft and sharp. "Ah, Ref," he said.

"Ah, Dave." She gave a soft, soft laugh that pierced Dave's heart like a feather flung by a tornado.

Dave was silent.

He listened to Ref's breath.

She lowered her eyes from heaven, into shadow. "Is there some way I can make this easier for you?"

Dave couldn't breathe; his vitals abandoned him. He felt a small wave of heat pass from her to him. He considered the merits and demerits of putting his arm around her – the arm in question entering its opinion with a single drip of sweat down his side.

Ref shifted her body to face him. "This is it, Dave."

"I know," he said, barely audible.

Ref placed a hand on his shoulder and Dave felt it through his shirt and jacket, amazed that he could differentiate fingers, feel settled by their touch. He cautiously sent one of his own hands up to touch them. It did and pulled back, and again, and pulled back. He settled his fingers on hers. They were soft. He slid his hand forward and soon their fingers were interlocked and they turned and faced each other, all four hands together on the bench.

"Ref –"

"Yes?" she whispered back.

"We can't be friends anymore. Not for long anyway. Someday, some lucky guy's going to take you away from me and marry you and that'll be it. Unless –"

"Unless – ?"

"Unless I – Unless I'm – But either way, we have an expiration date. And I don't want it to be somebody else if it can be me."

"What do you mean?"

"Ref . . . You're my best friend, okay? There's no doubt about that. But as best friends, we can't remain static. 'Best friends' has to turn into something bigger or something lesser. And I'd prefer bigger. All else being equal. 'Best friends' is too good to just let die."

"Dave, what, exactly, are you saying?" Her eyes were serious but warm and Dave realized he'd been looking into them for some time – a flash from passing headlights showed their greenish-brown sunfire as new and alive and exciting – Dave wondered if that had always been so.

"I guess I'm asking – wow, this sounds stupid, so, I don't know, old-fashioned, maybe – but I guess I'm asking permission . . . to court you. Ref, may I have your permission to court you?"

Ref raised an eyebrow and leaned back a bit. But before Dave could experience total breakdown, she laughed and with an "Oh, Dave!" hugged him and held on until he finally found the courage to hug her back – "Oh, Dave" – and he realized she was crying now. He pulled away just enough to return his eyes to hers, now slightly misted over. She blinked and a tear escaped. He reached up and brushed it from her cheek, but left his hand there.

"Ref? Are you okay?"

She blinked away a final tear, leaned her head into his hand, and smiled. "Yes," she said. "I am; it's strange, but I am."

"I just might love you, Ref."

She leaned back into him and rested. "I just might love you too."

EPILOGUE

Activities Uncharted

CURSES WAS, IT MUST BE admitted, glad to have been promoted to the position of Dave's Best Friend. That Ref had to be fired from that role to make it possible? Tragic. But to an Olai, every metaphorical death is a reason to celebrate, and Dave and Ref's end-of-friendship thus merited loading up on black crêpe paper and decking out the apartment. "Decking out" does not give justice. The apartment was paper-mâchéd black. It was dark and depressing and ready for partying.

X had married and moved out weeks before, and Curses had arranged for a hearing-aid outfitted Harron Crabtree and his mission buddy to move into Peter and X's old room. Harron and "Elder" (as Harron called him, and that was good enough for Curses) had a catalogue of awful BYU-themed songs to which Curses surreptitiously added melody and assigned animals.

Dave and Ref were still ostensibly involved with the project and, when Llew called once to ask about her rhyming dictionary, Curses drafted her as well. She dove into plotting and lyrics-writing and loved both Curses's singing animals and his accidental drug-trip ideas; and four days later – just six hours before his first final – Curses had a completed *Byuck* draft, a girlfriend, and the noisiest, most obnoxious, kick-in-the-pants roommates this side of the Alamo.

But now it was the last day of finals (another excuse for black crêpe paper!) and Curses could see Dave and Ref, hand-in-hand, approaching the apartment. Tomorrow they headed home to Fresno for the summer. And activities uncharted. Curses looked around the room and practiced the evil laugh Llew had taught him.

> *Falling in love*
> *Is a lot like death,*

he sang, words by Llew,

> *A bourne from which no polite traveler shall return.*

Curses laughed again and closed the blinds. He clicked on the red Christmas lights he had strung throughout the room and sat on the couch. Curses? Check. Dave? Almost check. Ref? Almost check. Llew? Presumably also an almost check.

"Yes," Curses told the glowing skull under the TV, "with Curses Olai in charge, even the deaths of friends, semesters, and adequate lighting can translate into the finest night of our petty little lives."

Then the door opened, and those dead friends walked in to the sounds of pealing demonic laughter.

CPSIA information can be obtained
at www.ICGtesting.com
Printed in the USA
LVHW111001181220
674503LV00010B/77